2000
A Literary
Afternoon

**THIS BOOK
BELONGS TO:**

Karen Bellamy

 Pierce County Library
Foundation
PROMOTING QUALITY LIBRARY SERVICES FOR ALL.

To Karen:

Many thanks! Let
me know about Rot
Bastards! x

kalikoff@
u.washington.edu

Dying for a
Blue Plate Special

Dying for a
Blue Plate Special

Beth Kalikoff

Five Star • Waterville, Maine

The characters in this novel are works of fiction, and Commencement Bay University is a product of my own imagination. The morning and afternoon newspapers I made up for Tacoma bear no resemblance to the excellent *News Tribune*. Lastly, I tinkered a bit with some local geography.

First Edition
First Printing: May 2005

Published in 2005 in conjunction with Tekno Books and Ed Gorman.

Set in 11 pt. Plantin by Christina S. Huff.

Printed in the United States on permanent paper.

Library of Congress Cataloging-in-Publication Data

Kalikoff, Beth.
   Dying for a blue plate special / by Beth Kalikoff.—1st ed.
      p. cm.
      ISBN 1-59414-297-1 (hc : alk. paper)
      1. Deans (Education)—Crimes against—Fiction.   2. Women in the food industry—Fiction.   3. Caterers and catering—Fiction.   I. Title.
   PS3611.A434D95 2005
   813′.6—dc22   2005000859

Dedication

To my beloved father

Stanley Kalikoff

1924–2004

Acknowledgments

The Seattle Police Department answered my questions with admirable patience.

I am grateful to the memory of Toni Mendez, quintessential New York agent, all ninety pounds of her in full-length mink and Rosalind Russell suit. I learned a lot from Ann Maurer. John Helfers of Tekno Books has been cheerful and professional. Pat Estrada is a fine editor whose exacting and creative suggestions improved Blue Plate considerably.

I thank Kima Cargill, Gene Edgar, David Morris, and Courtney Putnam for their encouragement and advice. Hans Ostrom is a wonderful reader and writer. I appreciate the unflagging support of Will Milberg, Connie Perry, Paula Tarnapol Whitacre, and Lisa Wood: talk about the long haul. Rachel May, great friend and prodigious reader, gave Jewel her rat phobia. My writing group, Ann Putnam and Beverly Conner, shepherded this manuscript from noisy birth into hard-living adulthood. Superb writers, they are also generous readers and friends.

Hedy Kalikoff, an excellent writer and inspired cook, provided great feedback. She's the sister I would have chosen if I got to pick. Architect Ray Studebaker, my dear husband, created one beautiful writer's nest after another for me.

Finally, I thank the City of Tacoma, where I've worked for the better part of twenty years. What richness!

Chapter One

Jewel Feynmann thought about taking off her clothes and standing buck naked in the storefront window of Blue Plate Catering. She'd never considered indecent exposure a marketing strategy, but things were getting desperate. Another slow month for her catering business in Tacoma, and she'd head back to New Brunswick, the longest three thousand miles in the world, to get the horse laugh from her family, who didn't believe that any good could come out of Jews moving so far from New York, the epicenter, unless they were crazy.

She wouldn't go back a failure. Crazy was looking good, but shaking her naked booty in the storefront window would bring the police rather than business.

Or Jewel could look for the rat in the wall.

The idea made her mouth dry.

Skittering sounds had come from behind the cabinets, at floor level. She'd heard them, off and on, for the better part of two weeks. There was a rat back there. Brown fur, yellow eyes, germ-ridden, teeth that could puncture skin like a balloon. She'd never seen him but knew he was there.

No one else had heard him. Better not go down that garden path. It was so unfair.

Or—hang on—she could check Blue Plate's month-old Web site. As of yesterday, the tracker had recorded only two hundred and fourteen hits in four weeks, and at least two hundred of them were Jewel, checking the tracker. On the bright side, the site had netted one e-mail asking for directions to Martha Stewart's web world and one saying, "Your site sucks."

The phone was ringing. Maybe this would be a big fat wedding for five hundred, bankrolled by the bride's parents.

"Jewel? This is Helena Moore. We met at 'A Taste of Tacoma.' You threw fried ice cream on my shirt."

"It was an accident!"

"I'm about forty, five-foot-seven, of Haitian descent—"

"I remember you. You were the only one I threw ice cream at that day."

"One never knows," said Helena.

Jewel had run into Helena at Tacoma's answer to big-city food fairs. Pretty hard, too. She had just gotten a big cone of fried ice cream from the Lotus Tree booth and was reconsidering her Taste of Tacoma game plan, which had been to eat a little bit of everything without throwing up. She swung around to check out the south end of Point Defiance Park just as the crowd surged forward. Jewel managed to hang onto the cone, but not the contents. As a result, the black T-shirt of a snappy-looking brown woman sported a third breast, this one of fried ice cream. It was a good look but not a great look.

Helena had been a sport about it. Jewel liked that in a person.

"So you ready to take me up on my offer? Dinner for two, catered by Blue Plate, your house?" asked Jewel.

"Generous," said Helena.

"Not really. I make the same offer to everyone I throw ice cream at."

"I wish that was why I called, but it's not. Have you seen the newspaper this morning?"

"Hang on." Jewel reached across the counter for the *Telegraph*, Tacoma's answer to the *New York Post*, still folded from delivery. She unfurled it for a quick look.

The headline screamed: "Woman, 20, Dies in Zoo U Kitchen Accident." Below the fold wasn't any better: "Campus Seethes With Sex Scandal." The article began: "Students chained themselves to the flagpole yesterday to protest . . ."

"Oh, no!" Jewel said. "That's awful. How are you? What happened?"

Helena worked at Commencement Bay University. Doing what, Jewel couldn't recall. The pricey little school by Point Defiance was oddly wedged between the Tacoma Zoo and the working-class neighborhood of Ruston, so everyone called it Zoo U.

According to the paper, the young woman had been found dead in the campus kitchen. On learning of the death, protesting students rattled their flagpole chains until around one o'clock, when they released each other and went back to class.

"I've been better," said Helena. "But as far as what happened goes, I can't tell you anything that isn't already in the newspaper. I'm calling you because the university needs an outside caterer."

Jewel was torn. Work was work. But— "Is something wrong with the ovens? Because—"

Helena sighed. She sounded as though she hadn't slept for a while. "No, nothing. Listen, can you come to campus this morning and meet the Dean's assistant, Muriel? She'll tell you about the job."

"This morning?"

"I know. Very sudden. But can you clear your calendar? It's an emergency for us."

11

As if Jewel had a calendar. She could memorize Blue Plate's commitments with room enough left in her brain for the collected works of Julia Child.

"I'm on my way." She hung up before Helena could change her mind.

Less than an hour later, she parked her cherry-red Dodge Duster in among the Hondas of the visitors' parking lot. The breathless *Telegraph* articles had her curious about what she'd see along the way. The reality was disappointingly sedate.

Jewel strode into a foggy postcard from some picture-perfect moment in the 1920s. The architecture was collegiate Gothic, red brick arches everywhere. The tall windows were etched with lead tracery. The cherry trees, heartened by the mild winter, were just about to bloom. In spring, they must look like heaven. All this luxury made her wistful for the college years she'd dropped like a burning pan. No one here ever thought about rats or car repairs.

She was homesick, but not for New Jersey. Who says you can't miss what you never had?

A brick building with a bell tower loomed out of the mist. It boasted huge wooden doors and Latin over the archway. A tiny sign was stuck in the herbaceous border for visitors. Darmon Hall. Muriel's office.

Several students in baggy shorts and cotton sweaters scampered down the stone stairs, giggling. If these were the flagpole radicals, they had lost their handcuffs along with their outrage.

Muriel turned out to be a petite woman whose desk commandeered the spacious outer office of the Dean. Muriel wore a flowery shirtwaist like the ones that kindergarten teachers used to sport. She had a good head of fluffy silver hair. Jewel wondered how she endured the institutional décor: oil paintings of balding white men in black suits.

"Oh, here you are," Muriel fluttered. "Thank you for coming on such short notice, Ms.—er—Feynmann." She pronounced it in the style of Midwestern Christmas-tree Jews, to rhyme with "bean." Back East, it rhymed with "wine."

"We don't generally hire outside caterers, as you probably know. But—" She stopped, then backtracked. "Have you read the newspaper today?"

Jewel nodded. Muriel sighed. There was a lot of that going around.

"The young woman was one of the students working for the university food service."

"How'd she die?"

Muriel's kindly face froze. Jewel jumped in before Zoo U cash flew out the window, heading north towards Winterset's Catering on Proctor, a fancy-pants competitor.

"I'm not nosy." A lie. Jewel was nosy. "My concern is with the kitchen. If there's been an accident with the kitchen equipment, I need to know about it."

Muriel's fluffy silver wash-and-set wilted slightly. She looked abashed. "Certainly you do." She took a steadying breath. "The student was found in the kitchens. Her death was not caused by any equipment failure or . . . anything related to her employment there. Nevertheless, several other students left their cafeteria jobs in protest. The food service is . . . restaffing."

Jewel wondered why the student died. And in the kitchens. And why the others quit.

"While they do that, we thought we'd hire an outside caterer to do a few special events. There are several Humanities Program dinners coming up very soon." Muriel seemed

13

heartened by her return to familiar ground. "The first is scheduled for next week. The Dean wants this dinner—all of the dinners—to go very smoothly."

"Yes, of course."

"This business with SSH has been extremely unfortunate. The Dean sees this as an opportunity to put it all behind us."

This business with—what? Muriel seemed to be hushing Jewel, or hissing at her. "What's SSH?"

Muriel looked unhappily over her shoulder at the closed oak door behind her. The inner sanctum. She lowered her voice. "Oh. That's Stop Sexual Harassment, an extremist group. The young women in it—there are even a few young men—are quite nice individually—they made coffee for me during their sit-in last week—but as a group . . . well, the Dean is very concerned."

Jewel tried to imagine a Darmon Hall sit-in of rosy-cheeked, coffee-brewing activists in cotton sweaters, but failed. "I want the dinner to go well, too. Will the Dean discuss the menu with me?"

"Oh, no, no. You and I will do that. Helena Moore enjoyed meeting you, and I've heard wonderful things about your work from Professor Underwood; you did the bridal shower for her niece. She's still talking about that cake."

Ugh. Complete catastrophe. The Duster had broken down on the way to the waterfront rambler. Then the guests only nibbled because they were dieting. They looked at the angel's devil cake as though it were made of slugs. "Oh, none for me, thanks." "No, I'm fine, really." "I couldn't possibly." What was it with women?

This Underwood must have been the one guest who asked for a business card.

"Great. Will you show me the kitchen?"

"No, the Dean wishes to do that himself. He's taking a special interest in this event because . . ." Muriel checked herself. "Well, he's what we call a 'hands-on' type of administrator."

Jewel had a sudden flash of handcuffs, but supposed that wasn't what Muriel had in mind. "Yes? What's his name, anyway?"

"Oh. Call him 'Dean Mulcahy.' Although he sometimes asks people to use his first name. It's 'Matthew.' " Muriel said it as though she were doing Berlitz Swahili—carefully and slowly. "Other times he asks people to use 'Mr. Mulcahy.' I expect he'll tell you what he'd like you to call him."

Won't that be a rush, thought Jewel. She struggled to keep her expression neutral.

Muriel checked her watch. "The Dean will meet you here in an hour to show you the Faculty Club kitchen. Perhaps you'd like to discuss the fees in the meantime?"

Jewel grinned, grabbing her satchel. "You bet."

"And of course if the dinner works out, we'll be eager to have you help on our other events, which we can discuss later."

"How many people?" Jewel asked hopefully. Her middle-of-the-line wedding dinner price was thirty-four dollars a head. This would go higher than that, according to the sanctified campus smell of nineteenth-century timber money.

"Ninety-six for the first event."

She did not fall to the carpet and kiss Muriel's sensible pumps. A matter of personal pride. Muriel named a figure. A high figure.

"It's quite a big celebration for us," Muriel continued. "The Humanities Program just received a sizeable two-year grant."

"Terrific!" Dollar signs danced in Jewel's head like sugar plums.

Muriel looked startled. "Oh yes. It was a national grant, highly competitive."

The older woman paused. Jewel smiled and nodded like an idiot while thinking about striped sea bass. Or maybe ham. Everyone loved ham. They pretended not to, for nutritional or religious reasons. Jewel knew better. Although once . . . salmon, then.

She thought about the stack of bills on Blue Plate's front counter. She could buy a new bedroom lamp instead of re-wiring the old one for the second time. Maybe get those ruby-red flats in the window of Second-Hand Rose's. They looked like lucky shoes.

Jewel didn't need a bank loan. She didn't need a college education. She didn't need to go back to New Jersey and compete for oxygen. She was Blue Plate. She had work.

"Er . . . Jewel?" Muriel smiled at her expectantly. Had she been talking?

"Yes?"

"Would you like to talk about the menu?"

"Muriel," Jewel grinned, "I thought you'd never ask."

Chapter Two

Clutching a note from Muriel, Jewel arrived at the University Personnel Office, which lived in a tidy little wooden house at the corner of campus. It reminded Jewel of Goldilocks and the three bears. But she was not one to criticize. The prim good taste all around spelled cash. She didn't work all those years as a waitress to sneer at cash.

Helena Moore was the only person in the office. She was enough, in her short, mocha suit-dress and big gold brooch. Jewel admired stylish women who were larger than a size eight. Helena looked worried but managed a smile. "You made it," she said. "Good."

They shook hands.

"How are you?" Jewel asked.

Helena rolled her eyes. "Do not ask." She eyed the paperwork in Jewel's hands. "Linda's at lunch, but I know how to make up a freelance contract. Won't take a minute."

For once, Jewel didn't mind waiting. She dropped languidly into a chair and counted her chickens, eggs, meatballs, and bills.

A lamp with a heavy brass base flickered. More faulty wiring, looked like. Jewel willed herself not to ask for a screwdriver. It was hard for her not to fix things that were broken.

That was how she'd gotten her first Tacoma wedding. Jewel's paperboy's mother's stepdaughter was getting married. The mother was nervous about the caterer who'd been hired. "Nouvelle cuisine!" she'd said, as if cursing. One thing led to another. Blue Plate's buffet trays of chicken cacciatore and new potatoes pleased both mother and bride. Jewel handed out business cards over the glazed carrots.

Three jobs came out of that slam-dunk wedding. Already a fine cook, Jewel slowly got the hang of the business. She'd tie on an apron for anything that paid more than ninety-nine dollars. What she liked best was the variety. One job would be a five-cold-salad buffet for thirty ladies from St. Leo's; the next a six-course anniversary dinner for two in some wealthy couple's greenhouse; then she'd head forty miles down I-5 to Lacey for a two-hundred-fifty-person high school reunion.

The trouble was that high school reunions didn't come often. Blue Plate's word-of-mouth was good enough for Jewel to rent a storefront, but she couldn't figure out how to crack the bigger markets. Maybe some big-league dinners at Zoo U were her ticket to prosperity.

Swiftly, Helena pulled a final sheet out of the printer and brought a pile of papers to the reception area.

"Here you go. Sign there on all of them. Don't forget your Social Security number, or you won't get paid."

Jewel smiled. "Trust me." She scrawled quick signatures, handed the papers over, and pointed to the flickering light of the lamp. "You know you have a wiring problem here? Oh, I talked to Muriel about the kitchen, but I still don't know what's going on."

"Consider yourself lucky." Helena rose and shrugged into an iridescent green raincoat. "I have to kick you out and lock up. I'm off to lunch. The cafeteria's open again."

She stopped abruptly and looked down to button her raincoat. Then she started over. "I've let the campus know that the dinner is going forward. Payroll will print up your check. Come by if you have money questions. Do you make scones? Bring scones if you come back."

Jewel jumped up indignantly. "I'd rather die. I do buttermilk biscuits."

"Even better. Goodbye, Jewel."

Helena opened the cottage door and disappeared into the mist.

Contract sandwiched firmly in her satchel, Jewel decided to check out the kitchen at the Faculty Club before her official tour. She studied the map Muriel had marked for her. The door of the building behind her swung open. The two grown-ups who emerged looked like they'd know where the Faculty Club was.

The fiftyish man, in a fancy blue suit and club tie, was doing all the talking. He had strong features and a ton of hair for a guy his age, the golden brown of a lion's mane. His voice sounded serious. Oddly, he had a small smile on his face. Not a nice smile.

"Sorry, Tom, a college isn't a charity. We can't let our personal feelings impede our professional choices. I'll want your decision by next week."

The other man, in his sixties, seemed lost in an oversized gray cardigan. His hawkish face had fallen in on itself years ago. He mumbled something that Jewel couldn't hear.

The suit interrupted. "Tom, I have very little to do with it. I'm only trying to meet my responsibilities. Even you can understand that, no matter how you might feel about my personal life."

He put a hand on the man's shoulder. The older man twisted out of reach. This time Jewel, beginning to feel foolish standing out in the rain six feet from a quarrel, did hear what the cardigan said: "You candy-assed, bear-baiting, scum-sucking bastard."

Jewel gasped. The men turned to stare at her.

She tried to look like someone deafened by a preoccupation with money worries. This was easier than she thought. She brandished her map. "Hi, do you work here? Do you know where the Faculty Club is?"

Recovering swiftly, the suit took a few steps towards her. "We're both currently employed by CBU," which seemed an odd way to put it. "I'm on my way to the Club myself, so I can take you. Care to join me, Tom? Or are you on the wagon these days? It hasn't affected your diction, still as colorful as ever."

The older man paled, turned on his heel, and headed towards the parking lot.

"Ah well!" The suit seemed buoyant. "You'll have to forgive my colleague. Sometimes we get so caught up in the world of ideas that we forget our manners. But I'm afraid you must be getting soaked."

The misty rain had turned serious. The man's gaze dropped to Jewel's silk blouse and then up to her wet face. That might have been solicitude—but she thought he'd probably checked out the goods well enough to win a bet on her bra size.

Maybe she was imagining things. From shock. No one had looked at her chest, with solicitude or anything else, since the Pleistocene Era.

"We'll walk and talk, shall we?" He led her off towards a cluster of smaller brick buildings. "Wretched weather, isn't it? Now I hope you won't be insulted if I say you don't look like an undergraduate."

"What? No. I'm thirty-four."

"Let's see if I can guess. You're not a faculty member. I know them all."

"I'm a caterer."

"No, no. You're a returning student, recently divorced,

going back for a bachelor's degree that your marriage inter-rupted."

It started to pour. She began to hurry. Her stride was long, but the suit picked up his pace, staying half a step in front of her. One of those.

"Here we are!" He waved in a perfunctory way at a pair of men scuttling down the stairs of the Faculty Club, throwing on REI raingear. "This is it. I admire returning students. They often do the best work. Their life experiences . . . I haven't offended you, I hope?"

They had reached the door of the stately white building at the western corner of the quadrangle, beyond the brick rect-angle of buildings. Not a moment too soon. She was lonely, but she didn't need any womanizing windbag to float her boat.

"Thanks," she said unsmilingly.

"I'm Matthew St. James Mulcahy." He announced it like a bridge player overbidding with a hand full of trump.

Shit.

"But please call me Matt. Only students call me Dean."

She bet that wasn't all they called him. This was off to a great start. She shook his proffered hand with a curse in her heart.

Chapter Three

"Jewel Feynmann. Blue Plate Catering."

Dean Mulcahy stopped shaking Jewel's hand. Finally. "Ah, 'Blue Plate'! I was just on my way to meet you. How serendipitous! That is, what a happy discovery."

Her pulse leapt to Code Red. If he thought she'd need an English-to-English translation, why'd he use the word in the first place? She bit the inside of her cheek to keep quiet. Maybe the grimace of pain would lend her a professional look.

Mulcahy gestured sweepingly at the wide white stairs to the Faculty Club, as though he were taking her to the Casbah. "After you, Jewel Feynmann."

She didn't like the sound of her full name in his mouth, but there didn't seem much she could do about it. She marched up the stairs, hoping that her long black jacket blocked a good view of her hindquarters, themselves good, if not small.

The Faculty Club could have been an arranged marriage of old-time Boston to pioneer Washington. Framed architectural drawings of early campus buildings hung tidily on white walls above a wainscot. The wall-to-wall carpet was the color of eggplant. It seemed to soak up unseemly noise. An antique pew was the lone furniture in sight, lending the hallway a New England church simplicity.

Yet two sets of mounted antlers hung in state. An old tree trunk, hollowed and varnished, held umbrellas. Not many—

Jewel understood that real Northwesterners disdained umbrellas, even when it was pouring. Mysterious.

Mulcahy strode past to lead her down the hallway. She peeked into the open doors to her right—the dining room. Plenty of space. Right now, the room was filled with white men schmoozing over coffee. There were a handful of white women and two black men.

Huh. Jewel knew for a fact that there were black women, Latinos, Latinas, Japanese-American men, and Korean-American women a'plenty in the Pacific Northwest. But they weren't eating in the Zoo U faculty dining room.

Mulcahy didn't dawdle. She found herself two steps behind and hurried to a coat check window.

"We'll only be a few minutes," Mulcahy said to the young woman at the coat check stand. "Could you put this," he gestured imperiously at Jewel's oversized black blazer, "close to the front?"

"Yes, Dean Mulcahy."

Mulcahy turned his paper-thin smile in Jewel's direction. "The kitchen's this way."

He walked smartly down the rest of the hall.

Jewel shrugged at the young woman, who rolled her eyes.

Mulcahy swung through white double doors at the end of the hallway with the confidence of a large man who made a lot of money. Jewel winced. Carelessly opened kitchen doors led to dropped trays and harsh words. Luckily, the staff worked at the other end of the room. One man was cleaning the flat-top grill. A big one. Good.

Mulcahy was a jerk. Not the first Jewel had met. You didn't have to be a university bigwig to be a jerk. You didn't have to be a Northwesterner, either. Plenty of jerks back East. New Brunswick alone was teeming with jerks.

Her ex-boyfriend Dylan, to name only one, a grown man

who went to work every day carrying a packed lunch made by his mother. Always the same lunch, too: pepper jack cheese, smoked turkey, whole-wheat bread, Dijon, lettuce, piece of fruit, bag of chips, white chocolate chip cookie. Not a terrible lunch, but every day? That should have tipped her off. Jewel had been distracted by his cabinetmaking artistry and virility. What about her cousin Nadine, the wedding planner? A jerk with an international reputation, since that reception in Toronto. And these were just the people Jewel knew.

No, jerks were everywhere. She had to keep reminding herself that New Jersey wasn't the promised land. That she'd rather put her head in the stove than return. The homeless caterer. Stranded on two coasts.

"Great kitchen," said Jewel.

"I have a meeting I must go to. Will you call me if any questions arise?"

"Thank you, Dean Mulcahy."

"You're supposed to call me Matt, now." He smiled and waited. The smile was genuine.

Those were the worst. Genuine smiles made her very nervous. "Right. Sorry." Dean, Dean, Dean.

"Professor Underwood says wonderful things about your work. I look forward to the dinner."

"Oh good," Jewel said, pushing damp hair from her forehead. That damned bridal shower.

"The timing of this event is particularly important. There will be a keynote speech of some significance."

"All right."

"I'll provide you with more details after you've had a chance to prepare for the evening. I don't want to interfere with the creative process. I write music in my spare time, so I know a little something about that." He said this as if handing

Jewel the keys to a new Jag. Comparing his job and hers was supposed to confer honor on her head.

But she already knew that cooking was an art. It took nerve, too, research, and improvisation. She doubted he'd ever even defrosted his own dinner. "Then I'll see you Thursday night," she said.

"I look forward to it." He extended his hand again. She shook it, although suspecting that he just wanted the low-voltage jolt of physical contact.

He strode from the room with his practiced air of unshakeable confidence.

No matter. Jewel wasn't here to find friends. She was here to find success. She wanted to dazzle Zoo U with Thursday's dinner so that she'd be hired on for more "events." If everyone at the dinner told one local friend . . .

Jewel had known in her bones that Blue Plate was a great idea and Tacoma was the city of her roasted dreams. Why doubt it? She couldn't sprout in northern New Jersey's toxic soil. Caterers bloomed and withered there by the hour. Everyone made the same lasagna. Everyone used the same garnish. And more caterers were cropping up every day, with no more vision than a cockroach on a Monday night, scuttling around with their sorry-ass potato salad and tired antipasto, people who thought that knowing how to eat qualified them to cook for a living. No, Jewel had been ready for a change. Tacoma was a chance to re-invent herself and her cuisine.

A swing by the Chamber of Commerce before she opened up shop confirmed her gut instincts. She learned there, to her delight, that the city's overreaching nickname was "City of Destiny." Tacoma's glory days had taken place in the sepia-tinted 1880s. The gallery in the Town Hall lobby had shown photographs of settlers standing tall and hopeful in front of Queen Anne houses with wrap-around porches. Back then, the brochures said, the lumber and railway industries were in a state of rude health. But that hadn't been enough to keep Tacoma from slipping into Seattle's shade.

No one really knew what Seattle had that Tacoma didn't. Both cities sported good ports and ravishing landscapes, wet winters and blue summers. But as the century got older, Seattle boomed. Its Pike Place Market, Belltown, and International District drew foodies from up and down the Pacific Coast. Tacoma found itself with a reputation for smoky taverns and the poisonous smell of industrial waste from the Asarco factory. By the time Blue Plate set up, the former glory hole had become the butt of yuppie jokes.

Yet Jewel, like the hopeful brochures, saw signs of a revival. The renovation of Union Station. The University of Washington's Tacoma campus downtown, with its renovated warehouses and commuting students. The Museum of Glass, drawing visitors from all over the world, possibly in hopes of seeing a vacation-making glass-blowing accident in the hot shop. The new Art Museum wasn't anything to sneer at, either. Movie companies filming on the water, spending money freely in local eateries. More local eateries.

That was a good sign. Tacoma had its share of fast food places with buckets of chicken and bags of burgers. Now it had been invaded by the overflow from Seattle's culinary excess. Sure, the Southern Kitchen, near Sixth Avenue, made the greatest fried chicken north of Arkansas, and their okra was good enough to curl your hair and straighten it out again. Harbor Lights, down on the water, also bucked the bohemian trend, offering joyfully huge, high-calorie fish-of-the-day servings. You ate lunch at Harbor Lights, you weren't getting any work done for the rest of the day. Still, though, these bright spots were exceptions to the foodie fashions all around her.

The city needed an antidote to the pesto-based cuisine of Winterset's Catering or the posh-mouth blue-corn Santa Fe cooking of The Armadillo Grill. Tacoma was a struggling American city that needed hearty, inventive American fare to claim its boomtown destiny. It needed Blue Plate. And Blue Plate needed business. That meant getting along with clients. Even when you wanted to club them with their club ties.

Jewel stuck out her chin. The Faculty Club kitchen awaited.

Chapter Four

Jewel tried to imagine her dining room table stacked high with serving platters instead of bills. Pecan-encrusted halibut, garlic-roasted whole chicken, tomato-red onion-feta salad, raspberry vinaigrette . . . her mind lingered fondly on the salad, so colorful and pungent, a salad that even toddlers ate, before she returned glumly to the cable bill. It was the second notice. Not a big bill. Double digits.

Was there a red border on the invoice? Nah. She could blow the bill off until next month. And if the cable people got snarky, she could watch snow on the TV for a few weeks.

Might as well. Jewel liked TV as much as the next Jew, and she didn't need HBO to fill her evening; basic cable was plenty good enough for her. But in truth there hadn't been anything good on since the half-time Janet Jackson tit incident, poor woman. Now *that* was unfair, Jewel thought, her eyes drifting to the twenty-inch screen in the living room. That could have happened to anyone dancing around in a costume on camera at half-time. Just happened to be Janet.

Why, Jewel herself had once gone through the better part of the day wearing a black sock underneath her white shirt, a laundry-sorting oversight instantly visible to everyone she met. No one had the simple kindness to tell her there was a black sock static-clinging to the inside of her shirt, above her bra, below her collarbone. Some sort of Northwestern pettiness masquerading as politesse. Fine. They could just be that way. Jewel herself was more charitable, always telling others who lived alone that they'd left a price tag dangling from their underarm or their fly open.

The rental house seemed to sigh. A kind of settling. The burgundy-colored dining room walls usually had a calming effect on Jewel. And she liked studying her collection of McDonald's plastic toys from decades of Happy Meals. The action figures, cartoon characters, tops, and other toys were judiciously displayed on the mantel over the fake fireplace. The spillover she put in basement storage. It was a rotating exhibit. She'd unearth the other red and yellow figurines when she got tired of looking at these. So many Happy Meals. She considered herself lucky to have friends and acquaintances all over the world pocketing fast-food trinkets and saving them for her.

Usually studying the collection or imagining a groaning table full of Blue Plate Specials had a cheering effect on Jewel. She never stayed low for long. But tonight she was restless.

Probably the prospect of the big Zoo U job, with more to come if she didn't screw up. Which she wouldn't.

The phone rang while she was deciding if she felt lucky enough to skate a couple small checks. The CBU down-payment she'd deposited, but the teller had given her some garbage about waiting for it to clear from a California bank. Why a California bank? Wasn't the state of Washington good enough for those over-educated Gortex-wearing Starbuck's-drinking sons-and-daughters-of—

"Took you long enough. What are you, coming in after milking the cows?"

Daphne's voice popped Jewel back into the moment. "Where are you, Daph?"

"Where am I? I'm in Hoboken. Where would I be—Paris, France?"

Jewel thought the Left Bank seemed unlikely. Her cousin Daphne complained more or less nonstop about traveling twenty-three minutes every morning to New York to fix computers for a bunch of young stockbrokers who looked like high school kids in a class play. Paris was even farther.

"You sound so far away," said Jewel lamely.

Daph snorted. Now that sounded closer.

"What took you so long to answer the phone, anyway? You slopping the hogs?"

"It's only three hours earlier here than there, you know." Jewel was tired of relatives who pretended to think she was in the same time zone as Australia and spent her time ranching and farming. "It's not morning, and Tacoma is a city."

"Spare me," said Daph. "So what are you, having sex this early? Did you even brush your teeth yet?"

"I don't have sex any more. I've moved on. I'm on a higher plane."

They both laughed. Jewel could imagine Daph's sea-green eyes and beauty-queen smile. People often expected her to be kind of genteel and ladylike.

"Well, I wish that fucking Patrick would move to a higher plane. Rain or shine, that man is ready for love at nine-thirty every night, falls asleep by nine forty-five."

"Hey, you married him. It's only fifteen minutes a day. Probably that's a normal amount of time, if you added it up and pretended you had sex once a week."

They laughed again.

"So how are you, Jewel?"

Jewel looked at the bills, then at her McDonald's Happy Meal trophies. "I'm fine. I got a new job today."

"Yeah? That's great. Good for you, girlie."

Daph's enthusiasm for Jewel's ventures was one of her many loveable traits.

30

"Yeah. It's at a university in town. A big dinner."

"Cool! That reminds me. Nadine—"

It was Jewel's turn to snort. Daph's older sister Nadine, the wedding planner, was as critical and pissy as Daph was warm and entertaining.

"I know, she's a pain in the ass, Jewel, but she heard about this job in the city, this hotel that needs a chef."

Jewel scowled. Nadine and the rest of her family couldn't believe that Jewel wanted to make her own way, and in the Pacific Northwest, no less.

"No New York hotel is going to hire me as a chef. They look for people who have been working underneath some big-name chef or—"

"It's a little hotel, Nadine says—new, and she thought maybe—"

"I don't think so, Daph. Tell her I said thanks, anyway."

"Oh, I'm not doing that. It'd just encourage her. I'll tell her you said for her to go fuck herself."

Jewel put her feet up on the dining room table, to settle in for a good gossip.

"Listen, girlie," Daph said, "I hate to do this, but I have to run. It's almost time for grandma to call to tell me how the nursing home is slipping shellfish into her kosher food."

"Oh, jeez, Daph. That's sad."

"It is and it isn't. You know grandma. She wouldn't say no to a little lobster. I'll call you tomorrow. And good luck with the new job, okay?"

The dial tone sounded like it was three thousand miles away.

Chapter Five

Late on Thursday afternoon, Del Troutman, Blue Plate's occasional employee, waited outside the storefront. He sat on the sidewalk, reading *Fire in the Belly* with a pink highlighter. His sack lunch looked empty.

"Del, lose your keys again?"

He jumped. "Jewel! I didn't hear you come up." He scrambled to his feet, a long trip for Del at six-foot-three. He seemed shorter than that to Jewel because he only weighed a hundred pounds. Maybe a few more. This was an odd trick of metabolism, rather than illness or starvation. Twenty-three-year-old Del ate like he was training for a season of triple-A ball with the Tacoma Rainiers. Hell, he ate like he was the whole team.

Jewel let them both in.

"I didn't lose my keys. I just can't find them." Del held up the paperback for her inspection, before he stuffed it in his baggy low-riders. He could have stuffed the *World Book Encyclopedia* in there, with room enough left over for a deck chair and a plasma-screen TV. "This is a great book, Jewel. It's about manhood, but without the mushy fake-Native-American bang-the-drum-slowly stuff."

"Huh." Jewel slung her blazer onto a hook behind the front door and headed for the refrigerators. She was pumped for tonight's dinner. The only other thing Blue Plate had on the calendar was a bar mitzvah, and Danny Mitznick had a small family. Or maybe a large family of people who weren't coming to his luncheon.

"Want to get your game face on and start unloading the trays? Then we'll carry them out to the car."

"Great!" Del headed for the refrigerators with a bounce in his long ponytail and his high-tops. The despair of his minister father, Del had dropped out of seminary so that he could spend more time reading. The rest of the time he was here and there—distributing clean needles on the street, dropping in at Mary Bridge Children's Hospital to make balloons into wiener dogs, designing Web sites for churches. He even did Blue Plate's web design, making Jewel wonder if he considered Blue Plate a nonprofit organization. Never mind. He had such a generous belief in what he called "faith in the universe" that Jewel thought his parents could relax: Del was heading for a ministry one way or the other.

He was also a natural genius in the kitchen. She watched him for a moment with satisfaction, as he stacked buffet trays laden with scalloped potatoes like they were a feather-light extension of his arms. He was humming something. What a happy boy.

Jewel loved competence. She pulled a tattered black scarf out of her pants pocket and tied her hair up. She loved competence in men and in women. It was seductive. It was too seductive.

Her thoughts skittered back to New Brunswick, where Anthony the Contractor still held sway over a gaggle of subcontractors. That man really knew how to measure, re-measure, and install. She saw his black curly hair rise up in front of her like a holograph. Hair all over, she recalled. A smile that could melt rubber. And his mother didn't make his lunch for him every day, either. Of course, there was the matter of the other women. Good thing she blew town. Anthony'd been well on his way to persuading her that he had more than enough to go around. ("Your piece of the pie won't be getting any smaller, I promise you.")

33

Oh, none of that. Now was no time to stagger down loser's alley, the rogue's gallery of Jewel's former whatevers.

"Jewel?" Del had already finished stacking the trays. He hovered, bright-eyed, by the computer. "Is it okay if I check the Web site for a second?"

"Why not?" said Jewel. They had a minute and, with a big dinner to cater, she hadn't checked the site for a couple of days.

She was looking forward to the dinner. Muriel, handmaiden to Deans, had answered Jewel's questions during the week. Mulcahy had materialized from time to time. She didn't entirely get him. A good-looking guy, in a prime-time TV sort of way. And an alpha dog: player, not spectator. But he reminded Jewel of a high school friend of hers who'd always looked around the room while talking, head spinning around like Linda Blair's in *The Exorcist*, working the angles, planning three moves ahead, never quite content to be in this place with this person. Yet the friend had worked at charming Jewel. Ditto Mulcahy.

Jewel was especially pleased to be able to use the Zoo U dinner as an excuse to check the farmers' market and begin filling the freezers. This dinner felt like a real chance to bring Blue Plate from a struggling to a going concern.

"Jewel. I'm sorry."

She wrenched herself from her cash-flow reverie. Del sounded odd. He was staring at the PC monitor.

"Something scary has happened."

"What, a virus or cookie or something?" Jewel's software knowledge was limited to hardware. "Don't worry about it, kiddo. You can figure it out later." She moved to the refrigerator.

"No." Del turned away from the screen. He was pale. "It's not technical. You better look at it now. Really."

She paused. For all Del's seeming scattiness, he had good common sense. He wasn't silly. Del got up from the computer, letting Jewel sit down.

Blue Plate's e-mail index was up. The list of messages and subject headings looked about the same as last time. Except—

"The new one," said Del.

The last message in line was from "Death-in-Life." The subject heading: "Read or Die."

Jewel blinked. She opened the message.

It was only a few sentences.

Someone died at CBU. In the kitchen. What if you're next? Save yourself. Save yourself.

She stared at the screen. She closed her eyes and opened them, but the message was still there.

Del's hand had come to rest on her shoulder.

She found her voice. "Some kind of joke?"

Del didn't answer.

"It's not funny," said Jewel. "Someone *did* die in the kitchen at CBU. A student. It was in the paper."

"I know."

"I don't get it." She studied the words as though she could pull them from the monitor and eat them. "A threat? It doesn't make sense."

"Maybe we should—"

Jewel stood up. "No," she said. "No. We're doing the dinner."

His face clouded over with worry.

"Look." She patted his arm. "We need the money. We'll call the police afterwards, okay? But this has got to be from a crank. Some sad-ass junior high student who reads the paper and sends screwed-up e-mail to strangers."

Del gazed dolefully at her. " 'Death-in-Life'?"

"We'll call the police," said Jewel. "Afterwards. In the meantime—" she checked her watch "—we have to get going. Anyway, who'd want to kill a caterer?"

At six o'clock, Jewel and Del fired up the ovens at the Faculty Club. Blue Plate's Sunday roast required a steady heat to warm it up again. Only an hour until showtime. Work, Jewel found, stuffed trouble into a back pocket. She refused to let the e-mail rattle her.

She didn't yelp when the double doors swung open. If one of the student waiters were swinging in like a drunken sailor, Jewel would give him a liberal-arts education that would last a lifetime.

Matt Mulcahy stood in the center of the kitchen, as if waiting for applause. "Blue Plate Catering at work!"

Jewel had to hand it to him. He looked like a so-young-to-be-this-successful banker in his pewter-colored suit, white shirt, and yellow tie. That leonine head and well-oiled smile would have won over elderly women with big savings accounts and little guile.

"Dean Mulcahy."

"Jewel, Jewel, what are we going to do about you?"

"Oh, right. I'm not supposed to call you 'Dean.' "

"Yes, Jewel, and this is—" He looked quizzically at Del, who was unwrapping the rhubarb pies.

"Del Troutman, Dean Mulcahy." Jewel gestured.

Del grinned. "Hey, man."

Mulcahy turned down the wattage on his smile. "If I could interrupt for a moment?"

She looked at the pies, the roast, the scalloped potatoes with Gorgonzola. "We're bearing down on seven P.M. But sure, what's up?"

36

He moved closer. There was something taut and excited in his face that struck Jewel as odd. "I'll be both keynote speaker and master-of-ceremonies for tonight's dinner program. That means I'll be too busy to offer you assistance. So let's make sure that you understand the importance of timing this evening." At least he didn't want to muck about with the meal itself. "I'd like there to be an hour between appetizers and salad."

"Oh. Are you sure? Usually people—"

His gaze didn't falter as he cut Jewel off with practiced expertise. "No doubt. But college faculty members tend to be great talkers. They linger over conversations, especially at the cocktail hour. And many of them have traveled in Europe and Latin America for their research, where dinner is taken much later than in the United States."

Jewel studied him for a moment, torn. Of course, he was a lout in Italian loafers, managing to imply in seconds that Blue Plate usually catered events for street gangs *and* that Jewel had only seen college-educated people in glossy magazines with articles about celebrity diets.

What threw her was that he had given three reasons for the long gap between courses. One would have been enough. Or really, none. Mulcahy didn't seem like the kind of guy who justified himself to caterers.

She willed herself not to ask why. The food would be all right. Although if he'd told her this last week, she could have done a ham, with a hazelnut glaze and winter squash. Hams kept forever. People loved ham, with its holiday air and frisson of nutritional taboo.

"Fine," she said.

Del slammed two aluminum pans onto the counter. Mulcahy jumped. He was certainly jacked up to "high." Maybe he, too, was getting crazy e-mails. Dinner, she advised herself. Focus on dinner. It was hard to take an e-mail death threat seriously in a kitchen full of people. Especially if you were from New Jersey.

"Well! Better go work on my speech. It's important. I confess I'm a bit strung up." He didn't look strung up. He looked secretive and glad, like he was going to pull down his best friend's pants in front of a girl. Probably nerves.

He wasn't the only one. There were going to be ninety-six people sitting down to a Blue Plate Special tonight, people who had brothers and sisters, parties and receptions. Jewel had even made a special effort to groom herself for the occasion, making sure that her eyebrows were headed in the right direction.

She wanted Mulcahy out of her kitchen.

"Good luck!" she sang out with desperation.

He smiled again and left without a backwards glance.

She stomped to the back counter, cursing softly.

Del looked up reproachfully. He had strong views about profanity.

"Sorry sorry sorry, and I'll squeeze lemons over the salads."

He beamed. The pies were arranged in rows like good little soldiers. He'd also stacked the dessert plates. The sight of Del's work calmed Jewel. He had a real knack. He had even tucked his long sand-colored ponytail out of sight.

"What was that all about, anyway?"

"He wants the seasons to change before the Sunday roast."

"Weird. Maybe he wants excitement to build to a fever pitch, like at a concert." Del made a roaring-crowd noise. Jewel laughed.

Later she would remember Del's remark with a shudder.

★ ★ ★ ★ ★

Blue Plate was ready at twenty minutes to seven. Del sat on an empty counter by the sink. The two student waiters, crisp in white jackets, huddled by the refrigerator. The tall, freckled one did most of the talking. The dark one with the cheekbones kept shaking his head mulishly, no, no, no. He looked haggard, that one, red-eyed. She hoped he was up to waiting tables.

Del watched Jewel prowl. "You should eat something."

"That's my line."

"It will calm you down."

Jewel shot him a dirty look, then reconsidered. He was right. "Okay, Mr. Mom. I'll see how many people are here, then I'll graze."

She hung up her chef's jacket by the kitchen staff's bathroom, then pulled at her pumpkin-colored sweater. A quick check in the window of the built-in wall oven showed her dark red hair curling to her chin like bubbles. There were sparkles of light in her brown eyes, or maybe it was just the oven bulb. She looked pretty good, for her. She liked work.

Slipping through the double door and turning down the hallway, Jewel almost fell on a delicate woman who came out of nowhere.

Jewel gasped. "I'm sorry."

The woman's heart-shaped face showed more distress than a bump into a stranger would warrant. Jewel thought that in the right light, relaxed, the woman would be a time-stopping beauty, with her olive skin and classic Italian features. Her long honey-brown hair fell in waves. Even the rotten mouse-colored jumper she was wearing didn't conceal a slender but womanly figure.

"Can I help you?" Jewel said.

"I'm looking for Matt Mulcahy."

39

This couldn't be Mrs. Herr Dean Little King Mulcahy. Too lovely, too young—not even thirty—and too poised, even in her agitation. Jewel had the Dean pegged for a pretty person his own age with a downtrodden, eager-to-please air. If this was the missus, Jewel had the final proof that God didn't exist.

"He was in the kitchen, but he left."

The woman wilted like a tiger lily on a radiator.

"Sorry." Jewel started up the hall.

"Please, wait." The tiger lily caught at her sleeve. "Do you happen to remember when he left?"

"Yeah, sure. A little after six." The woman's anxiety moved Jewel, but she didn't have time for human feelings that were unrelated to roast.

"Did he say whether he'd be back?"

"No, he just talked about when to serve." Jewel tried to come up with something that might make this woman buck up. Then go away. "He did say he was going to finish working on a speech. Lots of important announcements."

The woman went white, swayed slightly, and fell onto the eggplant-colored carpet.

Chapter Six

The woman lay still on the carpet. Jewel felt for a pulse at her wrist. It beat, if faintly. She pushed the long hair from the woman's face. So pale. The stranger's eyelids fluttered.

"Are you okay?"

Her eyes opened. So dark they were almost black. She stared at Jewel. "What—"

"I'm Jewel Feynmann. You fainted."

The woman opened her eyes wider. She looked about twelve years old. Her gaze moved to the hallway, then the front door.

"You're at the Faculty Club."

A ghost of panic crossed her face. Her marble features flushed pink. "What time is it?"

"Quarter to seven. Here, I'll help you up. Lean on me."

The woman rose with surprising speed. Jewel knew nothing about fainting, but she had always thought recovery took longer. Gripping Jewel's arm, the woman steadied herself. Iron grip. Jewel wondered if there'd be a mark. This lovely was strong, for all her fragile looks and faints. The stranger let go at once and stood straight as a dancer.

"Thank you. I'm all right now."

"All right? You just fainted. What kind of 'all right' is that? I'll get you some water."

"No. Thank you."

"At least sit down for a minute." Jewel pointed at the upright hallway pew.

The woman shook her head. Stubborn.

"It's not good, this fainting. Have you eaten? I bet you forgot to eat."

"Jewel. Thank you. I'm fine."

The woman looked like a fairy princess awakened from a spell. Jewel thought of that grip on her arm. She was no fairy princess. "Look, what's your name?"

"Frances Carlotti."

"Frances, I don't feel good about this."

"It's all right. I have to go to this dinner now."

Oh no. What time was it? She checked her watch. Six-fifty! She had to go too. There was no point loitering in the hallway, hectoring a wan beauty in ugly clothes. Years of meddling, matchmaking, and tinkering with appliances had taught Jewel that you can't help people who don't want your help.

"Me, too. I'm the caterer. Listen—come back to the kitchen if you want anything."

Frances smiled bleakly, glided away. She moved like she was walking back into a painting. A real beauty, but one worried potato.

Potatoes! Jewel fled.

Del stood solitary in the center of the kitchen, one man on an island. His usually beatific face was downcast. The freckled waiter, Ace, slouched against the far counter, hands stuffed in his pockets. They both looked apprehensively at Jewel as she flew in.

"What?" she said, taking in their mood at a glance.

Del looked at Ace, as if willing him to speak. Ace looked down.

"Hey, guys, we're t-minus ten minutes from liftoff. Talk to me."

"It's Tyler," said Ace, not quite meeting her eyes.

"*What's* Tyler?"

"Tyler!" he explained, like a four-year-old astonished that someone wouldn't know who his grandmother was. "You know. The other waiter."

Jewel scanned the kitchen. No one but tall, young Del and tall, younger Ace.

"Yeah, Tyler the other waiter, so where is he?"

"That's it. The thing is, he had to go."

"So what? A guy doesn't need a bathroom pass around here."

"No, it's not—he's really gone. He had to. He won't be back to do the dinner."

Jewel heard some of her smaller nerve cells fizzing and popping like roman candles. Maybe this was some college-boy type prank. The punch line had better be Tyler popping his sorry head out from behind the bathroom door. But no piece of Tyler popped out anywhere. Ace looked shifty. Del's eyes were sad.

"Ace?" Jewel said. *"Why not?"*

"I can't tell you."

"Has he gone nuts? Have you gone nuts? I've got almost a hundred people who need dinner, and he signed on to do the job."

Ace gave her a besieged but sturdy look as though he were Marine Colonel Oliver North and she the Senate Subcommittee. "I can't tell you. He's my frat brother. We're both Fijis, we took an oath. But it's really *really* important. Otherwise he'd be here. He needs the money, like, big-time."

Jewel glared at Ace, whose freckled face was screwed up in nervous determination, as though she might torture him to get him to reveal the secret of Tyler's defection. This sounded like a plan. Unfortunately, time was short.

"Del?" she said.

"Beats me. They were talking and Tyler just took off."

"Fine. Okay. Peachy. Super. I'll do Tyler's job. On top of mine. The next time I see him, he better be on crutches." She grabbed her white jacket and flung it on. Then she whirled back. "And Ace? You better do a damned—" Del flinched "—a darned flawless job out there tonight, or I will personally hand your Fijis to you in a jar."

Colonel North deflated into Little Boy Blue. "Yes, ma'am. Sorry, ma'am."

Silver tray of bacon-wrapped water chestnuts in hand, Jewel surveyed the Faculty Club dining room.

The place was a festival of mismatched garments. Some Zoo U faculty members must have forgotten why they were going out, costuming themselves for the opera, a kayak expedition, or a Ban-Lon nostalgia party. Others had apparently dressed in the dark. More tragically, Jewel judged, some celebrants had been forced to appear in whatever they were wearing when their houses caught fire.

Tweed jackets communed with blue jeans. Polyester pants topped off running shoes. There were prep school blazers and laughable ties, lumberjack shirts from *Seven Brides for Seven Brothers* and three-piece suits from the Reagan years. There was even a cowboy string tie, worn with a dress shirt. The women fared a bit better, but not much—jean skirts and Birkenstocks, tailored jackets with big, hippie earrings. One youngish woman wore anklets with penny loafers. Get over it, Jewel thought, but she was charmed by the eager fashion ineptitude all around her. It was like walking into a child's birthday party, where the guests had been allowed to pick out their own clothes. Maybe that accounted for the excited buzz of chat.

Or maybe it was the bar. Some people had white wine.

Most sported shot glasses. A knot of people crowded the bar at the other side of the room. The student bartenders looked harried. Loud laughter tinkled off the chandelier.

Jewel began threading her way through the crowd slowly, a smile on her face. Her unsmiling thoughts centered on Tyler and Ace and the entire concept of student waiters. While trying to decide which of the two was cemented more deeply onto her personal shit-list, Jewel saw a man who looked familiar. He wore a big, rumpled, black button-down sweater.

The cardigan. The older man who stalked away from Mulcahy in the rain last week. She hoped he wouldn't remember her. "Appetizer?"

Close up and out of the weather, he looked like the remains of a handsome man. He had striking light blue eyes. But his hawk-like features and grim expression said that the good years were behind him.

"What for?" he said.

"For food. Until dinner. You'll like them."

"I haven't liked anything at Zoo U for thirty years. You think these could break the streak?" He swept one from the tray and into his mouth. She waited.

"Don't tell me you're from Food Service, because I won't believe it. These are edible," he said. "You're a ringer."

"I'm Jewel Feynmann, Blue Plate Catering."

"Catering!" He snorted. "*Now* they hire a caterer. Too late for me, of course. After three decades of parents' receptions and alumni luncheons and English Department 'b-b-q's,' I have no sense of taste left. Of course that's a professional advantage, at Zoo U." He drained his glass. "I'm Tom Pearsall, by the way."

"Hi. Another appetizer?"

"No, another scotch. At least the liquor flows freely at

45

these shindigs. Just thinking about spending the night sober makes my fillings hurt."

"Pearsall! My man!" A sixtyish guy with a big beard and bigger belly waved his whiskey like a flag. Nearby drinkers were splashed.

Pearsall greeted the big belly with a high-five, then introduced Jewel while she was trying to escape. "You don't need to know this guy's name, he's only a philosopher."

The big belly laughed. Pearsall instructed him to take an appetizer, which he did. Jewel began to edge away.

"Come back here with those things!" commanded Pearsall. "I need something to soak up the alcohol. You could be liable."

"Great eats!" said the philosopher big belly through his food and beard. Jewel would have to hustle the tray away if anyone else was to get a mouthful. On the other hand, Ace was moving nicely through the growing crowd with his tray. Pearsall and his friend were old enough to have children old enough to marry. Maybe they'd need a caterer.

The big belly was gesturing hugely towards the noisy knots of professors. "A far cry from the barricades, right, man?" The big belly turned to Jewel. "We're a couple of old crocks now, but during Vietnam, we were down in the trenches together. We go back a long ways."

"You were in Vietnam?" Jewel was startled. They seemed too old.

"Hell, no!" Pearsall broke in. "We were here, doing sit-ins, open-mike rallies. In the fall of nineteen sixty-eight, the administration even brought in state troopers. The rest of these cowards were hiding in their offices, peeping from behind the blinds. Jesus! That was when protest meant something."

The big belly, working his way steadily through the appetizers, laughed again. "Yeah, you should have seen old Tom then. He was the angriest angry young man. Darmon Hall hated him. Tried to fire him, but he had them buffaloed. He packed students into his courses—Black Lit! War Lit! Radical! Prescient!"

Pearsall stared into his drink, unseeing.

"His classes were so big he had to use a microphone. When Darmon went after him, the students had their rich parents do a letter-writing campaign. And the groupies! Make love, not war, right, man?"

Pearsall looked up. Jewel couldn't read his face, but the big belly could: he stopped, hand poised over the silver tray. His face fell.

"So!" Jewel burst in. "You guys did good work on the appetizers. Do you want my business card?"

"Sure!" The big belly reached for her card, eager for a change of subject. "Thanks!"

"God." Pearsall roused himself from his reverie. "I need another drink to get through dinner tonight."

Jewel escaped, checking the ornate clock on the wall. Seven-fifteen.

She had barely reloaded the ravaged tray with franks in puff-pastry blanks when she spotted a dark face in the pale crowd. Helena Moore, stylish in a black blouse and brilliant multi-colored skirt. Her long golden earrings beckoned Jewel through the sea of people.

Helena was being lectured by a woman who looked like an underfed whippet in a pricey beige sweater-dress and pumps. The whippet appeared to be in her mid-thirties, but her hair was pulled back into such a severe chignon that it stretched her face into agelessness. "Really, Helena, I don't think we should be spreading rumors."

Helena laughed, a rich coloratura. "No rumor, Lesley. It was in this week's student *Herald*. Leo Wallinsky is definitely the new faculty advisor for SSH. And he wants them to hire a pit-bull lawyer from Seattle."

"Appetizers?" Jewel held the tray invitingly. The whippet scarcely glanced at it.

"Hi, Jewel." Helena greeted her warmly. "These look beautiful. Don't they, Lesley? Jewel Feynmann, Lesley DeLaMar."

"Hi, Lesley."

The woman flinched. "How do you do?"

"Lesley's an associate professor of French, Jewel's a—"

The whippet interrupted impatiently. "Helena, don't you see how paying all this attention to students simply encourages their misconduct?"

Jewel turned to fade back into the crowd when someone touched her shoulder.

"Do you have two seconds?" Helena said. Her voice was casual, her dark eyes serious. "I want to ask you something."

"All right," Jewel said reluctantly. She liked Helena, but she had real work to do, and didn't anyone at this place do small talk? She stood uneasily at Helena's elbow.

"Really, Helena." Lesley DeLaMar bared her teeth in a grisly little smile. "We can't keep . . . this person . . . from her work."

Helena went still. "Lesley," she said, carefully. "I understand your concern for the university, and I respect it. But the way to protect CBU is to follow university policy, to obey the law. We can't cover up a death."

Jewel's thoughts whipsawed in several directions. What cover-up, if the girl in the kitchen died accidentally? Who sent that e-mail to Blue Plate and what did he know? Or she? And whoa! Don't these university types know how to party down? And shit! She had to get going. Why had she told Helena she'd wait?

The whippet had turned a shade of fuchsia that Jewel thought would look good on toenails. She glared at Helena and, after a moment, found her voice. It was restrained, but barely, and the effort seemed to cost more than her shoes. "Excuse me."

Helena and Jewel watched her walk away, back as stiff as a broom.

"What did you want to ask me?" said Jewel, curious.

"Nothing." Helena's eyes stayed wintry. "I wanted a witness."

By seven forty-five, Jewel's adrenaline was pumping. She was pleased with how the Zoo animals had devoured Blue Plate's good, plain food. They were inhaling the salmon on rye toast. Ace had shaped up pretty well. His tray almost got away from him once, but Jewel had seen a wildly gesturing bald man careen towards him and was inclined to be merciful. She headed off for a final circuit. Then she saw Mulcahy.

Mulcahy was the center of attention in a big group by the bar. She edged around the group, offering an assortment of smoked salmon and franks in blanks to the spectators.

There were some familiar faces. Lesley DeLaMar, who still hadn't eaten anything. She was wholly focused on Mulcahy. It was curious how different she looked when she laughed—a real laugh, delighted, even girlish, nothing like the excuse for a smile she'd sliced at Jewel earlier. Now Lesley's face was rather pretty. Her hand was at her neck in an odd, protective gesture.

Jewel also spotted Frances Carlotti, the fainter, at the edge of the group. She looked lovely in a consumptive kind of way.

Various other Zoo animals were at the periphery. Mulcahy began speaking with a strong Russian accent as, Jewel gathered, part of a story. A few people laughed boisterously. Suck-ups, she thought.

Frances didn't laugh at all. Jewel wondered whether she was still waiting to talk to Mulcahy.

No one was going to get his attention while the woman by his side remained in the room. Maybe this was the real eye of the hurricane. The woman was spectacular enough to have weather named after her. In her forties, she had pale blonde hair, eyes the color of the ocean, a starlet's body in a drop-dead, simple, russet silk suit. Yet it wasn't the woman's features or clothes that compelled attention, striking as they were. It was an extraordinary sense of power under wraps.

Power over Mulcahy. She listened to his story with a civility that seemed to incite him. When others laughed, she smiled. When others smiled, her gaze traveled. Jewel saw that Mulcahy understood the insult of this abstract cordiality. He couldn't accuse the woman of rudeness, but he couldn't captivate her, as he had the others.

He launched into another anecdote. The white-blonde russet woman attended to it vaguely.

Suddenly Jewel was aware of someone by her elbow. Tom Pearsall, watching the blonde with frightening intensity.

Mulcahy noticed him, too. He let a silence fall. Others followed his gaze.

"Melisande." Pearsall sounded half-threatening, half-proprietary. "It's time to go. Could . . ."

The remarkable woman moved from Mulcahy's side, but he gripped her arm.

"Ah, no, Tom." The Dean smiled with odd gentleness. "You mustn't steal away your lovely wife so early. I simply won't permit it."

Chapter Seven

Spectators eyeballed the unfolding drama with voyeuristic rapture.

Melisande Pearsall broke the silence. "Oh, husbands take precedence over Deans." She sounded amused, but there was a note of warning in her voice.

Mulcahy seemed too provoked by the amusement to heed the warning. "Even though I knew you first? Did you learn more from him or from me? It's hard to imagine either of us teaching you anything, even back then. Who would have guessed what that brilliant twenty-year-old would become! Ah, Ms. Benoit, you should put your expensive degrees to work. Sorry—you prefer Ms. Pearsall, don't you?"

She broke from Mulcahy's mock-affectionate grip. Her face—spectacular, impassive—bore no sign of emotion. She moved through the guests to her husband as though the room were empty. People stared at her.

When she reached Pearsall, she kept walking with a smooth, untroubled stride. There was nothing provocative about her gait, Jewel thought, but somehow her white-blonde-russet self gathered and reflected all the light in the room. Pearsall hovered a half-step behind her, speaking into her ear.

Mulcahy watched the woman move further from him. Suddenly sensing that he was observed, the Dean wrested his gaze from Melisande to Jewel. Oh no. She thrust a sliver of smoked salmon and cream cheese on rye toast at the man next to her, who waved it away. Mulcahy turned back to the crowd.

"A tragedy, isn't it?" he said with a show of genuine concern. "I hate to see our best graduates simply settling."

"I agree completely," said Lesley DeLaMar in her high, piping voice. "Too many of them fail to use their CBU degrees to advance themselves professionally. That reflects badly on us."

The remark semaphored to spectators that the drama was over. Hastily, people began forming smaller groups. A few took smoked salmon from Jewel's tray. DeLaMar edged hopefully into the space by Mulcahy's side, into the void made by Melisande Pearsall's departure. The Dean seemed preoccupied.

"Will you be discussing that in your keynote speech tonight?" Lesley pursued.

Jewel disliked the girlish wheedling in the whippet's voice. Appetizers, she told herself.

"I will indeed," nodded Mulcahy regally. "In addition to making some critical announcements about the future."

The silver tray of appetizers was empty. Eight o'clock. If Jewel didn't tear herself away from the penny-ante Zoo U backchat, she'd find Ace gone, too, or smoking dope behind the kitchen Dumpster. The locals had probably used up their day's drama ration, anyway.

Del was a genius, Jewel thought. The artfully designed salads of assorted greens glistened on their plates like carnival glass. Individual dinner salads looked elegant on a buffet table, unlike community salad bowls, with their Tupperware party aura. Too, this way she wouldn't have to run back and forth to the kitchen for new preloaded bowls. Or worse, send Ace. Del could work back there in peace.

She stood at one end of the buffet table, ready to fling around business cards with abandon. Ace stood at the other end, fidgeting in his white jacket. He kept craning his neck to look into the hallway. Jewel prayed that he was not going to bolt. She was too promising a chef to spend the rest of her life in prison for murder. Although, given Ace's role as accomplice in the mysterious disappearance of Tyler, no jury of her peers would have convicted her.

Guests began scampering up to the serving table with merry determination. Most ignored Jewel, entirely focused on snatching plates of salad, as though afraid there might not be enough for everyone. But some people smiled at her. One man wearing half-glasses even thanked her: "It's nice to see a salad without any sprouts or wildflowers. I hate picking flora out of my teeth." Jewel gently helped the mob form a line.

Lesley DeLaMar reached the head of the line fast. Her sharply-angled whippet face looked overbred. While she painstakingly examined each individual salad for, perhaps, slugs, the people behind her on line grew restive.

"Hey, Les!" shouted a huge piratical-looking man about ten people away. "Pick up the pace! Or you won't get a seat by Dean St. James Cathedral!" He yapped wildly, a deranged terrier in the body of a beer-drinker. "You'll miss your lapdog treats, Les! Hurry!" A few people laughed. Most pinched up their faces in disapproval.

Lesley maintained a martyred silence worthy of Marie Antoinette heading for the chop. She made her salad selection. Jewel couldn't tell what the chosen one had that the others didn't. D.A.R. membership, maybe. She pictured the DeLaMar family studying delicacies on an antique table, while servants were flogged outside a picture window.

"That looks nice, Lesley," said an older woman at the whippet's elbow. She selected a salad for herself without fuss. Jewel saw that her hands were shaking. Odd.

The woman—mid-fifties?—was familiar, although nondescript. She could have been anyone. Yet her purple dress and elaborately knotted orange scarf indicated an attempt at panache. Her coiffure, long and looping, marked her as a sufferer of time-warp hair. This syndrome, according to Jewel, froze hairstyles at the moment in time when the person was happiest. In this case, 1975.

The woman was staring at her. Oh no—had Jewel gotten tagged for gawking? She took a deep breath to apologize.

A smile suddenly wreathed the woman's face. "Jewel Feynmann! How delightful! I suppose you don't remember me. The last time we met you were in rather a tizzy. So *eventful,* that night." She waited expectantly.

The god of new entrepreneurs smiled on Jewel, and she remembered: this was Professor Underwood, the giddy guest from the disastrous bridal shower. The only one who took a Blue Plate business card.

"Professor Underwood," Jewel said. "How are you? I have you to thank for this job. Thank you very much. I really appreciate it."

"Do you? I'm so glad. I thought you'd be just the person. Such a splendid cake you made for my niece. *Terribly* unfortunate about your car and the various other accidents. Especially as the food was so wonderful."

"Thanks. Thank you." Jewel's gratitude dimmed somewhat at the reminder. But Professor Underwood meant well. And she did help get Blue Plate this job.

"Now what marvels have you in store for us tonight, Jewel? This salad looks lovely. Most unusual. Just lettuce and cheese, how interesting."

"It's spinach and Oregon blue cheese. I was going for simple yet elegant."

"Were you? How charming! And Dean Mulcahy said—"

"Edith Underwood!" The big buccaneer roared from down the line. "A man my size needs regular feedings! Quit dithering!" People nearby tittered or scowled.

Professor Underwood colored with some embarrassment and more irritation. "Oh—that's Leo Wallinsky. Rather a personality. He's a playwright, you know." She said it as Jewel might say: "He's an organ grinder who has sex with his monkey, who is underage, you know."

"EDITH! Zip it up! We're not your students! They're trapped! By our cretinous religion requirement! But we're faculty! We're free! Free at last, free at last! Great God Almighty!"

Two red spots appeared on Professor Underwood's cheekbones. Her hands shook so much that Jewel grew concerned for the salad. Underwood, too. What was the deal? Wallinsky was annoying, but even so, the woman seemed tense. She must, after all, be used to the man.

Underwood collected herself, adjusting her scarf and throwing back her shoulders with verve. "He means well," she said. "But it's been rather a day. So many students." Her hands retained a tremor. She smiled brilliantly at Jewel and moved on.

Never had Blue Plate catered such an agitated crew.

Speaking of agitated. Jewel prayed that Ace had calmed down. People didn't enjoy a fidgety wait staff. She glanced down the length of the serving table to check on Ace.

Ace was gone.

No, here he was, hurrying back from the hallway. He returned to his end of the serving table and picked up a tray of appetizers to offer, fixing his gaze on the middle distance.

Jewel was unappeased. Professional smile intact, she bored her eyes into the side of his head until he took a peek in her direction. "Men's room," he mouthed.

Jewel wouldn't bet on it. Something was up: one waiter vanished, the other as skittery as a spotted owl at a logging camp. Never mind. Ace couldn't have been gone more than a few minutes. She'd decide later whether to strip him of his epaulets.

The dining room looked like a dance of human magnets. Hoping to bag the best seats, guests zigzagged between tables, attracted to this one, repelled by that one. The results were comical. What Jewel liked best was the way people pretended not to be scoping out the possibilities. One man with deep shadows under his eyes stood by the serving table, dousing his salad with dressing while surreptitiously checking the house for the optimum empty seat. The guy's dressing could be measured in tonnage. Poor spinach.

Across the room, a hand waved wildly at Jewel.

A flurry of conversation came to a halt when she reached the table. The hand belonged to a rugged man in a navy V-neck sweater. He had an outdoors look to him. He also had a lapful of ice. Not that Jewel would ever look in that direction, because she never would. But everyone else was looking, so it was her job.

He was simultaneously picking the ice out, putting it on the table, and drying his lap with a napkin. "Is there a towel?" the man asked. "I spilled my water. What an oaf." His eyes were as dark as his sweater. Either he just got back from the Caribbean or he was from an un-Northwestern ethnic group.

When Jewel moved to Tacoma, she had been startled by the number of people with great-grandparents from Sweden and Germany. But there were so many of them . . . blonde and blonde. This guy could be Puerto Rican or Mexican. Jewel felt a sudden stab of homesickness. Ah, New Jersey! It was a salad bowl of people.

"I'll bring another napkin," she said to him.

"Thanks a lot. Sorry to be trouble."

"No trouble. Happens all the time." Jewel hurried to the serving table. A truly professional caterer would mop up that sodden lap herself. Like a nurse. Yeah, right. She sped back, napkin in hand, ready to serve.

A low-level skirmish appeared to be in progress between Edith Underwood and the rest of the table. Jewel handed the napkin to the dark-eyed man. He smiled his thanks and stood. Nice. She told herself to nuke the pointless free-floating fantasy. It was a work night. Weren't they all?

A rosy-cheeked man was talking. "The rumor mill says that Mulcahy had that same couch in his office down in California, ever since he was an assistant professor." He spoke with the assurance of someone with a guaranteed lifetime job. "Do you suppose it has sentimental value? Or is it his lucky couch?"

Professor Underwood's eyes snapped. "That's *completely* irresponsible, as you well know. That couch is simply for conferences with faculty committees. Surely Dean Mulcahy can keep comfortable furniture in his office without being the subject of slander." She spoke at ten decibels, as though to drown out disagreement.

A nebbishy man in glasses said: "A couch! I can't fit a wastepaper basket in my office. I have to put it out in the hall."

Underwood ignored him. "You're as bad as Leo Wallinsky's cell of student radicals, perpetuating these rumors. As a historian whose work turns on accurate interpretation of facts, Henry, you should know better."

"But Edith," said the rosy-cheeked man, "why do *you* think Mulcahy's been dogged by the same 'rumors' all these years?"

"The students titillate themselves with these rumors, knowing them to be false," Underwood said with a theatrically patient sigh, as though instructing the unteachable. "It's like telling ghost stories. But they are too cunning to make their complaints official. It's quite infamous."

A round man wearing a tie with ducks on it said: "That's not what I heard. I heard that seven members of SSH have made individual complaints. If even one of them is true—"

Everyone at the table started talking at the same time.

"Shades of Monica—"

"The Salem witch trials—"

"Patriarchal privilege—"

"Senator Packwood—"

Under cover of this cacophony, the man in the navy sweater returned the wet napkin to Jewel. "Thanks!" he whispered. "Isn't this something? This always happens when you get professors together. We're all used to being the king of the classroom."

"Or queen," she said. He laughed, harder than the small joke would warrant.

On her way back to the serving table, she glanced back. Words erupted as if from a blender on high with the lid off. The man in the sweater seemed to be having fun. Professor Underwood did not. She glared at the jolly man, the man with the ducks on his tie, everyone. Jewel could feel the heat from across the room. Underwood might look like a dormouse in peacock finery—she might even be gracious to caterers—but she would, Jewel guessed, be no one to cross.

The officious clink of silverware on a wine glass drew everyone's attention to the podium. Jewel saw with alarm that

Mulcahy was standing there, full of natural dignity and confidence. He surveyed the diners, smiling.

Jewel stood frozen by the serving table. Mulcahy had told her repeatedly that the keynote address would take place after the meal. Had he changed his mind? What about the Sunday roast, the scalloped potatoes with Gorgonzola, the maple-glazed carrots? Questions chased each other around the hamster wheel in her head, moving fast, going nowhere.

She and Ace exchanged a panicky glance. Ace looked worse than she felt, which was bad.

The noise level sank from circus to hubbub.

"Colleagues and friends," the Dean began. "Welcome to tonight's celebration. We have much to celebrate. First, however, I must tell you that there has been a slight but unavoidable delay with tonight's entree, happily provided by Blue Plate Catering."

Unavoidable delay! Blaming Blue Plate!

"I thought I might preview tonight's keynote speech about the direction of CBU with a few relevant—celebratory—announcements."

If the room had been quiet before, it was now hushed. The sudden clatter by the serving table sounded especially loud. Heads whirled around to the source of the big bang.

Ace had dropped his tray. Jewel could see why. Tyler stood in the doorway of the dining room, the hallway behind him. He looked like he wanted to howl. With anger? With grief? Jewel couldn't read his face.

Tyler kicked his way through the fallen appetizers while the faculty stared. He stopped when he saw Mulcahy at the podium.

"You!" Tyler spat at Mulcahy.

"I beg your pardon, young man," said Mulcahy calmly. "Who—"

"How can you—how can everyone—'celebrate'? You killed my girlfriend, you son-of-a-bitch, you, you—" Tyler broke off.

Ace came up behind Tyler and put his hand on his friend's shoulder. The room was as silent as a photograph, except for a small, dry coughing sound. Jewel realized that Tyler was crying.

Mulcahy spoke, his voice rich with concern. "Young man," he said. "I'm genuinely sorry for your distress. But this is hardly the time or the place. The counseling center has trained psychologists—"

"You bastard!" Tyler said.

Jewel had to agree.

Chapter Eight

Frances Carlotti, honey-brown hair streaming down her slender back, appeared at Tyler's side with the otherworldly speed of a ghost. She put her arm around Tyler, and led him, as unresisting as a tamed bear, from the dining room. Ace trailed behind them like an anxious puppy. As they passed the serving table, Jewel heard Frances murmur to Tyler: "Be patient."

The crisis settled on the Faculty Club like a cloud darkening the sun. People began whispering in the breathy way usually reserved for funerals. They eyed the Dean, waiting for him to claim the moment. Mulcahy looked out at the assemblage, no flicker of anger, contempt, or triumph marring his regal features.

"We will reconvene shortly," he said, "after I attend to that unfortunate young man. The announcements and keynote address are postponed, not canceled. Thank you."

Mulcahy strode from the podium, pausing briefly at Professor Underwood's table to consult with her. His head bent to hers, with an odd intimacy. The red spots high on Underwood's cheekbones glowed.

As the dining room whispers swirled around her, Jewel's sense of purpose splintered. She should keep her post at the serving table, offering diners a picture of professional cool to balance what could be impending disaster. Yet waiters were dropping off the edge of the earth one by one, and Mulcahy was a liar, and what about Tyler? What happened to his girlfriend? What did the Dean do? Was Tyler crazy? The boy

61

needed help. He might not win the waiter-of-the-year award—she still felt like kicking his ass for him—but he was probably kind to animals, and guys his age didn't cry in public unless they were beside themselves. Mulcahy's ominous pledge to—"attend to that unfortunate young man"—rang in her ears.

And what about Frances Carlotti? How could she help Tyler? Not too long ago the pale beauty had been lying on the hallway carpet.

The thought of Frances fainting, Tyler going to pieces, Ace hovering, and Mulcahy pouring kerosene on troubled waters, while Del struggled to slow the meal for *who knows how long,* catapulted Jewel into the hallway.

It was empty. Where—

She found them huddled in the kitchen. Tyler was leaning over at the waist, hands on his legs like an athlete after a hard race. Frances Carlotti kept a steadying hand on his back. Del looked on sadly. Ace shifted from foot to foot.

Tyler looked up at the sound of the kitchen door. His eyes were holes in his face. He had wiped away signs of tears. "I'm sorry," he said to Jewel.

Apologies always worked on Jewel, no matter how mad she'd been. "Forget it," she said, a little ashamed. "I covered for you. I still can. Are you all right?"

He didn't answer. Frances shot Jewel a look, but the meaning eluded Jewel.

"Tyler," said Jewel. "You want to sit down?"

Del brought over a kitchen stool. Tyler dropped onto it like a dead weight. Frances watched him, then moved away. Jewel couldn't read the woman's doe eyes.

"What's going on?" said Jewel.

"His lover overdosed last week." Frances's voice was low and clear.

"That's awful." So she *was* the one in the newspaper. Poor girl. Jewel felt shame for having relished the lurid articles about CBU. It wasn't just newsprint. A real person died. Someone had found her. Someone else had to call her parents. Pack up her clothes, her souvenirs and trinkets, her secrets . . .

An overdose? Jewel found it hard to match up the pristine campus and its rosy-cheeked students with overdoses. A designer drug of some kind, maybe. "Cocaine?"

"Anti-depressants. They'd been prescribed by her family doctor."

"Oh no," said Jewel. "Poor thing. Poor Tyler . . . what a terrible accident. Why—"

Frances Carlotti spoke with a quiet fury that was not for Jewel, or for the dead student, or for Tyler. "It was no accident. There's been nothing accidental about this. Nothing."

Shocked into silence, Jewel looked across the kitchen. Del was offering Tyler some slices of Sunday roast. Ace took one, like an older brother trying to show that the medicine wasn't bad.

A faint roaring reverberated from the dining room. Ace's slice of roast slipped to the floor.

"He's coming for me," Tyler said with a strange calm. He stared at the kitchen door as if willing it to open.

"No, no," Frances said. "He's afraid of you. He won't come here."

Tyler shook his head obstinately. His face was so drawn that cheekbones seemed slashed on with a pen knife.

"Jewel," said Frances with quiet command. "Could you find out—"

"I'm way ahead of you."

Leo Wallinsky roared like a dying mastodon. "Don't patronize me with your clichés, you criminal fuck!" His pirate's beard pointed at Mulcahy, who stood rigid behind Edith Underwood's chair.

"Professor Wallinsky," Mulcahy said, his voice icy with disdain. "I insist that you conduct yourself in a professional manner. If you have charges to bring, I suggest that you make them through the proper channels."

"There'll be charges, all right, and seven kinds of national publicity! You'll get your fifteen minutes of fame, you parasite, and the rest of us will send you birthday cards in prison! Ha! I'd pay money to see it!"

"Dean Mulcahy," said Lesley DeLaMar, standing up as straight as if she were lashed to a mast, "Professor Wallinsky speaks only for himself. His unbalanced views do not represent the rest of us."

Jewel gaped from the dining room doorway. Was everyone going to go round the twist, one by one?

She noticed that Tom and Melisande Pearsall hadn't yet left, despite their earlier moment.

"I support Lesley's statement *completely*." Edith Underwood had found her voice, which sounded like an indignant trumpet. "This grotesque accusation is itself criminal, Professor Wallinsky. Have you no sense of shame? Can't someone remove this man?"

The big belly philosopher rose uncertainly.

Tom Pearsall, his hawkish face gray, began to shuffle towards the pirate, who stood his ground. "Hey, Wallinsky, man, forget it. There's no point. Let's get some oxygen."

Pity snaked across Wallinsky's face as he glanced at Pearsall.

Mulcahy commandeered the moment. "I imagine that Professor Wallinsky's grievance is less heroic than it is personal. If you have a complaint about the award of the Westerfield Grant, please take it up elsewhere."

Jewel watched Wallinsky, who had half-subsided, explode into fireworks again.

"Smoke and mirrors, you magic lantern full of pus! Members of SSH are ready to bring their charges! Don't forget to bring a toothbrush to court, because you're not going home from there!"

"Leo," said an older woman at a table close to him. "Bring it to the Judicial Committee. This isn't the—"

"No committee!" he said, sweeping his arm in a swashbuckling gesture. "He's got you all buffaloed!"

No one spoke up for the Judicial Committee, for Mulcahy, or for Wallinsky. A sense of exhausted confusion hung in the air.

Wallinsky surveyed the room with sudden amusement. "Are we tired after our excitement?" he said in a nursery voice. Then his mood changed again, contempt searing his features like a brand. He was the most volatile man Jewel had ever seen fully clothed. He swaggered away from his table and draped an arm over Pearsall's sunken shoulders. "You're right, Tom. Let's bust out of this pukehole."

Jewel swung back to the hallway when a choking sound arrested her.

Mulcahy. He had returned to the podium to wrest the evening back from Wallinsky.

Mulcahy convulsed over the podium, clutching at his stomach.

Someone screamed. Someone else shouted, "Christ! He's having a heart attack!" Jewel froze.

"Get a doctor!" cried the older woman, looking around wildly.

Wallinsky and Pearsall, stupefied in the center of the room, stared at the Dean.

"I'll call nine-one-one," the rugged man in the dark

65

sweater threw over his shoulder as he ran from the dining room.

Few people watched him. Most were transfixed by Mulcahy.

He slid down the podium, grabbing it like a lifeboat, his stamped-on-a-coin face slick with fever sweat.

Jewel broke from the doorway. Mulcahy fell to the ground before she reached him.

His arms and legs jerked convulsively. One of his wing-tips kicked at Jewel's shin so hard that tears came to her eyes. He made heaving noises. Nothing came up.

An elderly man was by Jewel's side, kneeling. "Loosen his tie." She obeyed as if hypnotized.

Mulcahy thrashed beneath her hands. His skull hit the floor with a sick thud. She grabbed a cloth napkin to cushion beneath his head, but he wouldn't—couldn't—keep still.

The elderly man reached into Mulcahy's mouth. Jewel cried out in protest, then realized he was feeling for an obstruction, food to dislodge.

Mulcahy turned his head towards them. His pupils were dilated. His legs jerked convulsively.

The room had become absolutely quiet. There wasn't even breathing. The only sound was Mulcahy's strangely high-pitched moan. The sound of a wounded animal with his foot half-severed in a trap.

The Dean no longer clutched his stomach. He could not control his arms.

His leonine head jerked away, then back. His hair shone obscenely against the oak floor like fool's gold.

"Coming through, please." Two good-sized men pushed through the crowd. The fortyish black man with a mustache carried a black bag. The white man, younger, had a face as flat and round as a pancake. He hefted an oxygen tank.

"Excuse me, miss," said the older man.

Jewel stepped aside. She was relieved to tears that medical help was there at last.

The man in the navy sweater who had summoned the aid stood breathless a distance away. He couldn't have been gone more than ten minutes—calling 911 and directing the medics to the dining room—but it seemed like years. She felt sick.

The medics checked Mulcahy's condition. The older man muttered something to the elderly faculty member as he pulled a syringe from his bag.

"Please, everyone," announced the elderly man unsteadily. "He says to leave. There are too many people. Everyone has to leave right now."

The faculty members, bewildered and stunned, began to move for the door. Jewel moved with them, turning automatically for the kitchen. Some people followed her. Others loitered uncertainly in the hallway. The older woman was lighting up a cigarette, Jewel noted irrelevantly.

Frances met her at the double doors to the kitchen. "I already know," she said.

"How—" Jewel began. An acrid smell from the ovens assailed her.

The older medic came into the hallway, moving as though his bones hurt. His medical bag dangled from his arm.

"Should we call a doctor?" asked someone.

"No need." He snapped the bag shut like a tomb. "He's dead."

Chapter Nine

The medic looked from face to face. "Did he have any family?"

A ghastly pause fell on the hallway crowd, as though some complex *faux pas* had been committed.

The elderly man who had tried to help Mulcahy fumbled with his spectacles. "I—I'm not sure."

Leaning against the corridor wall, Leo Wallinsky, outsized and unabashed, made a noise in his throat. Not a laugh, surely. But it sounded like a laugh. His eyes danced with pleasure. Several shock-bedraggled professors shot appalled glances at Wallinsky. He stared down at them until they looked away.

Still no one spoke.

The aid unit man returned his gaze to the elderly professor for a moment, not unkindly. "You've had a shock. Step outside the building for some air. I'll see how you're feeling on my way out." He put a guiding hand on the man's back, and gave him a gentle shove.

People parted to make a path. Their colleague walked through them and out the front door without looking back.

The medic turned back to the crowd of onlookers. His dark eyes were tired. "Next of kin? Anyone here know?"

The older woman blew out a cloud of cigarette smoke. "He wasn't married. But I had heard—"

A banshee wail almost lifted Jewel out of her shoes. People spun towards the sound. Jewel felt her own head jerk around like a marionette's.

Edith Underwood. She wailed as though she were alone in a forest. Her skin was mottled with tears. Her festive clothing looked grotesque, sucking the color from her face.

"No!" Underwood hit at her eyes with fists. "No, no, no, no!"

The people around her looked painfully embarrassed in the face of naked grief. Grief? Jewel waited for someone Underwood knew to comfort her, but the professors acted paralyzed, helpless.

Finally Tom Pearsall put a tentative hand on Underwood's shoulder. There was real sympathy in his eyes. "Edith." He patted her as though she were a frightened dog. "Take it easy."

She beat at her eyes and wailed as though Pearsall didn't exist. Jewel had never seen anything like it.

"There's a brother in San Diego," said Melisande Pearsall from nowhere. Her face was half-hidden by the chic curtain of white-blonde hair.

The medic nodded once. "Someone should let him know."

"I'll call," said Melisande. She turned for the front door.

"Why bother?" Tom Pearsall blocked her path. He spoke with new authority. "The bastard wasn't worth it. Not on the best day of his life."

Melisande nodded, less in agreement than in decision. The husband and wife withdrew together to the far end of the hallway.

Another silence fell like an anvil. People were stupid with shock. A few stared fearfully at the doorway to the dining room, although Mulcahy and the young flat-faced medic couldn't be seen from there. The crowd seemed to be waiting for the Dean to rise from the dead and tell people what to do.

Jewel felt claustrophobic, huddled among the professors

who were all strangers. Also confused. She couldn't concentrate on what was happening. She kept seeing Mulcahy dying. He had clutched at his stomach. His legs had convulsed. He couldn't control them. The sweat on that patrician brow. Like he was on fire with fever.

No wonder Edith Underwood had covered her eyes. The Dean had died in agony.

Jewel knew she should get back to the kitchen, where her dinner was charring. Poor Del. But she couldn't make her feet move. It wasn't as though anyone were going to eat the beautiful Sunday roast now.

And, to be honest, she didn't want to miss anything. Awful as Mulcahy's death was, she felt no grief or loss. She had barely known him, and that for less than a week. To be painfully honest, she hadn't liked what little she knew. To be shamefully honest, her breathing was almost back to normal. She didn't even feel sick anymore.

Jewel struggled to sort out her thoughts as the medic went into a huddle with the smoker. What could the other aid unit guy be doing in there? With Mulcahy. Who was dead.

Impossible. The Dean shouldn't have died. That's what she thought. Shock and fog were one thing. This was another. It made no sense. Mulcahy didn't seem like the type to peg out suddenly in high middle-age. Pearsall, the drinker and brooder, was that kind of guy, a born statistic. Or maybe even Wallinsky, one of those big, unrepentant french-fry-eating types, a guy in the code-red danger zone between thirty and fifty. Not Mulcahy.

The Dean was a survivor, bursting with rude health. The kind of person who played squash at dawn, when normal people were still dreaming about coffee. Who held business meetings while jogging, in order to keep his college weight and to humiliate the sedentary. The leader of the pack.

Even alpha dogs die eventually, Jewel reminded herself. But of old age, she answered herself back.

All this standing around stunned was wearing her down. Time to go back to the kitchen, check on the troops. If Tyler was okay, she'd send them all home . . .

"All right." The medic's voice, thick with fatigue and impatience, broke into Jewel's reverie. "This lady will call the Dean's brother in San Diego." The older woman walked down the hallway and out the front door, cigarette smoke trailing behind her.

"You," the medic pointed to the dark sweater who had called 911. "Call the police."

Amidst the gleaming surfaces of the Faculty Club kitchen, a wake of sorts was already in progress. Del bowed his head over the Sunday roast.

Jewel studied the meat with uncharacteristic detachment. It was dry and unforgiving. Yet the deep brown crackling of the surface told her that the succulent moment of perfection was a page of recent, not ancient, history. The roast was edible. Good. Wasting food was an abomination.

Then a thought struck her. "So, Del? What was burning?"

He shrugged slightly. "Beats me. Nothing spilled from the roasting pan into the ovens. It's funny."

"Ha ha?"

"Peculiar. You know. I always spoon out the excess. No way was there so much it would spill over." His voice was soft but adamant.

"Huh," Jewel said.

Del was a kitchen genius. Nothing had ever burned under his careful eye. On the other hand, he hadn't worked a three-ring circus before, either. On the third hand, he would never lie and say he had eyeballed the roast the whole time when he hadn't. Del wouldn't even lie to save someone's feelings. ("Oh gosh," he had once said to a friend in an ugly new shirt. "Is that color called puce?")

She peered inside the oven. No spillage. She poked around the pan.

Something was charred in the gravy. Not meat, not food. It looked like a scrap of paper.

Impossible. Pigs would fly before a grocery receipt would get into the oven without her spotting it on the way. This wasn't happening. Oh, to hell with it. She was suddenly tired. Her brain began shutting down, cell by cell.

"What's happening out there?" Ace asked apprehensively. He was sitting on the counter near the refrigerator. He sounded very young.

Jewel wrested her mind back to the program already in progress. "They're trying to find out the Dean's medical history. And waiting for the police."

Tyler, quiescent on a kitchen stool, leaped up like a galvanized frog leg. "Police!"

Jewel said, "Tyler, they always—"

"I'm gone." He hurled an unseeing look her way, then sprinted through the kitchen doors into the hallway.

"They always call the police for a sudden-death type of deal," said Del to the swinging double door.

"I got to go after him." Ace bounded off the counter. "He might do something stupid."

"Something *else* stupid?" Jewel said. "Is there prize money for stupid tonight?"

But Ace had fled, all arms and legs. She had a mental Polaroid of Mulcahy, flailing on the dining room floor.

She dropped heavily onto the stool Tyler had abandoned.

Jewel thought of pursuit. Of pulling Tyler and Ace back to the kitchen by their ears. But what for? She didn't need waiters anymore. Blue Plate Catering could clean up and pack up faster without the help of amateurs. And Tyler had already had a rough time. His girlfriend dead. Mulcahy. What was that about? He shouldn't have been working right after the woman's death. Although maybe he had to work to cut the grief. He needed the money, Ace had said.

"Gemini," said Del clinically. "They have mercurial temperaments. Big trouble keeping their feet on the ground."

"Del. Don't start." She pushed her hair off her face. "How could you possibly know Tyler's birth sign? Don't tell me you 'just knew.' I'll bite your nose off. Seriously."

"I asked him."

Jewel wanted to laugh. Giddiness from shock and stress. "We'd better pack up." She began ladling the carrots from their serving dishes back to baking pans.

Del found a spatula. He shoveled pie slices into the pie tins. "Second Harvest will take these pies. The roast, too. We can drop them off tonight. I have a key." Del volunteered at the food bank as well as the needle exchange and the children's hospital.

"Swell."

They worked in silence for a few moments.

"Where's the fainter?" asked Jewel idly.

"Frances had to make a phone call."

"Huh."

"She's really not weak," said Del, covering the filled pie tins in plastic wrap. "Virgos aren't. But their wills are stronger than their bodies."

"Del," said Jewel warningly.

At the door, someone cleared his throat. Jewel jumped, splattering the maple-glazed carrot juice onto her pumpkin sweater.

73

The pancake-faced guy from the aid unit. Standing behind him was a uniformed cop. The cop, fair-haired with a husky dog's light eyes, looked like he hadn't smiled since a Kennedy assassination.

"This is her," said the medic, ominously, Jewel thought. He left.

"Blue Plate Catering?" The officer squinted at each of them, trying to find the boss.

"That's us. I'm Jewel Feynmann. This is Del Troutman."

"You're the whole outfit?"

"We had waiters," said Jewel. "A couple students."

The officer waited.

"They left," Jewel said.

"No one was supposed to leave," he said, reaching for a small back-pocket notebook.

"No one told us to stay," she said, suddenly belligerent, hands on hips. "No one told us anything."

"What are their names?" said the cop, as though she hadn't spoken. "Why didn't they stay?"

Jewel wanted to lie down on the floor and go to sleep. But she needed to tell someone about that e-mail.

"Also," he studied the notebook, "I need to know exactly what you served tonight."

That woke her.

By midnight, Jewel was home in bed, under two quilts, a mug of hot chocolate with tiny marshmallows balanced on her chest. She wanted to call Daph in Hoboken. But it was three A.M. there. Jewel didn't have the heart to wake her cousin. It's not like Mulcahy was family—or friend, either.

The remains of a sizable buttermilk waffle topped with strawberries decorated a plate on the floor. There were late nights in a woman's life when only breakfast food would do. This, by God, was one of them.

The phone rang, causing Jewel to fling hot chocolate all over her chest.

If this was a wrong number—if this was an obscene phone call—she wiped the chocolate on her pajamas and prepared for battle.

"It's Helena. I called to see how you were."

"Oh." Jewel adjusted. Helena sounded warm and concerned. "Thank you. I'm all right."

"Is that so?"

"No, of course not. The police took the leftover appetizers and salads to their lab. To see if Mulcahy died from bad food. They carried away the salads in *plastic bags*." The memory of the imprisoned food agitated Jewel.

"I expect," said Helena judiciously, "that they're advised against carrying evidence in their mouths."

"Evidence of what? Why'd they have to carry it off at all? Nothing was wrong with any of it."

"They're investigating everything and everyone." Jewel heard a buzzing sound rise and fall. "They still have about six people over at the Faculty Club, answering questions." The noise again, rising and falling.

"Do you hear that? A buzzing noise?"

Helena laughed quietly. "My sewing machine. Beadwork is more restful, but I'm upstairs and the beads are downstairs and I am *not* moving . . . but I have to do something."

Jewel considered her chocolate-stained chest and pj's, the very picture of a selfish pig. "Helena, I'm a selfish pig. I'm sorry. This has got to be terrible for you. I didn't even know the man."

The buzz again. Then Helena eased up on the pedal. The

75

air was so quiet that Jewel thought Helena had hung up. But then she spoke.

"I knew the man. If he can make trouble from beyond the grave, he will."

Hours before dawn, Jewel padded downstairs to check Blue Plate's Web site and e-mail. Despite a whale-sized dose of hot chocolate and waffles, she couldn't sleep.

The teal and peach colors that Del had picked for the site came up on the screen.

Jewel had told the policeman about the e-mail message from "Death-in-Life." The man's blond eyebrows went up. He asked a lot of questions and wrote down her answers ("No," "I don't know," "Beats me," "I never met any of them until a week ago."). Now she was half-hoping that she'd dreamed it all, that the last message in the e-mail in-box was from a woman wanting to know about chicken pot pie.

"You've got mail."

As she stared at the cheery mailbox icon, Jewel got cold fast, even in yellow flannel pj's and robe, even in wool socks and clogs. She made herself open the in-box.

A new message awaited her from "Death-in-Life." Underneath the old one:

Why didn't you listen to me? You should have listened to me. He didn't listen and now it's too late. I'm sorry.

Chapter Ten

The next morning, Jewel rose, showered, dressed, and staggered into the wintry dark. She fell into the Duster, which, a moment later, roared into life.

Inside her store, Jewel whipped the funnel-cake batter like she meant business. And she did. She'd just never meant it so early in the day. The wall clock said five-fifty.

Outside Blue Plate's storefront, Pacific Avenue was as black as a lost planet.

After shutting down the computer a few hours earlier, Jewel had read in bed (a biography of Oprah) until an hour or so ago. Oprah's life story, even in its worst moments, was calming, because Jewel knew that Oprah emerged safe, rich, powerful, and muscular. Jewel just didn't feel like calling the police to talk about e-mail until she was up and dressed. She'd had enough for the night.

Work was the answer, she thought, looking with satisfaction around Blue Plate. The space was warm from the heater and the grills. The refrigerators hummed. Cinnamon and nutmeg from the funnel-cake batter filled the air. Coffee steamed from a pan, where she'd drained the ground beans through a thin cotton napkin. An Italian coffeemaker stood imperiously on the counter, but sometimes the simple ways were best.

Work was simple. She beat the batter with renewed vigor. If you worked hard, there was always a payoff. You became a better cook. You got smarter in business. And you massaged and kneaded and pummeled problems until they got small enough to put in a bread pan. Then you cooked them.

Today's problem, besides too little sleep, was how to bounce back from a threatening e-mail correspondent and a nightmarish dinner that ended in a man's grotesque and terrible death, with the whole dinner left over. The Dean's death throes haunted her. He was the person who kept returning to her head this morning.

That wouldn't do. Jewel had her own ghosts. There was no room for new ones. She dropped a dot of oil on the grill. It sizzled.

She poured the batter in a slender stream that landed in the shape of a pretzel. The batter hardened into cake under her gaze. She flipped it over.

Work kept new ghosts out and old ghosts at bay. She never heard the rat when she was working. Coincidence, maybe. A glance in the rearview mirror had given Jewel a glimpse of corkscrewy dark red hair and Samsonite under her eyes, but baking refreshed her. She flipped the cake from the griddle onto her plate. A little confectionery sugar on top.

The funnel cake was almost right. Light, crunchy, hot. But it tasted a little too much like a funny biscuit. Scrambling for vanilla in the cabinet by the refrigerator, Jewel concentrated. What happened the night before didn't make sense. She didn't know anyone or anything about Zoo U. Why was she singled out to get bad e-mail? Who was she? Also, Mulcahy hadn't looked like a man with a condition, although some ailments were invisible to the naked eye. But it wasn't just that. He took up a lot of space at Zoo U. His death left not just the usual void but a king-sized vortex. Even in Jewel's sense of the place, limited as it was.

She poured out a new, vanilla-enhanced funnel cake.

She needed more coffee.

Mulcahy. He seemed like a big guy, but wasn't, really. Hadn't been. Somehow, though, he'd had the aura of celebrity that made certain people act stupid around him.

The dark began fading into gray. A few people scuttled down the sidewalk, on their way to work, or the First Gospel Mission. You couldn't always tell.

Jewel decided to give away some funnel cakes to passersby. If they liked them, and they passed Blue Plate every day, maybe they'd come back for a bigger bite. She didn't run a deli, but food was food. Who knew what would happen with these next Zoo U dinners? Maybe they'd be canceled, now that the Dean was dead. She'd check. No one wanted to be ghoulish, or foolhardy, but the living must go on and pay rent on their storefronts.

Another few people, wrapped warm against the dank and wintry morning, hurried by the window.

Jewel poured eight funnel cakes onto the grill. A great hissing noise rose into the steam. The cakes began to pop with air bubbles.

Someone tapped on the door.

She yelped.

A man stood outside. He ducked his head a little, apologetic.

Jewel came out from behind the counter. The man held an ID up to the glass. Government, badge, photo that looked like him.

She trusted her instincts, except in romance, and let him in.

"Sorry to startle you." He was a middle-sized man in his forties, wearing a weather-beaten brown wool jacket.

"That's okay." She slid her eyes to the wall clock. Not even seven yet.

"It's too early, but I saw your light on." He unzipped his jacket a little in the heat of the kitchen.

"I'm not really open. You're just lucky. Hang on."

She turned back to the grill, where the cakes were almost at the point of no return. She flipped them in the order she'd poured them.

When she'd turned back to the counter, the man stopped watching the grill and met her gaze directly. He had chocolate brown eyes. A watcher, this guy, like he was studying up on cooking. Maybe he was a spy from Winterset's on Proctor. Industrial espionage, she should be so lucky.

"Are you Norwegian?" he asked.

"Are you kidding?"

"Those look like *krunkaka*."

"Like what? These are funnel cakes. What's krun—?"

"*Krunkaka*. A Norwegian funnel cake, I guess." He smiled a little. "My grandmother made them on Christmas morning. She'd fold them up into cones and put whipped cream inside."

"A cone, that's interesting." She kept one eye on the grill. "I don't do Christmas, but that's a great idea." She flipped the cakes into a stack on a big plate. "Am I Norwegian, come on."

"Well, you were making *krunkaka*."

Jewel took a closer look. He was built solid. His hair was halfway between receding and history. The little left was brown and short. Somehow it made him look intelligent and self-possessed, like he didn't care that he was within spitting distance of bald. He looked like he knew how to rewire a lamp.

"Try one." Jewel put the plate on the front counter and sprinkled confectionery sugar over the top of the first cake. He took a bite. She waited.

"Oh man," he said. "This is great."

She groped for a pen and paper under the counter. "Could you spell that cake name?"

80

"Just the way it sounds, all k's. Did you put vanilla in this?"

Her pen stopped mid-scribble. She looked up into his face, with its strong mouth and Hershey's eyes. Her eyebrows shot to her hairline. "Just barely. How could you taste that?"

"Like you said, I'm lucky." He worked his way through the cake in a fast and tidy fashion. "That was the real thing."

"What are you, a caterer? Picking out vanilla like that? What's with the badge?"

His eyes darkened slightly. "I'm a policeman. Detective Ben Hartsock. You're Jewel Feynmann?" He pronounced it correctly, to rhyme with "wine."

Her heart sank, then, unaccountably, soared. He was probably here about those traffic tickets. "Officer," she said almost joyfully. "Those parking tickets? I can explain—"

"No." His chocolate eyes remained watchful. "I'm here to ask you a few questions about the dinner last night at the university." He continued to study her.

"Oh, terrific. Oh, peachy. There's nothing I'd like better than talking about last night's disaster, all day long. But you know, I answered a bunch of questions from a policeman last night."

"He wasn't a detective from Robbery and Homicide."

Her eyes widened. "Mulcahy was murdered?"

"There's a chance it was an accident. We're checking every possibility. I have some questions."

She cursed herself for thinking the long night had ended.

Hartsock pulled a pad from his back pocket and opened it onto the counter. He studied his notes for a moment, with an air of quiet concentration. "Roast, potatoes, carrots, rhubarb pie, salad, appetizers."

Jewel leaned over the counter from the other side, trying to read his notes upside down. "He didn't eat half that stuff. No one did. We only got a chance to serve the appetizers and salads before he died. And there was nothing wrong with any of it."

Hartsock's eyes met hers steadily. "We haven't got a lab report yet. But it seems possible he was poisoned by something he ate at the dinner."

An imaginary band of steel tightened around Jewel's skull. It felt like every headache she ever had all at once. "Officer, Mister, listen."

"Detective Hartsock. What I want to know is where and when you bought the ingredients for the salad."

"Poisoned salad?" Her mind was a runaway truck. "That doesn't make sense. Greens don't do botulism or anything. They just go limp."

"Is it Miss, Mrs., or Ms.?" he asked mildly.

"The salad? It's totally neuter," she said, her voice careening up about an octave.

"What to call you," he said. He sounded like a dog-trainer who wanted to calm some lunatic poodle. He remained watchful, his face suspiciously unjudgmental. Jewel realized she'd better jack down. The man—Hartsock?—didn't appear to be ready to drag out the handcuffs. Mulcahy, murdered. Or, she amended, killed accidentally. If someone poisoned Mulcahy, accidentally or not, of course the police needed to know about it. Plus she didn't want this vanilla-tasting guy to think she was a moron. He didn't seem to be a moron.

"I'm sorry." She ran her hand through her hair. "Ms. Feynmann is fine."

"Ms. Feynmann, did you know Matthew Mulcahy before taking the job at CBU?"

"No."

"Did you get to know him well in the week you worked for the university?"

82

"No, I only spoke to him a few times."

"Then you'd have no reason to kill him unless you were crazy, would you?"

"I'm not crazy."

"You're not sending yourself threatening e-mails, are you?"

"Of course not," Jewel said, in a huff.

He smiled briefly, too quickly for Jewel to tell if he was patronizing her. He waited.

She got the point. "So I get salad stuff down at the Muller's Market on Twelfth. It was only spinach."

"Parsnips?"

"No, I don't like them with greens. They're too bitter. They tend to dominate."

"Can't have that." He looked at her without expression.

She narrowed her eyes. Was this some sort of police joke? She wasn't going to bite. "Why do you ask about parsnips?"

"How long's this—" he glanced down at his notes "—Del Troutman worked for you?"

"Del! But he's—"

"Ms. Feynmann? I just want to find out what happened." His tone was mild, his gaze unblinking.

She regrouped. "Del's worked part-time for eight months. He also works over at Mary Bridge and at the needle exchange near the Mission. He seems ditzy, but he's not. He's careful. He doesn't buy the ingredients, I do."

"Your student waiters, um—" he consulted his pad "—Tyler Seito and Bill Birney?"

"No Bill. Oh, is that Ace's real name? Yeah, Tyler and Ace."

"They were in the kitchen while the salads were prepared?"

She felt a sudden stab of concern for Tyler, the geek. "No, they arrived afterwards."

"But they were in the kitchen with the prepared salads?"

"Yes, but—look, did anyone else get hurt? No one else did but Mulcahy?"

He waited.

"I'm sorry, it's just that there's no way anyone could know who'd get what salad. It was a buffet, not place settings. Any guest could pick any salad."

Hartsock took a few notes, then read back what he'd written—"Muller, Troutman, parsnips, buffet"—and folded the pad into his pocket. "That's it for now. Thanks. I'll get back to you after I check out what you've told me."

"Not so fast." She sighed. "I got another e-mail."

"When?"

"It was sent around three A.M. I opened it maybe an hour after that."

He pulled his pad back out from his pocket.

Her face was hot with fatigue and fear. "What do you mean you'll get back to me after you check out what I told you? What's to check? I told you there was nothing wrong with anything I bought, and greens—"

Hartsock unzipped his jacket. "We rushed the lab and got a preliminary report. Odds are good Mulcahy died from ingesting poison, in a plant that would have resembled wild parsnips." He met Jewel's eyes. "I check around to find out if he died through Blue Plate's criminal neglect—"

Her snarl did not stop the flow of his quiet voice.

"Or he died because someone committed first-degree homicide. You say you didn't use parsnip, you don't know how it got there. Fine. If your answers check out, I move on."

She began to protest again. He cut her off again, politely and firmly. "You saw him die?"

84

The wind wilted in her sails. "Yeah, I did. It was terrible. You think someone did that on purpose?"

"More terrible than waiting for me to ask a few questions at Muller's?"

A pause fell like a block of ice.

"This is a police investigation. You can see that your word isn't good enough. Nobody's word is. Now tell me about this new e-mail."

Much later, Hartsock made for the door. He opened it and turned back. "Thanks for your time. Thanks for the funnel cake, too. You have powdered sugar in your hair." The door swung shut behind him.

Jewel stood behind the counter, immobile.

Automatically, she touched one of the funnel cakes on the plate by her elbow. It was as cold as death.

Criminal neglect, criminal neglect. The phrase echoed like a sadistic nursery rhyme in Jewel's head as she parked the cherry-red Duster near Darmon Hall. E-mails scrolled down her brain: *"Save yourself." "I'm sorry."* Who was writing this stuff? Favoring rage over fear, Jewel veered back to Hartsock. That damned cop. That Hartsock. She thought of many cutting things to retort in the hour after he'd left Blue Plate, but she couldn't get his little lecture out of her head.

To hell with him. She hadn't meant to suggest that her word was the Ten Commandments. Okay, she had, but she hadn't meant to get nailed for it. How repulsive for him to be right in that mild, clear-headed way.

After shaking the sugar out of her hair—Christ! she'd looked like KoKo the Clown—she gave away the icy funnel cakes to stunned passersby and made a batch of biscuits to hawk in office buildings at midmorning. Then she decided to return to the university. Maybe she could find out about the next dinners. And she was curious, in a sick sort of way, about Zoo U's morning after.

She loaded a sack of biscuits, because you never knew, clicked on the answering machine, stopped home to change clothes, and hightailed it for campus.

High noon and Darmon Hall was moribund. No bird-chattering students, no fighting faculty members, no rebels chained to the flagpole.

Inside the Gothic building, Jewel hesitated. This was a bad idea. She couldn't go to the Dean's office. What would she say to Muriel? Jewel's concerns about future dinners were petty and her curiosity worse. At least she could give Muriel the biscuits.

Jewel halted in the hallway outside the Dean's Office. The door was closed. Women's voices came from Muriel's ante-room. One, a brook-like murmur, was too low to hear. It murmured in a tone of timid protest.

The other was high-pitched and bore no protest. "No, take them to recycling, Muriel," said the woman, with the command of a born general. "I certainly won't be needing his personalized letterhead stationery."

The door swung open. Muriel emerged as if propelled by a boot in her butt, listing under the weight of several brown stationery boxes. Her eyes were red-rimmed. She swept past Jewel unseeingly.

"Er, I made—" Jewel extended the bag of biscuits towards Muriel's back. The older woman seemed not to hear, almost trotting down the hallway. She was wearing a dark blue print dress. Jewel thought it was probably as close to black as she owned.

"What's this?" The general's voice came from behind Jewel. She turned to face Lesley DeLaMar.

The French professor, greyhound-sleek, was quietly re-

86

splendent in a narrow gray suit, matching hose, and white blouse. She looked too big for Muriel's outer office, although she was only middle-sized. Her straight, brown hair was twisted back into an elegant knot. Diamond studs glittered from her ears. Jewel was glad she herself had changed out of her rumpled clothes into narrow, brown pants and a fitted 1940s jacket.

But even in all DeLaMar's dress-for-excess splendor, it was her expression that hit Jewel hardest. Her narrow features—thin mouth, patrician nose—were flushed with something other than Estee Lauder.

DeLaMar's perfect brows raised inquiringly.

"May I be of assistance?" She gave Jewel a smile that seemed intended to be friendly. It looked like a baring of incisors. The woman extended her slender hand. Another diamond glittered there, like an evil eye. She doesn't remember me, Jewel thought.

"I am Acting Dean DeLaMar."

Chapter Eleven

Jewel's hand was grasped so firmly in DeLaMar's cool, dry grip that she almost yipped in pain. Jewel liked a woman with a real handshake, but this was ridiculous. "Hello, Dean DeLaMar. Jewel Feynmann. We met last night."

Lesley DeLaMar released her, smiling in disapproval and annoyance.

"Of course," she said. "The caterer. Please come in." She turned her narrow-shouldered gray silk back in Jewel's face and strode past Muriel's desk to the reception area outside the Dean's inner sanctum. With a gesture more military than graceful, DeLaMar ushered Jewel to one of the forest-green wing chairs, intended no doubt for wealthy parents and alums.

Yellow police tape blocked the doorway to the inner sanctum. The door was open, though. Jewel's eye was snagged by a long couch against the south wall, in a burgundy brocade of painful good taste. "He's got a couch in his office." Who said that last night? She wrested her gaze away.

An open packing box sat on the floor outside the sealed door: "Mulcahy's Effects." Barred from the throne room itself, DeLaMar had apparently contented herself with packing the framed outer-office photographs of her predecessor. Business as usual. No grass growing under those slender suede pumps.

Queasy, Jewel took the armchair indicated by DeLaMar's open palm. The Acting Dean lowered herself into the other wing chair. She leaned back and crossed her legs. Sitting outside her new office seemed to relax her.

"You understand, Ms. Feynmann, that you find us in sad disarray this morning."

Was this an apology or a rebuke? "Sure, of course. I'm very sorry about Dean Mulcahy's death. It was terrible."

DeLaMar nodded her neat head in acceptance. "Yes, certainly. A very tragic accident. Shocking for all of us. And a great loss to the university community."

"Yes."

"He was in the prime of his academic career. He was only fifty-two, you know."

"No, I didn't."

"It would have been years before he retired. In the academy," DeLaMar explained graciously, "people need not retire at age sixty-five, if they remain hale and capable. Dean Mulcahy had many years to contribute to the university, perhaps as many as twenty years. A tragic loss."

Jewel felt a rush of sympathy for the dead man. Unpleasant though he had been in life, he should have lived longer. She felt sorry for anyone whose life was only a job, even a high-paying fancy-pants job like this one. But maybe that was only DeLaMar's take on him. Mulcahy's life might have meant more to him than that.

Leaning back in the wing chair, DeLaMar looked years younger than Mulcahy. She said all the right things about tragic loss. Quick learner. But the words barely hid her triumphal ease outside his office. Hers now. She hadn't wasted any time hanging up her shingle.

Jewel wondered when she could work this peculiar conversation around to Blue Plate's dinners.

"Tragic," she echoed. "And tough on you, huh? Moving in so quick?"

DeLaMar inclined her head again, as if accepting a clumsy compliment. "It was my responsibility, and I accepted it. I was of course astonished to receive the phone call from the Board of Trustees first thing this morning."

"I bet. May I ask, did—"

"They expressed gratitude. Of course I was happy to serve CBU in any capacity."

Too weird. Jewel didn't give a shit about the Board of Trustees. DeLaMar was actually chatty, she of the snooty asides and manicured talons. Last night she'd considered "the caterer" beneath notice.

Suddenly Jewel realized that she was one of the Acting Dean's first guests. That was it. DeLaMar so relished her spanking new job that she'd even b.s. with a caterer to wallow in it. Jewel's curiosity was getting the better of her.

"So were you in line for the job already?"

"There is no 'line' for a Dean's job per se. Especially one as far from retirement as Dean Mulcahy had been. When appropriate, there are always a number of candidates for the Board of Trustees and the President to consider."

"Oh."

"The President is fundraising in Silicon Valley, but he phoned very early this morning to express his complete confidence in me."

Suddenly DeLaMar tired of practicing Dean backchat on a food person. She sat forward, posture-perfect. "Thank you for your condolences at this time. Was there anything else?"

"Yes, there is. Muriel had said something about future dinners to cater, and I wondered—"

"I see. Yes, there are two more university dinners to arrange. You understand, I'm sure, that it is out of the question for us to rehire your firm at this point."

90

Jewel counted to three. "No, Dean DeLaMar, I guess I don't."

"Don't you? I suppose not, given your lack of familiarity with university life. The police were here this morning to interview me at length. They implied that Dean Mulcahy died as a result of something he—ingested—at last night's dinner."

Jewel counted to five. "His death had nothing to do with Blue Plate Catering. Our—"

"Perhaps not," conceded DeLaMar. "The police did not suggest that your firm bore responsibility for the tragic incident. Obviously, however, we cannot rehire Blue Plate. It would be a public relations disaster. As it is, the local press—" she permitted a sneer "—has been grossly inconsiderate, calling Board of Trustee members all morning with completely inappropriate questions. Were they to learn that we rehired the same firm that catered the dinner at which the Dean was poisoned . . ."

Her cultured soprano voice trailed off.

Jewel stopped counting. "Dean DeLaMar, I understand that CBU doesn't want any more bad publicity."

Lesley DeLaMar's face hardened.

"But my business depends on word of mouth, and if—"

The Acting Dean checked her watch.

Jewel started over. "Look, if you had evidence that Blue Plate had nothing to do with Mulcahy's murder, would you—"

"His *death*," snapped DeLaMar. She regained control instantly and appeared to consider Jewel's suggestion. "I do take your point. You would like the opportunity to prove your 'innocence.' " She paused.

"If you wish to return to my office with 'evidence,' I will reconsider my decision." DeLaMar smiled, as though indulging a billionaire aunt's deathbed longing for Disneyland. "Needless to say, I will decide at that time whether the 'evidence' is sufficient."

She rose.

Jewel counted the number of times she would like to slap the Acting Dean back to grade school. She rose, too, gagging on the words she couldn't say. Blue Plate was too important to risk in a few impulsive home truths.

"Thank you, Dean DeLaMar."

The Dean had already turned back to the packing box, smooth head bent over the pitiful "effects." She reached up to the wall to pull down another memento. Her hands were claws. Vulture, Jewel thought. DeLaMar looked back. For a terrible moment, Jewel was afraid she had said the word aloud.

"If you see Muriel in the hallway, Ms. Feynmann, would you be so kind as to send her back?" She returned to her work without waiting for a reply.

On the way out of the office, Jewel had a mental flash of Mulcahy's oversized couch, blood-red in the weak midday light.

Muriel stood, sunken-shouldered, in the hallway. She seemed lost.

"Muriel," said Jewel.

The grandmotherly woman gave Jewel a vacant look. Then her gaze cleared. "Oh, Miss Feynmann."

"It's Jewel." She held out the little white bag. "These are for you. Sourdough biscuits. I'm sorry for your trouble."

"Thank you, dear. That's so thoughtful." She forced a wan smile.

"Were you and Dean Mulcahy—" Jewel started over. "Will you miss him?"

"That's . . . not easy to say."

"I'm sorry. I didn't mean to pry." A lie. Jewel forgave herself.

Muriel glanced at the door to the Dean's suite. "No, dear. I mean: that's not easy to *say*."

"Oh!" She couldn't talk here, not with Lesley DeLaMar at the helm. "That reminds me, your new boss wants you."

Muriel said nothing. Her face, as she scurried back to the Dean's anteroom, said everything.

The leafy quadrangle was still deserted. Its beautiful landscaping pissed Jewel off as she steamed across campus, heading for her car. She felt like throwing McDonald's wrappers all over the well-tended grass. Or used condoms. Where would she get those? Her mood went from fury to despair. Then, remembering Lesley DeLaMar's snotty death knell for Blue Plate, back to fury.

Across the green, a solitary figure waved at her. Compact, in a brown jacket. Hartsock. Goddamnit. He was also headed for the visitor's parking lot.

She veered the other way around Darmon. She'd had enough of him for the morning.

Last night was bad enough. Now she'd lost two other big Zoo U dinners. Worst of all, Blue Plate would get a toxic reputation. Bad word of mouth killed caterers as fast as—well, poison.

Blue Plate's kitchens were spotless, its methods sanitary, its food delightful, but none of that mattered. "Blue Plate" now meant "accidental death." Rumors about bad food or sloppy preparation were like fungus. When every person from last night's dinner learned that Mulcahy'd been poisoned by a Blue Plate Special . . .

Jewel kicked a stone out of her path. But he hadn't been,

she thought. He died from something else. That's what she had to remember. Start from there.

There was still a chance. DeLaMar—Jewel paused mentally to loop a lariat of obscenities over the head of the Acting Dean—had left open a back door. If Jewel could prove to her that Blue Plate was completely innocent . . . if she could bring evidence . . . Jewel suspected that Missy Acting Dean just liked the idea of being beseeched, that she'd turn down Blue Plate even if Jewel showed up with testimonials from Ralph Nader and the entire cast of "Law and Order." She kicked another stone.

Finding evidence to exonerate Blue Plate was only one migraine-sized problem. The e-mails were another. They were an utter mystery. Why Jewel? Jewel had nothing to do with any of the Zoo U scandals. Who cared whether she worked temporarily on campus?

Never mind. She'd gnaw on that leg-bone when she got to it. Finding evidence to clear Blue Plate might uncover the e-mail writer. Or not. But she had a better shot at focusing on Blue Plate. Focus, she told herself. Evidence. Get evidence.

"I need evidence." Jewel liked the sound of her own determination.

She came at the parking lot from the south end. Squinting, she could see Hartsock leaning against her car.

No escape.

He was watching her.

This was a moment she loathed, walking towards someone too close to ignore and too far to talk to. It didn't seem to bother him. He watched her.

Some weeks later, she reached the car.

Hartsock peeled back the lid of a Styrofoam coffee cup. The lines on his face were deep with fatigue, or maybe just the steam from the coffee. His eyes remained alert. "You're kicking up a lot of gravel."

"It's not a crime," she said belligerently, then felt stupid again.

"You need detective shoes." He didn't smile. Jewel forced herself not to look at his feet. She'd been fool enough for one day. At least he wasn't treating her like public enemy number one. Maybe he'd already checked her story.

"How'd you know this was my car?"

"It was the only car parked outside your business before the sun came up." He watched her unhurriedly. "What are you doing here?"

"I'm trying to save my damned business." She forgot her mortification. Words spilled out of her in a rush. She told him everything. "So I have to find some evidence to nip this rotten word-of-mouth in the bud. Rumors *slaughter* caterers, any food business."

"What kind of evidence?" He asked as though he were really interested. She had to remind herself that he wasn't. This was a technique to get criminals to talk.

"I don't know!" She had an inspiration. "When you find out that Blue Plate is clean, completely innocent—could you tell DeLaMar? She'd have to believe you."

"If or when, I'd do it, but I don't think that'd help."

"But—" she half-danced in frustration. "Haven't you gone to Muller's yet?"

"Ms. Feynmann, I'll get to Muller's today. But rumors haven't waited, if that's your worry. Mulcahy died in front of a hundred people, and he died of something he ate. There's also the matter of these e-mails. Someone has singled you out. They're not random."

"Aren't you the little merry sunshine!" she snarled. "Thanks for nothing."

He took a sip of coffee, undisturbed. "I'd say you're just going to have to ride this one out."

"Ride it out! I can't just sit around and wait. I can't wait for a *bus*. Blue Plate's in trouble *now*. I have to do something."

"Without you, there is no Blue Plate." He finished his coffee and pressed the Styrofoam cup neatly into a cube, then stuck it in his pocket. "You don't strike me as a stupid person. Stubborn, maybe. Be careful. You can't beat this if you're dead."

Jewel marched around to the driver's side of her car without a sound, Hartsock's laconic words stinging her ears. How dare he say that she wasn't stupid. No. How dare he say that she was stubborn. What if she was? She would be damned if she was going to sit around waiting for Prince Charming—no, for Detective Hartsock—to rescue her business, and she sure as hell wasn't going to let a few e-mails scare her into immobility. No way.

She was going to draw up a campaign strategy to rescue Blue Plate from oblivion. She slammed the car door so hard that small plastic bits of dashboard came off onto the seat.

By the time she returned to Blue Plate, she still felt like making noise and gave the door a good whacking slam behind her.

Del sat mournfully at the counter, the afternoon paper spread out in front of him. "Oh, Jewel. Hi."

"Del! Cheer up!" She flung her winter coat on a hook. "We have work to do."

"I don't think so, Jewel." He began closing up the newspaper carefully.

"What do you mean, you don't think so? I have an idea about how to nip these damned—darned—rumors in the bud. You and I are going to volunteer at some Career Day—

type stuff at high schools. Then we're going to get a license to work the Tacoma Mall, in the center with all the popsicle stick-jewelry stands. A cooking demo thing? Then—"

"You haven't seen the afternoon paper, huh?" He finished folding it so that it looked untouched by human hands.

Jewel never read the afternoon paper. She preferred the lurid *NY Post*–like morning rag to the sedate *NY Times*–esque evening news.

He turned over the front page, showing the headline below the fold. "University Dean Dies of Poisoned Salad."

"Fuck!" she cried. "I mean—"

"It's okay, Jewel," said Del. "You can swear."

Chapter Twelve

Jewel devoured the front-page article. When she opened the *Tacoma Times* to the inside, where the article continued, the crackles of the pages might as well have been gunfire.

Moments later, she replaced the newspaper on the counter with ominous calm. Sensitive to personal vibrations, Del retreated further within the kitchen, where he hoisted himself onto the chrome counter by the double sink. "Jewel?"

After wrestling her feelings to the mat, she turned back to him.

"There's more," he said.

"More?" She wondered whether her heart would leap right through her chest onto the tiled floor, like in *Alien*. "More? How could there be more? Are the villagers heading this way with torches? Is my cousin Nadine the wedding planner coming out to live with me? What more, Del?"

"On the answering machine. The Mitznick bar mitzvah job is off."

"Any reason?" She knew she was grasping at straws, hoping that Danny Mitznick had skipped town to join the big-money bridge circuit, where a mathematically-minded thirteen-year-old could clean up.

Del leaned over to press a button on the answering machine. A bubbly voice filled the room.

"Jewel, hi, this is Courtney Mitznick, Danny's mother? Listen, I'm really sorry, but I have to cancel the bar mitzvah luncheon. I'll pay you the cancellation costs, your expenses, or whatever. I know last night was an accident, but I just can't risk it, Danny's my only child."

There was a long pause. Del hung his head. Jewel stared at the answering machine, as though she could rip Courtney from the spooling cassette by her tweezed eyebrows.

"Not that I wouldn't like you to make whatever you made last night for my sister-in-law, the woman is driving me crazy. God, what am I saying, I'm just kidding, that's sick, I'm sorry, don't tell anyone I said that. Listen, Jewel, is there anyone else you'd recommend? My number—"

Del turned off the machine. He sat down again, drawing his knees up to his chin.

Jewel flew to the planet Mercury for a full minute. She stood motionless while gears and pistons and tele-trans-porters whirred.

"Jewel?" Del asked softly. "Can they say that about Blue Plate in a newspaper?"

"You better believe it." She came back to earth with a thud. "Look," she grabbed the paper and waved it like a flag. "They don't say that Blue Plate killed anyone or that I delib-erately, or even accidentally, put anything rotten into the salad. They only say that the dinner was catered by Blue Plate and that the police were going to question me and people who were at the dinner and blah blah blah."

Del dropped his chin to his knees. "Oh. So—"

"So they haven't told any lies. But anyone reading this will figure we're over here cooking up botulism and e-coli and who knows what. This is a word-of-mouth deal. We'll have trouble getting someone to drive past the place, let alone hire us."

"Maybe the police will find out what really happened."

"Yeah, maybe. But they'll be dotting the i's and crossing the t's while Blue Plate goes under. That Hartsock said—"

"Who?"

Jewel filled Del in on the events of the morning. He drooped at her account of the DeLaMar ultimatum, but brightened on hearing about her encounters with the police. "He just made that stupid comment about my hair to intimidate me. And the detective shoes. It's a power thing, like big-belly businessmen sitting you in a chair lower than theirs so they can look down on you. Where does he get off? He pretends to be all mild-mannered Clark Kent, when he's really—"

"Superman!" Del said happily.

"No! That wasn't what I was going to say! When he's really—"

"The Incredible Hulk!"

"Will you quit it?" She took a deep breath to ready herself for a savage attack on Hartsock's appearance, character, and ancestry. Del's face distracted her. She narrowed her eyes. "What have you got to look so perky about, little mister?"

"I've never heard you talk that much about a guy before."

Unfairly, Jewel exploded. "Of course you haven't! My life is passing before my eyes like what happens to people in plane crashes! He's the last face I see! He's the black box! He's—"

"Never mind, Jewel. Tell me what we're going to do."

She put her hands on top of her wavy red head, as though trying to hold the lid on. Del was right. Now was no time to burn out on side trips. Every minute counted. "We're not waiting for *him* to solve the crime, that's for sure." Her head cleared. "We're going to find out who did it ourselves. I'm going to investigate. And come up with the bigfoot monster who did this. Then Hartsock can tell DeLaMar and we'll get the next two university dinners and I'll go to the newspaper and they'll interview me and everyone in town will know! We'll be back in business!"

"Cool!!" said Del. He unfolded himself from the counter. "What do we do first?"

"You, you get your ears flapping. At all those community deals you do. Mary Bridge Children's Hospital. The Needle Exchange. And what's that parade thing?"

"Oh yeah! The annual Tacoma Daffodil Parade! We're meeting this coming Saturday. And how about the Men's Alternative Reading Group?"

"Yeah, all of them. You go and ask around about Zoo U, about the murder, about the scandals before the murder, anything you can scare up—people who work there, used to work there—anything."

"Great!" He began to pack up his gear. "And what'll you be doing?"

An hour later, Jewel hovered on the threshold of the Tacoma Public Library's main branch, her brain green with parsnips. Parsnips. What kind of death could hide in a salad, disguised as parsnips? The first step was to find out what was in Mulcahy's salad.

Maybe it was some dangerous rare growth that was only found in captivity, and someone she'd met at the dinner raised nasty fungi as a hobby. Or maybe it was some murderous weed that came from Bolivia, where someone at Zoo U had recently spent a year studying insects.

All Jewel's ideas sounded like she'd been eating too much brightly-colored children's breakfast cereal, but she needed to start somewhere. Her first choice was starting with food, or fake food. The plan was to figure out what killed Mulcahy and then see whether any of the Zoo animals at the dinner had a special way of getting it. One thing was sure, Hartsock wasn't going to tell her a thing about it. Fine. He would be mightily impressed when he learned that she'd found out on her own. Not that she cared what he thought.

The first floor seethed with bookish activity. Two women

in cardigans and khakis marshaled a school group through the distractions of the video section. A man in multi-color-rimmed glasses checked people through the electronic gates. A handful of men, some in suits, some in jeans, sat at large tables, reading the day's paper. Oh great, people were sucking up the *Tacoma Times* all over town.

She let the thought propel her to a second-floor reference librarian, who didn't seem to find her fumbled request—"Poisons? Or, um, anything that would be poisonous?"—suspicious. As the chunky Japanese-American woman let her fingers do the walking over a computer keyboard, Jewel surveyed the old card catalogues and huge reference works set up on stands. She seized up in memory.

The last time she'd done any research that wasn't about food was in college. Poli Sci? Sociology? Who remembered? What came back was the strangely comforting blend of quiet and noise inside the Rutgers library, hush and rush. She remembered how she liked finding things out, traveling through pages like a pioneer woman on the front of a wagon.

Jewel had gone to school part-time, worked full-time, and bucked her family's critique of her life double-time. Daphne always had faith in her. But it wasn't enough. She'd go to the library, with people reading all around her, or looking things up in the card catalogue, and words swirled in front of her eyes. She was tired all the time. While she struggled to stay awake and understand the high-flown language of, oh, Comparative Political Theory, she heard only her mother's voice: "What do you need college for? You're a terrific cook." Or her father's: "Drop the cooking and go for nursing. Nurses never starve." It was funny. Not all that funny, really. She dropped out.

Blue Plate Catering was her life's blood, her heart, soul, and liver, but she sometimes wondered what would have happened if she had stayed in school. Maybe she wouldn't feel so desperate at the moment. Talk about putting all your apples in one—

"Are you okay?" The sturdy librarian waited for a reply. Her glasses magnified the concern in her eyes.

"Yes, sorry, I'm fine."

"Oh, good. Here are the call numbers for the books you asked about . . . you'll find them in medical reference, by the college catalogues."

"Thanks a lot."

An hour later, ensconced in a plastic bucket chair, her reference books spread out across a table in front of her, Jewel paused to rub her eyes. She sure knew a lot more about pesticides than she had before. Also rat poison. Although you'd have to be using some serious spices to disguise the taste of Rodent-B-Gone. Five-star curry would be the best bet.

But this was a waste of time. Mulcahy had been poisoned by a plant, not a pesticide or Rat-Away. She reached for the *AMA Handbook of Poisons and Injurious Plants*. Flipping through the table of contents, Jewel had a nervy flash of wondering who'd read this book before her. Had the poisoner come to the library to do research on his method? Or hers, she amended. DeLaMar's vulpine smile came to mind. Also Frances Carlotti's powerful hands, pulling herself up after her faint.

Concentrate, she told herself. The man wasn't strangled.

She brooded over the introduction to the *AMA Handbook of Poisons*. It wasn't *Silence of the Lambs*, but it had her attention. The book said that most adults who died from poisonous plants cashed in their chips by eating the stuff in a salad.

Her page-turning hand hung suspended over the entry.

The top three killers were bad mushrooms, tree tobacco leaves, or a species of *cicuta* mistaken for wild parsnips. Bingo. She let her hand drop.

"Trivial names," added the medicos, "are water hemlock, beaver poison, children's bane, and death-of-man."

The air left Jewel's lungs with the suddenness of a body blow. "Symptoms show anywhere from fifteen minutes to eight hours after ingestion. They include convulsions, stomach pain, and fever. Death may occur before medical attention becomes available." No shit, Jewel thought.

But the next paragraph thrust her into the slough of despond. The section on where water hemlock was found dashed all her hopes of grabbing a fast clue to the identity of the person behind Mulcahy's death. Not Bolivia; not the steamy greenhouses of the rich and infamous; no, it could be found everywhere there was wet or swampy ground.

That narrowed Jewel's investigation to the lower forty-eight and Alaska. She closed the reference tome with a dull thud.

An older woman in a nearby armchair moaned in her sleep. Jewel knew how she felt.

Everyone Mulcahy had ever met had the means to kill him. All it took was a couple of hours in the public library—less, if you were some fast-fingered university type—a healthy tramp on local wetlands, and a quick reach into a coat pocket during the salad course, to grab the hemlock and drop it into Mulcahy's salad.

That took nerve. Anyone might have noticed. Nerve or desperation. Or a fury that blotted out the fear of being caught.

"The library is about to close. Please check out or return all books in use. The library—"

Jewel leaned her head on her hand. The means of murder

didn't rule out a single person. She'd have to go at this another way. Death of man. The e-mail lunatic was "Death-in-life."

"Motive," she said out loud. The armchair woman snored.

Tyler, Jewel thought. Damn it. Tyler and the dead girl.

The Fiji house stood stately on a corner of Fraternity Row, just south of Zoo U. It nestled in a cluster of huge pine trees. With its white pillars and wrought-iron balconies, the building looked like a rough draft of Tara, except for the toilet paper hanging bedraggled from the pines.

Ace had said that he and Tyler were Fijis. It was a half-an-hour business to get the address from the Student Center and pick out the place from the rest of the fraternities. In the cooling gray light of dusk, the house had a deserted Gothic air, as though boys lived in the basement, year in, year out, without ever climbing up into the sunlight.

She rang the front bell hard.

There was shouting from within, then silence, then more shouting. Finally, Jewel heard feet stomping down stairs. The front door was flung open by a big-faced boy in a Homer Simpson T-shirt. He looked startled.

"Oh," he said.

"Hi," she said. "I'm looking for Ace Birney."

He looked even more startled. "You? Really?"

"Sure, me, really, why not?"

He looked stymied. Jewel was beginning to think his range was limited.

He squinted at her. "It's just that, no offense, but you're not . . . Ace tends to go in for sophomores. No offense."

"None taken," Jewel said through her teeth. "We're not an item, okay? I just want to see him."

"Hey," the boy said, giving her a sly smile. "Don't get mad. That's just the way Ace is. *I'm* not like that."

Jewel liked him better when he was stymied. "What's your name, son?"

"Dave. What's yours?"

"Dave?" Jewel leaned forward. "Get! Ace!"

He leaped backwards. "I'm *getting* him." Dave shot a surprised yet surly look at her over his shoulder and headed up the stairs. She thought she heard him mutter something about "time of month," but she wasn't sure.

It was getting cold out on the stoop.

Ages later, freckle-faced Ace bounded down the stairs. He looked relieved. "Jewel!" he said. "Boy!" he said. "Am I glad it's you!"

"Why?" Jewel asked, nonplussed.

"When Dave said there was an older woman on the steps freaking out, I thought it was my mom." Ace laughed, worry-free. "She's started making these drop-in visits. It's, like, a major pain."

"Ace," Jewel said, beyond insult. "What happened to Tyler's girlfriend?"

Ace didn't register the swift change in subject. "It's also really, really embarrassing." He seemed to catch up. "Tyler's girlfriend? Leilani Summer." He made another leap forward. "Jewel—what are you doing here?"

"I'll be happy to tell you. Could we go in? I'm freezing."

He gave his forehead a bruising whack. "Oh, sure! God! I'm sorry! What a geek! Come in!"

The foyer of the Fiji house boasted royal blue wall-to-wall carpeting highlighted by piles of old newspapers, a pizza box, and a ballet slipper. Jewel tried not to think about it or about the trophy case on the far wall, which didn't appear to contain athletic awards. At least it was warmer in here, and lighter.

"Ace," she said, "I'm trying to find out how Dean Mulcahy got killed."

"But I thought—they said that he ate—" He blushed a fiery brick and stuttered into silence.

"It looked bad," she said pleasantly enough. "But Blue Plate had nothing to do with it. What I'm doing now is finding out how Mulcahy *did* die. I want to find out who did it. Then the police can take care of it, and everyone in town will know that my business is clean."

"You're going to find out yourself?" Ace looked excited. "Like 'The Equalizer,' except a woman! This is so great! My dad put all those on video, and I used to watch them when I stayed home from elementary school. You know? This guy, the Equalizer? He doesn't think that cops—"

"Ace, could you try to bear down? This is important. Blue Plate's reputation is on the line here."

"Oh, wow." Ace returned to the previously-scheduled program and nodded solemnly. "I can see that. You don't want people saying, like, you're total killers."

Jewel thought briefly and with sympathy of Ace's parents, taping TV shows, buying Little League uniforms, saving money for a pricey little college, so that their beloved Ace could stumble his way to graduation before going to work in the family business as an overpaid, elaborately-titled office boy. Christ, she hoped they had a family business. "That's right, Ace. So what was Tyler saying about Mulcahy and Leilani?"

Ace went from brick to beige.

"You're not thinking that *Tyler?* That what he said at the dinner, about how the Dean killed his girlfriend? He wouldn't hurt the Dean! Or anyone, never! Jewel, if you knew him— he's like this total Buddhist. He took this course—"

"Did I say he hurt anyone?" Jewel bit back a scorching

criticism. Keep calm and slow down, she told herself. Slow way down. "I'm asking you, because I need to find out everything that was going on that night. If I know for sure that Tyler had nothing to do with the Dean's death, then I'm that much closer to finding out who did. Why did he leave the dinner, anyway?"

The question, like the line of reasoning, eluded Ace, who seemed lost in thought. He then reached a decision. "Tyler wouldn't hurt Dean Mulcahy, no matter what he said, and you know why? Because Leilani broke up with Tyler, like, three weeks before she died. It just about killed him. Man! After that—he couldn't—she broke up with him *before* she died. It *ruined* him. They'd been together for *two years*. So," he finished up triumphantly, "he wouldn't have any reason to kill the Dean."

Chapter Thirteen

Ace managed to look both woeful and triumphant. His Hardy Boys' face was bright under the frat house foyer lights.

"Huh?" said Jewel.

"Leilani left Tyler," explained Ace. "Not because of him. They were like this total love thing. But she was flunking out of school and got really stressed about it. She just didn't want to have anything to do with him or anyone. Boy, did that—I've never seen a guy so messed up about a girl."

Jewel thought.

"They met during freshman year. It was like, whoa! First sight love." Ace looked at his shoes, respectful and silent in the face of the real thing.

"That's sad," said Jewel.

"Major sad."

"How is Mulcahy a player here?"

"I don't know. I mean, I know, but I don't know if I should say." He struggled mightily. Something about his features reminded Jewel of castor oil, but maybe that was how Ace wore ethical dilemmas.

"Listen, Ace, the police are going to find out about what Tyler said at the dinner, if they haven't already. If he had nothing to do with Mulcahy's death—"

"Jewel!"

"Oh, sorry." She liked Ace's faith in his friend. "Since he had nothing to do with Mulcahy's death, he needs some help.

Talk to me. Face it, Tyler makes a death threat, Mulcahy dies, Tyler disappears. It's not *Heidi*."

"Who?"

"Ace, please tell me. Tyler's in trouble."

He blew out a faceful of air. "Okay. See, Leilani was flunking out of this physics course she needed for her major. To be an engineer? Although I think that was more her mom's idea. Leilani wanted to be a kindergarten—"

"Ace."

"Oh yeah. So she files a petition to take the course over and, like, wipe the F off her record. The Dean needed to sign the petition. But he wouldn't do it, or he wouldn't do it right away, or something. I never got the whole story, because Leilani swore Tyler not to tell."

"Tyler blew up at the Dean about some physics course?"

"It was a big deal, Jewel. She needed to pass it before she could take the rest of the stuff for her major. And her parents didn't want her to go to summer school. It's a lot more money."

"Huh. So why did Tyler disappear from the dinner?"

Ace looked grave. For a moment, Jewel could see what he would be at forty. Not bad. Educated by life.

"Oh, that. He hadn't decided until the last minute whether he was going to say anything to the Dean in front of everyone. Then he said he had to do it, for Leilani, like. But before he could, he had to do something else."

"What?"

"Um. He had to burn something. A letter she wrote him."

"But—" The acrid smell in the oven. The charred scrap of paper she'd found. "Ace, I found burnt paper in the oven last night. Was—"

For once, Ace was ahead of her. "Yeah. He'd gone back to his room to get it."

110

"Why? I mean, why'd he burn it, and why burn it in the kitchen? I'm not tracking here."

"To protect her memory, Tyler said. Is why he burnt it. And the faculty kitchen is like—well, they both had worked for the food service. That's how they met. In the Faculty Club. Also they worked in the student cafeteria. So to him—both places were like these major symbols. He was really mad that they were going to go ahead with the dinner, even though Leilani was dead. He said it was like, you know, sacrilege or something."

Jewel looked at Ace but saw her computer screen. *"Someone died in CBU's kitchen." "He didn't listen." "Save yourself."*

Tyler Seito was one of the few Zoo U people she knew, a little. He worked for the cafeteria service. So did Leilani. She had been found in the kitchen. Who else cared about the kitchen? But that didn't make sense. Was the e-mail from the killer or not? Was Tyler worried about Jewel, maybe? A comforting thought, but senseless: the first e-mail arrived before she'd even met Tyler.

She had to find Tyler. Suddenly, irrationally, she felt afraid for him. She was also becoming afraid of him.

"Thanks, Ace." She buttoned up her coat. "You don't know where he is, huh?"

Ace shook his head glumly. "I wish. Jewel—will—can you help him?"

"I hope so. I'll let you know."

He smiled wanly. Then stopped. "Leilani was so pretty. But shy, like she didn't—I don't know—I never knew anyone who died before."

Jewel was afraid to cut through Darmon Hall on her way back to the Duster, so she did it, stomping up the stairs and

111

swinging open the big, wooden door. She didn't believe in ghosts. She wasn't afraid of cops.

A good thing, as Ben Hartsock was leaning over the second-floor balcony. "Hey," he said. "Are you still here? Or here again?"

Jewel stood in the spacious lobby, looking straight up at him. She didn't like the Romeo angle. "Here again. What about you?"

"Still here." He turned from the balcony and walked down the sweeping staircase to the foyer. "What are you doing?"

"Nothing," she said. Romeo. Ridiculous.

He seemed not to notice. Now he was standing by her side. His dark chocolate eyes stayed on her. His voice stayed casual. "I was over in Personnel, going through Mulcahy's paperwork."

"Job records, you mean?"

"Uh-huh. Nothing to speak of. Hard to say what matters yet." He nodded towards Darmon's front door. "You going through?"

They started walking out together. He held the door for her, almost absentmindedly. "What do you mean by job records? Insurance? Benefits and all?"

"Yep. As in: 'Who benefits?' "

"Was he rich?"

"Rich enough."

"For what? How rich is rich enough?"

"Now you're asking the tough ones," said Hartsock. "Richer than me is rich enough."

"But how rich is—" She stopped herself, realizing that she was about to ask the man his net worth. Ridiculous.

They both laughed.

The visitor's parking lot was closer to Darmon than she'd remembered. "Who inherits his money?"

"That's the question, all right," said Hartsock.

The cherry-red Duster was the only car in the lot.

"Is it hard to park a car that size?" he said.

"Not anymore."

"Where'd you learn to drive?"

She laughed. "New Brunswick. I'm used to parallel-parking in front of a crowd of stoop-sitters. It toughens you up." The advice she used to get ("Cut your wheels! Look out for the Toyota, girlie!") got up her nose, but now she missed it.

They stood a moment by her car door, and for a moment she forgot what brought them there.

Then she remembered. Death, *"save yourself,"* poison, Blue Plate, bankruptcy. "Gotta go." She unlocked the door and got in. "See you."

He only smiled. As he walked away, unhurriedly, she realized that he hadn't answered her question. Who benefits?

Jewel swore meditatively behind the wheel of the Duster. Why hadn't Hartsock answered her? What now?

In the staff lot across the alley, a patch of iridescent green glittered like Aladdin's slippers. Helena's raincoat.

Even in the black February dusk, this looked like a plan. Beat thinking about Hartsock.

Jewel hotfooted it across the alley. A few dark-coated overtimers scuttled around her to their cars.

"Helena!" Jewel shouted. "Wait up!"

The green figure froze by a Ford Taurus.

"It's me, Jewel Feynmann."

Close up, Helena relaxed a little, but her face was still watchful. It was hard to tell in the dark. "Hi, Jewel."

"Sorry if I scared you." She gulped for breath. "Can I talk to you? It's about last night. Did you see the article—"

113

Helena made a small motion with her hand. She unlocked her car and tipped her head towards the passenger seat. "Get in."

Jewel slid into the front seat. Helena sat beside her and put her key in the ignition. She didn't turn on the heater.

"I saw the paper. Heard the story on the radio, too."

Jewel moaned.

"I'm sorry, Jewel. But I don't know how I can help."

"Me neither." Jewel sang her sad song, finishing with DeLaMar's request for evidence. Even to her own ears, her mission sounded stupid. "I'm a caterer, not 'Magnum P. I.'" The memory of Ace's boyhood couch-surfing lingered. "But I have to do something. So I'm out beating the bushes."

Helena stared. "Not a good idea, Jewel."

"It's a pitiful idea," agreed Jewel. "But what can I do? I can't wait for the police. Two weeks is a lifetime in catering. So can you tell me what happened with Leilani Summer and Dean Mulcahy? Ace Birney said that the Dean was holding some physics course over her—"

Golden temple-bell earrings rang lightly as Helena shook her head. "I can't help you."

"Oh, no. Why not?"

"My job. I'm ombudsperson."

"What?"

"I mediate, solve problems—between faculty and staff, students and faculty, administration and the community."

"So?"

"I also hear complaints. Grade, wage, promotion, sexual harassment, discrimination. But all that's confidential." She stared at a distant horizon invisible to Jewel. "My position is a new one. I helped create it. A lot of people hope I'll screw up so they can fire me. Without me, things will get worse. If even one person thinks that I've been talking—"

114

"I promise I wouldn't tell—"

"Jewel. You're out beating the bushes. Anything confidential you learn will help you decide what to do next, right? It'll get around, whether you tell anyone or not."

Jewel sighed. Confidential. Wouldn't you know. She rejected a Watergate break-in of the Personnel cottage. She wasn't the type that wound up at a country club prison.

A young man with a badge and a notebook hovered by a nearby car. He seemed to be writing up a ticket. Helena studied him for a moment, then shook her head slightly, like she was shaking off water, or a presentiment.

The women sat in the cold car. Jewel tried to figure a route through Helena's resistance.

"Isn't there anything that isn't confidential? Aren't there—not secret things, but things a townie wouldn't know?"

Helena's strong brows came together. Then she smiled without reserve. It was a glorious sight, the prize at the bottom of the Crackerjack box. "Mmmm. No harm in telling you what's common knowledge."

"So what's common knowledge? About Mulcahy?"

"That he'd been Dean for years. Before that, he was a professor of music. Originally he came from the University of California system."

"Yeah? Why'd he leave?" Jewel had sudden hopes of a trail in the sands of history.

"Too big a pond. A small place like CBU gave him a better shot at an administrative post."

"Is it that Deans make more money?"

"He liked money. No mistake. But he seemed to like power better."

Jewel wanted to mull this over, but she was afraid to let a pause set. Helena might get out of the talking mood. "Did he have a lot of enemies?"

"Yes indeed. He was autocratic and devious."

"Devious? Like—"

"He never went from A to B when he could go round the houses to Z first. Dishonest, too, just for the fun of it. Would rather climb a tree and lie than stand on the ground and tell the truth."

Jewel filed this away for future use. What she wanted now was a list of suspects. She could hardly sit still. "So he had enemies, like who?"

Helena shook her head.

"Well—well—what about his personal life?"

"His family was from San Diego. He never married."

"What was common knowledge about his personal life?" This was like playing Mother, May I.

Helena chose words like stepping through a minefield. "He was said to be having a long-time affair with a married woman." Jewel opened her mouth. "Sorry, I can't say who." Jewel closed her mouth. "And even that may not be true. It's only what people say."

"It's something, anyway. And what about Leilani Summer?"

Helena sighed. "She never made a complaint to me, formal or informal. But I knew her. She interviewed me once for a sociology class, a paper about 'difference.' " She rubbed her palm over her eyes, sounding more tired than angry. "She was fragile. Afraid to say boo."

"Was she in that flagpole group, SSH?"

"Oh, no. She wasn't a joiner. But Tyler Seito was. The first man to join. The student *Herald* quoted him in an article, before Leilani died. He said that SSH was around to protect women from predators, middle-aged lions who preyed on lambs." The music in her voice turned flat. "One of the Dean's nicknames was Leo, for lion. His hair and all."

"Oh."

"It made a stir. It's a small campus. The members of SSH knew that Leilani had left Tyler. After her death, they said it was murder, that Mulcahy had killed her. His defenders said that Leilani had been emotionally unstable."

Jewel thought about the dead girl. A picture of her was emerging, blurred like a delicate silk. She wanted to be a kindergarten teacher, but her parents pushed her into engineering. Her family doctor had her on anti-depressants. She was pretty, and shy, and fragile, and so upset about her grades that she broke up with Tyler, her true love. What had Mulcahy done to her?

"I have to go home now."

"Oh! I'm sorry! Listen, thanks." Jewel patted Helena's shiny green arm, then opened the door.

"Jewel." Something smooth and hard in Helena's voice made her turn back fast. "There's a lot involved here. Let the police investigate."

"My business—"

"If something happens to you, you have no business. Two people are dead. You be careful. I mean it."

Jewel searched Helena's face in the dark car. The February night blotted out nuance, and Jewel couldn't tell concern from warning, warning from threat.

Back at Blue Plate, Jewel picked up the phone, then put it back. She had to do something. But what? Helena was right. Jewel was swimming blindfolded in shark-infested waters. Helena was the third person to warn her off, after Hartsock and "Death-in-Life." Jewel couldn't stand thinking of her anonymous correspondent. Tyler? No. But— A scratching in the wall stopped her dead. The rat.

Jewel's breathing came fast. She felt like yelping, but fought the urge. That's all she needed, someone reporting her

117

shouts, a visit from the police and then the Health Department. A rat-infested catering company could declare bankruptcy right now. She'd have to change her name, change Blue Plate's name, move away, fight nuisance litigations, become an urban legend, like the beehive hairdo that doubled as a nest for cockroaches.

No yelping.

But rats terrified her.

She stomped over to the closet, loud in her big black boots, and grabbed a broom. Jumping up on the front counter, she sat, facing the kitchen, with the broomstick over her knees. Watching.

Her knuckles glowed white. But she didn't hear any more scratching. Had her stomping silenced the rat?

Sweet Jesus, what if there were two or three of them? Don't think about it.

Jewel concentrated on breathing. In. Out. Slower. In. Out.

Some phobia book on sale at the Safeway had recommended breathing, thinking about your breathing, and visualizing something calm. Jewel's visuals focused on amaretto tea cake with raisin sauce. First, pulling down the sugar from the cabinet. Then . . .

By the time she had the sauce on the boil, her pulse was almost normal. She allowed herself to leave her image of the tea cake, although mentally she turned off the heat and put Saran Wrap on the saucepan first.

Helena's face came into her head. The last person she'd seen. Her warning.

Jewel returned the broom to the closet and was drawn to the computer as to a child's loose tooth.

"You have new mail."

Goddamnit. What she wouldn't give for someone writing for a free recipe.

But only one message was there, and it was from him. Her. Damnit, she didn't even know the sex of the person. She was so damn helpless.

The message was the shortest yet:

I didn't mean to hurt anyone. I don't want to hurt you. Goodbye.

She speed-dialed Del.

"Del, I—"

"Jewel!" He was amazed and delighted. "I thought you were Uncle Lyle. Did you know that he—"

"Hold that thought." She filled him in and heard herself saying, "I'll call Hartsock."

"Hartsock?" Del's voice rose. "I thought you were mad at him. Or something," he added.

Jewel rose above it. "I don't have time to be mad. I have a new e-mail and I have to tell him about it. And he has to tell me something. If he thinks I'm mucking up his investigation, wouldn't he have to tell me something just to get me to stop?"

Del hesitated. "No," he said.

"But I was there the night Mulcahy died. He'll have to trade information with me, like it or not!"

"You know what I think?" Del was as merry as Santa. "I think you could really report this to any cop, but you want to—"

Jewel hung up.

Chapter Fourteen

"Grapes," said Hartsock.

"Yes," said Jewel.

He sat at the work table behind Blue Plate's front counter, watching her open the industrial-strength-size oven. Today he was white-shirted, in dark jeans. He looked completely comfortable.

Del, lolling all over the side counter, had taken to him with disloyal speed. Blue Plate looked pristine and uninfested.

Jewel found it hard to believe that it had only been yesterday that she'd met Hartsock at dawn, or that she'd witnessed Mulcahy's death the night before that.

"On pizza," Hartsock said, as she pulled it out of the oven.

"Yes." She wasn't going to make a fool of herself today, not two days running, not with him. She was prepared to bite her lip until it bled. She slid the pizza onto the table.

"Original."

The compliment was ransacked for evidence of sarcasm. None found.

"It's a sweet, white pizza," Del said proudly. "No tomato sauce, four different cheeses, Bermuda onion, and green grapes."

Hartsock gave Del a smile that could melt rubber. Jewel refused to notice. He turned back to her. "Where'd you come up with the idea?"

She couldn't grind her teeth in impatience while biting her

120

lip. "Ray's Pizza off Central Park. They serve a tomato, egg-plant, and pineapple number. I like the fruit and veg together, but pineapple's too sweet."

Hartsock nodded again. "What job is it for?"

Del jumped in to head off a diatribe from Jewel on their underemployment. "It's for practice, like a dress rehearsal. Cooking is a performance art, really. That's what Jewel says. You know who else says it? This Spanish guy—" He began rummaging in his knapsack for a book.

Jewel handed a slice of pizza to Hartsock. She did not admire his chocolate eyes—chocolate was trite—or his clean-planed face. His anonymous good looks irritated her. It was typically tricky of him. People should be either anonymous or good-looking.

He was built solid. She'd remembered him being more slender.

"Jewel gets these great inspirations," Del continued, leafing through a book. "Once—"

She couldn't stand it anymore, listening to him talk about her like she wasn't there. "Here, Del." She thrust a slice at him. "Eat up."

He tucked the open book under his arm and filled his face obligingly. Jewel turned back to Hartsock with some belliger-ence. He was sitting there as if—as if— "Okay, so thanks for coming, now you know about the third e-mail, here's the pizza, and have you found out anything more on Mulcahy's death that clears Blue Plate?"

Hartsock negotiated the four cheeses gracefully and reached for a napkin. "For now."

"For now?" The hell with good impressions. "What do you mean? Blue Plate—"

"Unless new evidence comes in, Blue Plate's cleared."

"Oh! So you talked to the grocer and to—" She saw his ex-

121

pression. It was suspiciously patient. "Okay, I don't need to know the details."

"True." He looked like he wanted to laugh.

"Okay, good." She was determined not to thank him, it was just his job. "So what's that mean?"

"It means he didn't die by accident. He was murdered."

Murder. No surprise there, as she knew he wasn't accidentally poisoned by Blue Plate, and Hartsock was from Homicide.

Then why did she feel so queasy on hearing the word said out loud?

"So are you any closer to finding out who did it? Because until you do, Blue Plate still looks like Deadly Nightshade Catering."

"I'm working on it. You said on the phone you had information."

"Yeah, I do. I'll tell you, and then you tell me what you found out."

Hartsock eyed the pizza eloquently.

"Take," she said.

While he steadily polished off two more slices, Jewel reported her library findings, a shade defiantly, then her conversation with Ace and with Helena. "Do you know where Tyler is? And have you talked to Pearsall? He was at the dinner and he was really pissed at Mulcahy. They had this fight a few days before."

"What fight?" Hartsock sidestepped.

Jewel detailed what she could remember of the fight in the rain—actually, the Dean had seemed calm and content; it was Pearsall who was fighting. It all seemed a long time ago.

Hartsock listened, raising his eyebrows at Pearsall's bitter complaints. "You have a good memory."

She shrugged. She knew she had a good memory. "So—"

"I heard something." Del slid onto his feet. He was very limber for someone who'd just eaten his weight in white pizza. "At the Daffodil Parade Meeting."

"Yeah?" Jewel said.

"Yeah, a graphic designer who works in the Zoo U print shop. He didn't know the Dean, but the word on the street was that only two people would cry at the guy's funeral."

"Was he talking in general, you think? Or did he mean two people in particular?"

"I asked him. He said the new Dean and what's her name, you know—the lady who recommended Blue Plate for the job. Underwriter?"

"Underwood." And DeLaMar. Figured.

"What's the name of the man you spoke to?" Hartsock said.

"Andre. He's part-Basque."

Jewel paused briefly to marvel at Del's capacity for irrelevant data. But he was a sunny, helpful boy and a fine sous-chef. "Thanks, Del. Keep digging, okay?"

He nodded, eyes sparkling. "The Triple-A Artwalk is coming up. I'll ask people there."

"Automobile—"

"Artists Against AIDS."

"Good." She turned back to Hartsock. "Your turn. What did *you* find out?"

"What I told you. Blue Plate's in the clear, unless something else turns up. I don't expect it to," he said in what Jewel would have considered a friendly way if she wasn't already closing in on a fresh outrage.

"That's all you're going to tell me? What else have you found out about who wanted him dead, and how come, and his health and his family, and the whole enchilada!"

Del had worked his way swiftly through four pizza slices

and now sat enthralled, in the lotus position on the chrome counter, as though he were watching a particularly fabulous visiting circus.

"I can't tell you details of this investigation. We need to keep them under wraps in order not to tip anyone off about where we're headed. You're right about the method. It was water hemlock. This is very good. Tarragon?"

Percipient bastard. "Yes. But on the phone you said—"

"I said I'd listen to your information and that I'd tell you something, which I did."

"I spilled everything I had!" She sounded like a child, but she couldn't stop herself.

"And I appreciate it. I called Acting Dean DeLaMar to tell her that as far as I'm concerned, Blue Plate is off the hook. But it's your responsibility to tell me what you find out. Otherwise, you could be withholding evidence. It's a crime, whatever your intentions."

Jewel rose abruptly to turn off the oven. Mainly she wanted to hide her face, which tended to show everything at once. She stewed in an odd masala of mixed feelings.

She feared he saw her as playing detective, like some overage Nancy Drew. On the other hand, he had called DeLaMar. On the third hand, he wasn't going to come across with what he'd found out. On the fourth hand, even pissed, she knew that he couldn't just spout off about police matters to anyone who asked, even a concerned, intelligent, victimized, yet totally guiltless person such as herself.

"Jewel." Hartsock was right behind her. She jumped a foot. He put a steadying hand on her arm, then withdrew it quickly.

The touch, momentary, innocent, on a generic body part, in front of Del, decompressed her like a diver coming to the surface.

She stared at Hartsock as if he'd stepped off a UFO.

Something moved behind his eyes. He probably thought she was a neurotic, pathetic, lonely woman who had not had a man's hands on her, even on her arm, since dinosaurs roamed the earth. She wanted to touch him.

He spoke first, evenly. "You're a good witness. Do you remember more conversations from the dinner?"

She nodded, afraid to give herself away with breathlessness.

He checked his watch. "I'm out of time, but I want to talk to you about what you saw and heard. You're good on detail, and you're not employed by CBU."

Del slid off the counter to his feet. "Jewel is *super* on detail! She never forgets any ingredient or amount, and she's unbelievable with names and faces. Has she ever told you about that word contest she won when she was a kid?"

Hartsock smiled at him and put on his jacket.

"We've worked together for almost a year, but there's nothing between us; we have a Platonic relationship, like brother and sister. So I'm real objective."

Her horror knew no bounds.

"Good," said Hartsock. "We like objective." He turned back. "How about tonight? I'll call from the station."

"How perfect," she said as neutrally as she could manage. Del was a dead man.

The soon-to-be-deceased party-in-question grabbed his serape and stuck his book in the backpack. "I'm going, too," he said, avoiding Jewel's death-ray eye. "I have to be at the Children's Hospital. I'll walk you out, Detective Hartsock."

"Ben's fine."

The two swung companionably out the front door. It slammed shut with the awful, adhesive thump of male bonding.

★ ★ ★ ★ ★

There were bathroom stalls bigger than Frances Carlotti's office. The young historian looked like Rapunzel stuck in a tower prison. The windowless cell of an office smelled funny, like dirt and incense. Jewel had expected better of Tewkweiler Hall, catty-corner from Darmon and splendid from the outside.

At least Carlotti's jailers had given her plenty to read. The walls were jammed with books. Jewel had to step carefully to avoid the stacks of books on the floor as she picked her way to the visitor's chair.

"Isn't this like working in a broom closet?" She cursed her own rudeness.

But the slender historian didn't seem to notice. "The best offices are for those who've been here the longest. This is only my second year."

"Oh."

"As I said on the phone, I'd like to help. But I don't know what I can tell you." Both women sat: Carlotti lightly, in the desk chair, Jewel heavily, like someone who'd had white pizza for lunch.

Faced with the choice of going over the Hartsock lunch meeting five hundred times in her head or doing something useful, Jewel picked useful. It was bad for her health to dwell on her humiliatingly vivid response to the cop's neutral touch or on Del's matchmaking attempts. Why didn't he just offer Hartsock two goats for a dowry?

Her mental arrow had spun through a list of Zoo U people she wanted to talk to and landed, almost accidentally, on Frances Carlotti. No way was Jewel going to sashay up to Tom Pearsall and ask whether his wife had been playing hide-the-salami with the Dean. She couldn't even imagine it. Melisande Pearsall was so gorgeous and so much in charge.

Yet fabulous women fell for all sorts of unworthy men. Jewel ought to know. She'd thought of seeing Edith Underwood, who had been friendly to her and who'd liked Mulcahy. No, give her another day to cut the grief.

Frances Carlotti, olive-skinned beauty, fainter, friend to Tyler.

"How do you know Tyler Seito?"

"He was in my American History survey."

"Leilani Summer, too?"

Carlotti seemed to brace herself, as if for a body blow. Her ramrod posture, incongruous in a long wheat-colored sweater and skirt, was that of a ballerina's. She focused hard. Maybe she did everything hard.

"She wasn't one of my students. She came by to talk to me once."

"About her trouble with physics and the Dean?"

Her delicate features did not change. "I can't talk about that."

"Confidential?"

"Not anymore. Dead women have no secrets, no rights, no honor. I can't talk about it without screaming."

Fury came off her rigid body in waves. Jewel almost flinched. "I'm sorry."

Carlotti waited, tight as a viola bow. How long had she been this tense? Was all of it because of Leilani?

"Why were you looking for Mulcahy before the dinner?"

"Do you think I killed him?"

Flummoxed, Jewel began backpedaling and stammering. "I—I'm sorry, I didn't mean—"

"Don't apologize. Women apologize too much." Carlotti leaned forward. "I didn't kill him. I don't believe in violence. It only breeds more violence." She took a deep breath. "Malcolm X said of President Kennedy's assassination: the chickens are coming home to roost. The violence of racism, sexism, poverty—they erupt in revolutionary counter-violence. Mulcahy's chickens came home to roost. I see his murder as a political act."

Sweet Jesus. Jewel was in over her head.

"The Dean was violent?"

"Yes. He was a bully and a sadist. He enjoyed provoking confrontation, especially with the powerless. As an educated white male at the top of the university's pyramid, he held most of the traditional cards. However, he hadn't counted on insurrection."

"You mean the articles—"

"The student protests, by SSH. He understood how to subdue individuals and groups, but SSH caught him by surprise; he never understood the dynamics of protest. The students had nothing to lose—their numbers protected them— and everything to gain, including publicity that brought pressure on the university to change its sexual harassment policy and practice."

Jewel admired the force of Carlotti's opinions. She wondered if Mulcahy had. Or what else he'd admired: even in the no-nonsense, boring clothes that the historian favored, her Pre-Raphaelite prettiness was as clear as glass.

"Like with the whole Anita Hill thing?"

"Yes, Jewel!" Carlotti nodded, her dark eyes lit from within. "Not to mention classic Northwestern cases such as Packwood's and those at Boeing. The legal debate on sexual harassment is evolving, even since the Monica Lewinsky debacle. We talk about it in all my History classes. It's a legacy of shame."

Jewel felt hammered by data and intimidated by the woman's intensity. "Did the Dean know what you were teaching?"

The light in Carlotti's eyes turned to heat. "He knew. That's one of the reasons he'd decided to 'downscale' the Women's Studies program. He was going to announce the decision at the Humanities dinner, but he died first."

Judas Priest. No trouble getting *this* informant talking.

"How'd you know—"

"Everyone knew. I have a joint appointment in History and Women's Studies. He'd met many times with Women's Studies faculty to discuss the program. He called it 'a sixties leftover that had no place in the rigorous academic community of the twenty-first century.' " She quoted like she was spitting glass. "He met with us for months, demanding comparative studies from other programs on two weeks' notice, requiring us to convene at night or on the weekends, stipulating that we demonstrate how the program met the newest specious requirement for 'rigor.' "

"So—Mulcahy was willing to listen, at least?"

"No. He just liked making us jump through hoops."

What a prick. Jewel thought of an assistant manager from the restaurant where she used to wait tables. He'd hold stupid meetings where he'd go around the table and ask people what they wanted their schedules to be like and why. Then he'd go ahead and do whatever he wanted. The meetings were his hobby. Jewel used to bring a newspaper. Drove him crazy, but he couldn't afford to fire her. She did the work of two people.

Carlotti was talking again. "He was looking forward to killing Women's Studies." The word hung in the air like a noose.

Being a murder suspect was evidently one of Carlotti's career goals. Jewel couldn't believe it.

"Why are you telling me all this?" she blurted out. That strange, pungent smell must be getting to her. It wasn't food. What was it? A gas leak?

"Women should help other women. You helped me the night of the dinner."

"Oh, yeah. Are you better now? How come you fainted?"

For the first time, Carlotti was nonplussed. "Oh—I'm fine—it was nothing. I was just . . . dizzy for a minute."

"Did you ever find Mulcahy?"

"Yes. I asked him to reconsider his decision about Women's Studies. He said that if I were worried about losing my job, he'd give me a position as special assistant to the Dean." She broke off the words like snap peas.

The other shoe dropped. The Dean couldn't have expected to get anywhere with Carlotti. He was mean, not stupid. "Did he really think that you'd—"

"He had no sexual interest in women with Ph.D.'s. He just liked the idea of having a tame feminist at his beck and call. I doubt the job he offered would ever exist. He wanted to have something I wanted."

Jewel thought for a minute. "If he wound up cutting the program, what would have happened to you? You'd still teach History, right?"

"No, I expected to lose my job if the Women's Studies program was axed. I'm untenured. The school is always trying to find ways to cut back."

"You could find another job, though, right?"

Carlotti's face hardened. "Wrong. In History, hundreds of people apply for each position. I was lucky to get this one. I intend to keep it."

So if Mulcahy had lived to cut Women's Studies, Carlotti would have lost a job she valued. How far was she willing to go to keep her job or to punish the wicked? "Did you talk about anything else?"

The historian rose in one graceful motion, fluid as fresh

honey. She was really lovely, if you liked the long-haired lithe type. Who didn't? Was Carlotti telling her everything?

"I have to grade papers."

Jewel got to her feet. "Thanks a lot. One more thing—what's going to happen to Women's Studies now?"

"Something different, I hope. DeLaMar's no feminist, but she knows that reputable universities have Women's Studies programs." Carlotti's mien of grave satisfaction was unmistakable. "Good luck with your business."

"I'll need it." From the doorway, Jewel sniffed. "Excuse me, but your office smells like musk or something. Perfume?"

Carlotti smiled, without putting much into it. "I wear no cosmetics. You're smelling cuttings from my garden." She gestured to pots on the floor, half-hidden by stacks of books. "They purify the atmosphere up here."

"Flowers? At this time of year?"

"Herbs. I grow them behind my garage. Organic vegetables, too." She lifted her chin. "Mulcahy made a 'joke' about it once. He said I was a witch."

Chapter Fifteen

A chill wind blew the gray water of Puget Sound into white-caps. Gulls screamed overhead. From her picnic-table lookout point at one of the tiny parks along Ruston Way, Jewel could see a speck of boat. Maybe it was the ferry on its way to Vashon Island. She wished she were on it.

Overwhelmed, suddenly, by the pungent small-room smell of organic herbs and witchery, Jewel had fled the campus for the great outdoors, driving downhill to Ruston Way on the water. The park, pier, and picnic table were less than a mile from The Spar (beer, burgers, billiards) and Starbuck's (why didn't they just colonize Mars?), but after a few days in Zoo U's hothouse, it felt like actual nature.

The wind invigorated her. She wondered if Captain Vancouver had felt the same way when he first sailed into the Sound two hundred years ago. Of course, that was in summer. If educational television could be trusted. Vancouver would have been nuts to sashay into town in February. They didn't have wrap-around camel coats to ward off the afternoon chill back then.

Frances Carlotti had her thinking about history.

No, no, no, she'd come down here to get away from college professors, however smart and female and forthcoming. Carlotti was so forthcoming it gave her a headache. But it wasn't history that threw her. Jewel might not have a college education, but she rode the bus, she made transfers. She liked finding things out. It wasn't being lectured at by a college

132

professor that freaked her out.

A loon landed on a dock post and folded its wings.

Carlotti was admirable, if not warm or funny. A college professor so young. A woman who wore no cosmetics. Uncompromising. Even Jewel of the Jungle, as kids used to call her in elementary school, when they weren't calling her Mailbox Mouth, wore a little foundation. Of course, Carlotti was gorgeous, with or without makeup. Still, she got the points for brave. Not to mention her opinions.

There were plenty of them. She hated Mulcahy, to name six opinions right there. He was gunning for the Women's Studies program, which she supported and which supported her. Carlotti also held him responsible for Leilani's death. Suicide. Death. Suicide. She just about vibrated with fury when Jewel asked about it. Yeah, her opinions were passionate and she hated Mulcahy.

All told, she was a hot favorite for the Suspect of the Moment contest. Although her office was too small to hold the prize statuette. But did people kill for political reasons? Of course they did. Jewel watched CNN.

The speck of ferry, if that's what it was, had disappeared. A huge tanker sat motionless out in the Sound. Jewel dug her hands deeper into her camel-coat pockets and sat down on a wooden bench attached to a picnic table.

Frances Carlotti had laid out her own motives for murdering Mulcahy like a fillet of flounder. To protect her job. To avenge Leilani. To save Women's Studies. To make some other kind of political point. You'd think a person would try to soft-pedal her motives for murder. That's what gave Jewel a headache. She didn't even want to think about water hemlock and organic vegetables. But she couldn't bypass Carlotti as a possible murderer just because she admired her or because she was a woman.

The loon dove into the water.

Yet Carlotti said she didn't believe in violence, and she didn't seem to believe in compromise, either. Jewel couldn't see her violating one of her own principles. If she didn't compromise on anything, her love life must be pretty inert. But maybe beautiful young women with Ph.D.'s made other people do the compromising. Was she married? Probably not. Life was simpler without men.

That was Jewel's latest philosophy, anyway. She planned to put romance on ice for a few more years, deep-freeze it, while she put work on the front burner.

But. Easier said. There was no getting around that moment at Blue Plate with Hartsock. The ice was thawing.

Hell. She'd just have to refreeze it. She needed a clear head to figure out what was up between Leilani, Mulcahy, and Tyler—or Mulcahy and the Pearsalls. Jewel had no sense yet of what this was about. Sex and power, power and politics. Helena said the Dean had made a big salary. Who scored the most from Mulcahy's death?

Lesley DeLaMar's smug possession of the Dean's armchair came to mind. Her grisly smile. And there was more than one way to score. Tom Pearsall wouldn't be bringing lilies to the funeral. He won Christmas in February. What were he and Mulcahy fighting about in the rain, anyway?

There were too many possibilities.

No, this was no time to think about men. Look at what happened to Daph, back in Jersey. She thought about men while everyone else thought about school or hair or friends or sports. Now she had been hooked up with Patrick for twelve years, Patrick the reliable, the Chevy Buick of men. But Jewel always suspected Daph of blowing smoke, complaining about Patrick to mask her embarrassment at having a love affair with her own husband.

No, no married men, no cops, no nothing. Blue Plate was going down the tube at warp speed. She needed all her energy to save it. Hartsock wasn't helping. Not at all. So what if she responded to him at some low beast level? She didn't even know him. He could shoot quail in his off-hours, for all she knew. So what if he had a good palate? That meant nothing. Every time she saw him, she wound up mortified. Forget that. Think of something else.

The e-mail. The last e-mail. Something about it bothered her. Beyond the fact that she could be the next target of a murderer called "Death-in-Life."

The voice. The sound of the voice in the last e-mail. It wasn't frightening. Or not only frightening. It was sad, that *"Goodbye,"* full of despair. Despair, guilt, grief . . . But if it were Tyler, why guilt? Surely he didn't kill Leilani. Grief could cover guilt, though . . . Jewel's thoughts spun.

This detective business was much harder than catering class reunions.

Jewel dug deeper into her pockets and stared out to sea.

"Chef Boyardee! I remember you from that awful dinner."

Jewel turned and searched for the speaker.

A rugged, dark-haired man stood a picnic table away. He looked familiar. That was impossible. Good-looking men didn't pick Jewel up in the park. She goggled at him. "I spilled my water, like a fool, and you got me a napkin?"

The navy sweater. Dark-skinned. How could she forget? He was the one who ran for the medics.

He looked fine outdoors, too, leaner and younger than she'd remembered. His dark-green windbreaker and hiking boots made him look more like a forest service man than a college professor.

"Oh yeah, I remember," she rallied. "I'm Jewel Feyn-mann."

135

"I know. Nick Mariani. The food was terrific, by the way. I meant everything else was awful."

"Oh, thanks." She did a double-take. "How do you know my name? Do you want to sit down?"

He climbed over the bench on the other side of her table. "Edith Underwood in Religion. She spoke up for you this morning. She said that she liked you *very much* and helped get you the job and that she was *absolutely positive* that you hadn't murdered the Dean *on purpose.*"

Too agitated to laugh, Jewel let out a strangled yell. "I didn't murder him at all! The police—"

Mariani shook his head. "Don't worry about it. That's Edith all over. She really means well, but a lot of times you'd rather have her on the other side than on your own."

"Who'd she say that to?" Jewel had hopes of a Latinate hallway conversation between two Religion professors on a pipe break during Bible study.

"Oh, just the Curriculum Committee, before the meeting started. There weren't more than twenty-five people there."

She moaned.

"Anyway, *I* know Mulcahy wasn't murdered by you or your company." His teeth were very white.

"And how do *you* know that?"

"Leo Wallinsky told me."

She took a moment to place the name. The big guy with the beard who blew up at Mulcahy after Tyler did. "But how does *he* know?" Her voice was loud, even louder than the gulls in the wind. The only way freewheeling, obscene Leo Wallinsky would know that Blue Plate was innocent was if he knew who was guilty. Zoo U's gossip internet—did they all have wrist radios and cell phones?—made Jewel want to throw herself into the Sound and let the gulls peck her head off.

"The policeman told him. What's his name? The quiet one."

Ben! No, Hartsock.

Jewel jumped up, electric with new energy. There was no time for loon-gazing or self-pity. There was work to do. Before "Don't Help Me, Edith" Underwood "defended" her any further.

"Nick, do you have a minute?"

As they walked with the wind at their backs, Jewel told Nick what she was after, thinking to herself that she should put her sad story onto cassette for easy listening. In turn, she learned that Nick was an Art Historian who'd been headed for Johnny's Seafood, near Old Town, when he spotted Jewel at the picnic table. She also learned that Mulcahy had been one of his squash partners.

"He was really competitive. Played a great game. I didn't have to cut him any slack, even though he was ten, twelve years older than me."

This was the first person besides Edith Underwood she'd heard say anything nice about Mulcahy. Of course, most guys would admire Attila the Hun if he'd beaten them at squash. It was a dick thing.

"So, you liked him?"

"No, I didn't. He wasn't interested in ideas for their own sakes, only as something to use. We used to get into big fights about art and music. Mulcahy didn't care about ideas, he just wanted to beat me. It was boring."

Boring, but better than the mean-spirited cat-and-mouse game he'd played with Carlotti, jerking her and her Women's Studies program this way and that for cheap entertainment.

"He wasn't a disastrous Dean," Nick continued, "because he was a hard-working guy, energetic. But he didn't see CBU as a community. He was the artist, the school was his canvas, and the rest of us were colors or tools. Oh, look—the mountain's out today." Mt. Rainier loomed before them, gigantic, as though it were two miles away, instead of sixty. It was white and shadowy, a ghost mountain, the more impressive because it wasn't often visible in February. On overcast winter days, Rainier disappeared. Jewel squinted at it, then at Nick Mariani, who seemed rapt in the face of living art. He had good insights. Mulcahy'd been pretty nice to him, but it hadn't blinded him. Jewel wondered whether a good squash game had been enough to bring the Dean's grudging respect. Embittered Tom Pearsall and piratical Leo Wallinsky must be rugby players.

They walked for a few moments in companionable silence. Nick was easy to be with. Good-looking, too, although lean. Jewel herself was not lean. She had life-sized hips. She preferred men in scale: solid, sturdy, dark-eyed. Like Hartsock.

"Judas Priest!"

Nick looked concerned. "What is it?"

"Nothing." She gritted her teeth. When had she started comparing all men to Hartsock? It was cold-shower time. Nick was still looking at her. "I just don't understand men." She hoped he would think they were still talking about Mulcahy.

He laughed, rueful and relieved. "I know what you mean."

"How come Mulcahy didn't pick on you? Was he only tough on women?"

"No," Nick said slowly. "Not that he wasn't tough on women. He didn't like women. Womanizers don't, I guess. With men, it was different. He competed with men. For top-dog status, for women, in games. You know."

Jewel knew.

"But he could be tough on men, too, if he thought they

were after his turf. I'm gay, so he didn't know what to make of me. I wasn't part of his equation."

Jewel stopped. Her headache was gone. It had been replaced by a gallon-sized mental tornado. "He—you—"

Mulcahy had been a bully and a powermonger, full of old-fashioned ideas. Even in the science-fiction world of male friendship, she couldn't see him getting along with a gay man. She had to pull herself together. Nick had stopped, too, and was looking at her. "He knew you were gay and he—"

"Everyone knew. It's on my vita."

They began walking again.

"I chair the Gay and Lesbian Studies section of the National Art History Association. I'm the faculty advisor of the Pink Triangle Union, a student group on campus. Undergraduates come out to me in my office about once a week. It takes so much time that I put it down as 'university service' when I went up for tenure."

"I don't mean to be a moron here, Nick, but Mulcahy sounds like he was always looking for an advantage, that he liked to jack people up, just for fun—I don't get—"

"He was exactly like that, but he couldn't find a purchase on me. The most he could do was beat me at squash once in a while and trot me out as a Diversity Poster Boy when it suited him. Actually, he liked my being gay. It meant I wasn't a contender. On younger heterosexual men, he was death."

He registered the word at once and stopped walking.

They were back in front of Johnny's Seafood. Nick checked his watch. "I have to run. Got a seminar, and a meeting before then. Good luck."

"Thanks for talking to me, Nick."

"No problem. We're all talking nonstop about it. This is the third conversation I've had about Blue Plate in two days."

"Great. Who else besides Underwood?"

"Your colleague, with the ponytail. Del."

"You know Del?"

"Sometimes I see him at the Triple-A Artwalk."

"Oh." Del got around. And why not? It wasn't as though he had any work at Blue Plate these days.

"Well, hang in there! And remember the university motto: the truth will set you free. See you!" Nick waved and turned towards Johnny's.

When she returned to Blue Plate, Del was still gone, showing his innate good sense, the little weasel, and the answering machine light was blinking. Jewel's spirits rose like soufflé. Work! She almost skipped to the machine.

"This is Ben Hartsock. Could you come to the station as soon as you can? It's at Pacific and Sixth. We found Tyler Seito."

Chapter Sixteen

"You okay?" The Hispanic police officer didn't wait for an answer. She led Jewel down a hall, stopped at a door, knocked, smiled, and left.

Good. Jewel was planning to throw up all over the station hallway. The fewer witnesses, the better.

Tyler Seito. She was all wrong about him. She thought he'd written those e-mails to her. He hadn't. But he'd known what happened to Leilani and why. He wanted to avenge her, to expose the killer. His rage at Mulcahy made it clear that he thought Mulcahy killed Leilani. But then who killed Tyler?

Jewel's head pounded. Tyler had just been a boy, just a broken-hearted boy. She should have known, should have done something. . . . Because she hadn't, she would have to identify his body. A grim goodbye.

"Goodbye." The last e-mail:

I'm sorry. Goodbye.

She almost staggered in front of the closed door.

She was wrong *again.* Tyler was a suicide, not a homicide. He did write those e-mails to her. Sick with guilt and grief. Then he killed himself. Why hadn't she figured it out sooner? She could have saved him. Instead, she was so concerned to pretend she wasn't frightened . . .

The door swung in and she was eye-to-eye with Hartsock. "Hi. Tyler Seito's in here. He's been asking for you."

Jewel sagged with relief, bumping into the door frame.

Tyler sat hollow-eyed, elbows on knees, on a metal chair behind a wooden table. He straightened up when she came in. The small white-walled room looked like an old-movie mental institution.

"Jewel." His voice sounded ragged. "You took so long." He was wearing the same clothes he had worn under his waiter's jacket. He might have slept in them. His dark eyes and high cheekbones sucked all the color from his face.

Relief flooded through her and turned at once to lava. "Tyler, I just got the message! I rushed right over here! What have you been playing at? You head case! Ace was scared for you! And what about your poor parents, goddamnit! Do they deserve to have you pinballing all over the place, instead of in school? You wasted Detective Hartsock's time! You kept him from looking for the real killer!"

Hartsock, leaning against the far wall, looked surprised, but only for a second. Tyler took the barrage stoically. "I *am* the real killer."

"Oh, bullshit! You're a liar is what you are! But you wrote me those e-mails, didn't you?" Jewel felt like throttling him.

Hartsock's eyebrows rose. He'd probably arrest her for bellowing at Tyler, some sort of Northwestern noise pollution ordinance, even though Tyler scared the living life out of her with those crackpot e-mails, not that she'd admit it. Jewel felt like throttling Hartsock, too. The pair of them.

She put her hands on the table and leaned over at Tyler. "Well? Didn't you?"

Tyler blinked. He must have expected Jewel to be the good cop, not the bad one. More fool he. Goat. E-mailer.

"Yes. I'm sorry."

"Sorry?" Jewel was suddenly tired. She dropped into the

chair opposite Tyler's. He watched her apprehensively. She glowered back.

"We found him," said Hartsock, "hiding out at a friend's house in Lakewood. A frat brother who graduated last year. Tyler here says he murdered Dean Mulcahy, and he sent you those e-mails, but he wouldn't say anything else unless you were here. He doesn't want a lawyer."

She took a deep breath, the better to explode at Hartsock and at Tyler both. Then she wondered at Ben's calm. Back flat against the wall, he looked weary. Also irritated. Tyler was not in handcuffs. There were no other cops in the room to subdue him, in case he decided to rush for freedom. It didn't look like the crime bust of the week.

She put her elbows on the table. "Why'd you want to call me, Tyler?"

"My parents are in Hawaii." He sounded a little apologetic. "I didn't want them to get upset and come flying over here. They can't really afford to."

She rolled her eyes, ready to ask whether they could afford to hire Johnnie Cochran to defend their son, when she saw Hartsock, leaning just out of Tyler's line of vision, shaking his head. All right.

"Okay. But why me? Why not Frances Carlotti? She's a kind of friend, isn't she?"

"She's cool. But she works for the university. They're all still afraid of him. Even though he's dead." He sat up straighter, like a Foreign Legionnaire in front of the firing squad. "Because I killed him."

"Will you quit saying that! It's getting on my nerves."

"It's the truth. I have to say it." He coughed a little. "And Ace said you would help me."

"You—when did you talk to Ace?" If the Hardy Boy had been holding out on her, she would go back to waiting tables.

143

His dark eyes warmed at the memory of the conversation with his friend. "This afternoon. He said you came by."

"He *knew* where you were? I'll—"

"No, no, he didn't." Tyler defended his friend in a stronger voice than Jewel had heard him use so far. He glanced apprehensively at Hartsock. "I called him to find out what was going on, but I didn't tell him where I was. I wanted to keep him out of this."

"Okay, okay. But why'd you write me those e-mails? What the hell were you doing? And where's your lawyer? You need a lawyer, Tyler, not a caterer. This is serious. It's not like having a bad day at Alpha Beta Soupa."

"Phi Gamma Delta," he said with dignity. "Fijis."

"Whatever!" she snapped.

"I'm not a child," he said.

Her blurry mental picture of Leilani came into focus, swift and heartbreaking. Long, black college-girl hair. Little pearl seed earrings. The look of a puppy who has been hit, hopeful but afraid.

Tyler was old enough. He lost a girl—woman—he loved. He lost her not to the ravages of age and illness, a grief everyone two-stepped with sooner or later, but too soon, before he could even recover from the miracle of falling in love with her.

"I know." She ran her hands through her hair.

Hartsock, looking tired and intent, moved his hand in a circle. It was a "keep it going" gesture. She realized that he wanted her help.

"All right." She leaned over her elbows. "You wanted me to be here because I'm objective—I hardly knew Mulcahy and didn't work for CBU—and because Ace said I was okay and because you didn't want to bother your parents. So . . ."

"I wanted to tell someone why I killed him."

144

A confession. After desperately wanting to get information about Tyler, Leilani, and Mulcahy, Jewel, on the verge of getting a wad of it, had a perverse stab of fear, a cowardly impulse to race from the room before she heard what turned Tyler into a fugitive.

The fact is, she thought, as she watched him struggle with his memories, she didn't want him to be the killer any more than she wanted Frances Carlotti to be. How was she going to save Blue Plate if she didn't want to believe that anyone she questioned was capable of committing a crime? Tyler had already admitted to sending those threatening messages.

He rubbed his eyes.

Ben Hartsock waited. He knew how to be quiet.

"Tell me, Tyler." She found her voice. "I know the part about how Leilani had flunked physics. She went to the Dean about taking the course over . . ."

"Yeah." His voice faltered. "I said I'd go with her—she was shy around people she didn't know—but she said no, she wanted to do it herself, because that's what anyone else would do. Leilani—some things were hard for her. She was really smart but she'd get kind of panicky. Like with this physics.

"So she went to the Dean's office by herself. She told me he was really nice, that he took a lot of time with her." His face darkened when he spoke about the niceness of the Dean.

"He sign her off on physics?"

"No. No. He said he would, but that she'd have to come back and talk to him again. He wanted her to bring a study plan for him to go over. So he could help her organize her time. Leilani thought it was amazing that an important guy like him would want to help her like that." Tyler's voice clogged with anger and frustration.

"So . . . she went back."

"She went back." He took several deep breaths. In the stillness that followed, the past iced the present over like frost. Nobody moved.

"I went to her room that night to see how it went. She was crying. She said she was sick, for me to go away, but I knew she wasn't sick. She—" He struggled to keep the tears from his voice. "Leilani wouldn't—she couldn't tell me everything. Not then. But a week later, she broke up with me. In a letter. She wrote that she wasn't good enough for me, that she'd done things that were bad . . . she wrote . . . the letter said . . . that she loved me so much she had to break up with me. Because . . . because . . ."

He covered his face with his hands.

Ben moved off the wall and handed Tyler a handkerchief from his pocket. Clean, Jewel noticed.

"Thanks," Tyler whispered.

"Did you know what she meant?" Jewel said.

"Yeah," he said. "She and I . . . we never did all that much. Sex, I mean. She kind of wanted to. But her parents had told her that if she did bad things—like, like sex without being married—that people wouldn't respect her anymore. She was afraid of me not liking her anymore, so we didn't. . . . It wouldn't make a difference to me. We were going to get married, after graduation. I thought it was fucked up, but—" He blushed. "Oh, excuse me, Jewel."

She shrugged it off, opening her palms to the heavens.

"But it meant something to her, so . . ." He gathered himself up. "So I knew that, to her, bad things meant sex. And everyone on campus had heard the rumors about Mulcahy. I just never thought—I should have gone in with her, I should have made her let me—"

Jewel reached over the table, grabbing his forearm. "No, Tyler. It's not your fault."

He folded his hands, gripping until his knuckles turned white.

Hartsock slid into the metal chair beside Tyler. "Then what?"

The boy seemed to welcome the prod as a brief release from guilt. "Then . . . I tried to get her to change her mind. She wouldn't see me or return my calls. She begged me to stop calling. I tried everything I could think of . . . she looked bad, afraid and stressed out. Then I got this letter from her."

He looked sick with the memory.

"Still have it?" Hartsock's voice was just audible. He didn't seem like a cop. More like a, a—Jewel wrenched her head from the end of the thought.

"No," Tyler said. "I burnt it. The night of the dinner. That's why I left, Jewel. I wanted to get rid of the letter so that no one would ever read it. She would've hated that. She'd asked me to destroy it, but I just couldn't."

"When—" Jewel began.

"I got it the night she died." Tyler seemed empty of tears, of rage, of frustration. Grief had emptied him. "She said she was going to kill herself. Because she knew she was a bad person. She'd had sex with the Dean. He said if she told anyone about it, he'd tell her parents it was her idea. He said that if she kept doing it, he'd sign off on her physics course before the next term. She hated it, she hated him, but she was afraid to stop. She was afraid that her parents would believe him."

Jewel wanted to mutilate Mulcahy's dead body, to put his head on a stick.

"She told me she loved me. She told me to stay away from Mulcahy, that he could find a way to hurt me. She said . . ." He looked at Hartsock. "Do I have to say everything?"

"Not now."

"I ran over to her room, as soon as I got the letter. I got security to open it up, but she wasn't there. She was in the cafeteria . . . we used to work . . ."

"You found her?" Jewel was horrified. No wonder the boy was unstrung.

"Campus police did."

"So you decided to kill Mulcahy," suggested Hartsock.

Jewel shot him a poisonous look, which he ignored.

"Yes." Tyler turned to look Hartsock in the face. "Yes. I executed him."

"Tell me how."

"I poisoned him, his dinner that night. I came back and dropped the poison onto his plate when he was moving from table to table, talking to people."

"Uh-huh. Where'd you get the poison?"

"I don't want to get anyone in trouble."

Jewel held her breath.

"It was rat poison. I got it at a garden store in Puyallup. It wasn't their fault, I told them I was going to use it on rats."

Hartsock sighed.

"I did, I did it! He deserved it! I'm not sorry, either. No matter what happens to me."

Jewel sat back in her chair. "Oh, Tyler."

Hartsock never stopped looking at him. "He didn't die of rat poison."

Tyler's eyes widened. "But I thought—well, maybe I got the name wrong. Maybe it was something else."

"Maybe." Hartsock never took his eyes off the boy's face. "And maybe this confession is a bunch of moose shit. Maybe you're wasting taxpayers' money and keeping me another hour away from finding the real killer. Maybe I should throw you in jail for threatening Ms. Feynmann and obstructing justice. I say, let's get your parents to the mainland to bail you out."

"Please—they don't—"

"They don't know what you've been up to? They don't know you want to see your story on the six o'clock news? I bet they don't."

"Ben—" Jewel thought this was a little rough, although five minutes ago she'd been ready to pull Tyler down Pacific Avenue by his ears.

"I'm sorry." Tyler bowed his head. "I wish I had killed him."

"No shit. I figured that part out already." Ben Hartsock's tone was gentler than his words. "This is a homicide. Do you understand me?"

Tyler nodded. "Yes, sir."

"You find some other way to take the weight." He kept his face close to Tyler's and his voice low. "You committed a real crime in sending those e-mails."

"Yes, sir. I'm sorry, sir. I'm sorry, Jewel."

"Tyler!" Jewel burst in. "Was it—something to do with the kitchen?"

Tyler looked over at Jewel almost gratefully. "Yes. When I heard that they were going to have this big dinner anyway—right after Leilani died—this big 'celebration'—" he spit the words out, "—I tried to get them to stop it. It was so wrong. No one would cancel it. They all said that Mulcahy wouldn't hear of it."

Jewel remembered Tyler's written words: *He wouldn't listen.*

"I knew you were the caterer they hired. Ms. Moore sent out an announcement. I thought that if you quit—if they couldn't find someone else to do the dinner—" He held his hands over his eyes. "That was before I met you. I wasn't going to hurt you. I just wanted to scare you off. I'm sorry. I felt bad, afterwards."

Jewel was stymied. But not for long. She jumped on the one fact she knew for certain.

149

"Tyler," she said. "You're a mess."

Hartsock stood, perhaps fearing a little amateur psychology from the resident caterer. He gave Tyler the hairy eyeball. "Don't run away anymore. I'll need a statement from you."

"Yes, sir."

Hartsock stood by the table. "Stay at your Fiji house. For now. I might still come by tonight to arrest you. I'll see how I feel."

"I—I can go?" He rose uncertainly.

"Get!" Hartsock waved him away like he was batting flies.

"Tyler!" Jewel rummaged in her elephant-sized bag. "Have you eaten?"

"No, Jewel." His look was dazed.

She pulled a Jonathan Gold apple from the inner reaches of her purse, then a small sack of banana-walnut muffins. She shoved them his way. "You have to eat. Your blood sugar is in your boots. That's why you're carrying on."

"Thanks."

"Call Ace to come get you. I hate to think of you driving, you'd be a menace. Also, you need a shrink, no lie."

"Okay." He clutched the muffin bag. "Thanks, Jewel. And," he turned to Hartsock, "I really—"

"Get!"

He got.

Hartsock sank back into a metal chair.

Jewel whirled. "The guy lost his girlfriend! He had to stand by and watch, practically! You don't have to be so mean!"

He laughed. "You're the one who called him a head case. I thought I'd have to offer him police protection."

She couldn't believe it. "I'm serious!"

"So's murder. Look. Mulcahy might have been the

world's biggest bastard, but that doesn't mean his killer gets to go free. Thanks, by the way."

She stood over him, angry and confused. "For what?"

"For what you said to Tyler. 'You wasted Detective Hartsock's time—you—' "

"It's not funny!" But she laughed anyway.

Her relief at Tyler's boneheaded confession was tremendous. The idiot.

Her laughter faded as she thought about Mulcahy and Leilani, his murderous power games and her terror. The only escape she could find was death. And Tyler, sick with helplessness, love, and rage. If only he'd been older—if only she'd—

Jewel felt a rush of emotion welling up like a geyser, all the feeling she didn't permit herself while Tyler was talking.

"Love sucks!" She slammed her bag onto the table. "Love is hell! What'd it get Tyler? What'd it get Leilani? All it does is drag you into a poisoned well!"

Hartsock studied her for a moment, then looked at his watch.

"Oh, excuse me so much! Am I taking too much of your precious time?"

"Yes and no." He stood. He was close to Jewel, suddenly. He smelled like bubble gum and athlete's sweat. "I'm going off duty. I'll drive you home."

Chapter Seventeen

Joy, fear, and suspicion played bocce ball in her brain. She hoped it was her brain. "My car is here," said Jewel. "Thanks, anyway."

"You're welcome. When was the last time *you* ate?"

"I—what?" She preferred bristling to retreating. "What's it to you?"

"*Your* blood sugar. You told Tyler he shouldn't be driving, if he hadn't eaten for a while."

This was true. She hadn't eaten since the white pizza seven or eight hours ago. What with Frances Carlotti and Nick Mariani, Dean Mulcahy and Captain Vancouver, she'd forgotten to eat, a fail-safe sign of crisis.

"I'm fine," she said.

He raised his eyebrows.

The planes in his face were strong and clean, like they'd been drawn in India ink, without an eraser. A solid guy, not tall, someone who worked outside, not on a Stairmaster. He had laugh lines and thought lines.

Quiet-spoken. But not shy, not this potato. Self-contained.

She had to admit he'd given her pretty free rein with Tyler. He hadn't made fun of her burning ambition to rescue Blue Plate, either.

Hartsock watched her gravely.

"What?" she said, grievance just a heartbeat away.

"I didn't say anything."

With a flurry of motion, she gathered up her bag and threw on her coat. "Thanks for letting me talk to Tyler. I'm glad he didn't do it. Have you talked to that Tom Pearsall yet? He was really mad. Oh, I told you that at lunch. Anyway! I'll let you know if I hear anything else—I'll find my way out."

He almost laughed again. "I make you nervous?"

"No!" She forced herself not to look skyward for the bolt of lightning. Fortunately, there was no God. "Don't be silly."

"Uh-huh."

"It's just that if you drive me home, I'll be leaving the Duster on the street all night."

He laughed hard, startling her. This laugh she hadn't heard before. It was a swashbuckler with the sound turned down, low and deep and full of mischief.

"Good point," he said when he got his breath. "There's a big gang of car thieves looking for seventy-nine Dusters."

Still laughing, he opened the door. "Come on," he said. "I dare you."

A funky yarn and lace thing about the size of a seahorse hung from his rearview mirror. Jewel was afraid to ask.

"What's that?" she said.

"A good-luck charm."

He drove like the car was part of his body. He must have learned on farm machinery when he was six.

"Yeah? Does it work?"

He smiled. "Here you are."

She felt something stir inside her. This wouldn't do. Not at all. "So, who do you think killed Mulcahy?"

"Who do *you* think?"

For once she didn't mind his side-stepping. This was, after all, the million-dollar Blue-Plate question.

"Frances Carlotti had about six reasons to hate him."
Jewel told Hartsock about the historian's hyper-articulate
fury. "Also, she has a garden full of organic stuff at home."

Jewel was surprised to feel no guilt over giving up
Carlotti. She trusted Ben Hartsock not to nail the wrong
person.

"I haven't spoken to her yet. She have the nerve?"

The night of the dinner came back to Jewel in a rush.
Frances's grip on her arm as she pulled herself up off the
floor, her faint half-forgotten. Her championship of Tyler,
in front of everyone. That took some sand. Then today, in
her campus cubicle, Frances Carlotti had spoken with the
white-hot passion of a true believer. Uncompromising. Fanatical?

"She has the nerve," said Jewel. "And she almost wants to
get tagged for the murder. Go left here."

Hartsock spun the car around Wright Park. Closed after
daylight, it had the eerie effect of a deserted fairgrounds far
from the city. The park wasn't deserted. Two men, one in a
flack jacket, stood by the edge, below the greenhouse,
smoking.

"She wants to go down in flames for a good cause?"

"I don't know. I wouldn't peg her as a martyr type. Did I
tell you she fainted at the dinner?"

She felt rather than saw him raise his eyebrows. The car
drove down K Street and pulled up by her pint-sized
Craftsman bungalow before she'd finished her rundown.
"Thanks for the ride. I guess I'll tell you the rest tomorrow."
She grabbed the door handle and tried to bolt.

"You're welcome. I also want to know what you heard at
the dinner itself."

"Okay. Did someone give you that good-luck charm?"
Jewel couldn't believe herself.

154

"Uh-huh." Hartsock smiled in the dark. "Like it? I bet she'd give you one, too."

A wife. A lover. Of course. She should have known. One of those wretched craftswomen she'd met a year ago at the Women Entrepreneurs' workshop downtown. No, not wretched. Happy, creative, hard-working, normal. Blonde. Norwegian. Outgoing. Ilsa. She probably made dried flower arrangements and volunteered at the Teen Runaway Hotline. A nice, good woman.

The electricity between Jewel and Hartsock was all invented. She'd short-circuited.

"Do you have a fever?" he asked.

"No. Why?" She hoped her face wasn't flushed.

"You're usually so nosy." He showed no impatience to be on the road. "Aren't you going to ask who made it?"

No way. "So, who?"

"My daughter, Sara."

"Oh!" Better ask. "How old is she?"

"Seven."

He was a family man. It was too much.

Suddenly, the night closed in on her and she had to get out of the car. She wanted to make something difficult, delicate, and time-consuming. Baked Alaska.

"She lives with her mother in Minneapolis. I'll walk you in."

Hartsock stood on the porch, watching her struggle with keys. Finally, she turned to say goodnight.

Instead, she kissed him. His mouth was warm and sweet. Jewel put her hands on his shoulders to steady herself.

When she pulled back to look at him, strong and intent in the dark, he moved closer, so near she could feel waves of heat radiating from him, or maybe it was her.

He kissed her, once. Twice. Light. Careful. She felt his

Beth Kalikoff

hands on her waist. At her back, somehow, was the door frame. Ben Hartsock had pressed her up against the house. She dropped her bag.

They kissed again.

The seasons changed.

Someone must have moved, because the air between them disappeared. His chest big against hers. Jewel gasped at the feel of him, at every pressure point or inch of skin, as though her clothes had melted off.

She slid her arms around his waist, moved them up his back, and down again, measuring him for scale, caressing him, grabbing his shirt, back and front, to make sure he didn't fade away into the night or memory.

His breathing came unevenly.

She couldn't breathe at all. She didn't want to breathe. She could breathe later. They kissed again, this time long and hard.

Without breaking from her, he slid his arms inside her jacket. His hands, light as silk, brushed over her breasts, so that she had to pull her mouth from his to gasp. He closed his mouth over hers again.

She put her arms around his neck, then took them away to unbutton his shirt. Beneath it, she saw through a fog, he was wearing a sleeveless white undershirt, like a minor-league ballplayer from the 1940s.

He worked her blouse out of her pants. His hands were warm on her stomach. The two brain cells that had not yet become hot mush sounded a faint warning, like a fire truck three miles away. She'd only met Ben Hartsock a few days ago. She hardly knew a thing about him. This was the twenty-first century. There were things a person had to know.

Determined to take a firm stand, she stopped unbuttoning

156

his shirt and put her palms on his chest with determination. "Birth control."

"In my wallet."

"Do you shoot quail?"

"I want to smell your hair," he said.

That sounded like a no to her.

She slid his jacket off. It fell to the porch. Stepping back to kick the jacket out of the way, she saw that the hairs on his chest outnumbered those on his head. He put his face in her hair and made a noise, deep in his throat. She peeled off his shirt. Somehow he maneuvered her slowly into the house without letting more than a centimeter separate their bodies. She began to tear at his undershirt.

He pulled her blouse over her head, fast. Her breasts came half-out of a toast-colored underwire job, evidently not built for punishment. He made another noise at the sight of her and bent to cover first one nipple, then the other, with his mouth. She shivered. Then reached for his belt. Damn buckle.

They were definitely inside the house now, the porch behind them. He kicked the door shut.

Jewel arched her hips to his. She felt his hand at the small of her back. Solid ground disappeared beneath her. Am I fainting? she wondered. But no, Ben was guiding her to the bare oak floor, which looked tough on a guy's back. His eyes were almost closed.

"Are you okay?" she said.

"No," he said.

She bent down to kiss him: his mouth, his neck, his chest. Lying on top made it easier to open his belt. He was faster, though, and already had her zipper down. Jewel heard a high-pitched electronic beep. Maybe I'm having a coronary, she thought. I shouldn't have waited so long.

Ben said a very bad curse word.

"What?" she said. Her voice seemed higher than usual.

He arrested her hands. "My pager." He sat up, holding her so she wouldn't fall. She found herself in his lap, facing a grim half-naked policeman. He swore again, under his breath, but she heard him. You learn something new every day, she marveled. And she thought she knew it all!

"Hurry up and turn it off."

He did, but that's all he did. "I have to go."

"You have to *go?*"

"Yes. Something's happened."

He silenced her protest with a swift, hard kiss on the mouth, but she was still complaining when he pulled away. Suddenly she was half-naked and alone on the hard wood floor.

"I'm sorry."

"*You're* sorry?" She glared up at him while he buckled his belt and brought his shirt in from the porch. "Why does it have to be your pager? Why can't they call another cop?"

"Must be one of my cases. I'll let you know." He was dressed, his hand on the door.

She scrambled to her feet. "When? You promise? Really?" Gears shifted with a clank and a screech. "If it's about Mulcahy's murder—you'll call me? Because we have to find out who did it. My business is going under."

"I'll call when I can." He took her in, her slacks open, her bra askew, her hair hurricaning crazily around her head. "Don't pick up your car like that."

"Coitus interruptus," said Del's Uncle Lyle in his Okanogan County twang. "Lord, that brings back memories." After a sleepless night, Jewel had tracked Del to Lyle's barber shop, spoiling for a fight. Instead, she found herself telling the story of her last thirty-six hours, including the rat-scratchings in the wall, while Lyle cut her hair.

She scowled into the mirror facing them. Usually she enjoyed Lyle's cowboy tales, but his seventy-year-old memories of eastern Washington cut no ice with her today. "It was *not* interruptus! We never even got our pants off! Haven't you heard a word I've said?"

Unoffended, Lyle snipped at Jewel's wild hair. "I sure hope you weren't planning to have yourself some unsafe sex."

Del smiled from the other client chair, his long legs hanging over the side facing Jewel.

"That's another thing!" Jewel pounded a fist into her armrest. "We were thirty seconds away from showtime and he hadn't said a thing about birth control! How come I had to be the one to ask?"

Del considered her question, his brow furrowed. "How come *he* has to be the one to ask?"

"Because he's—"

"You don't quit jumping around," said Lyle, "I'm going to cut you."

"Anyway," said Del, "at least he had condoms with him."

"Oh fine! He carries condoms! He's ready for action every day of the week! Lucky me! I was condom number three in his wallet! Wonder who number four is!"

"Of course," Lyle's voice was reflective, "back then in Okanogan County, the rhythm method was all the rage."

"Lyle!" shouted Jewel.

"Jewel!" said Del. "What are you going to do next to solve the murder? So we can get back to work?" His sweet face was wreathed in concern.

Jewel scowled, this time in thought. "Talk to the other people. Tom and Melisande Pearsall. Something's really wrong there. Leo Wallinsky. He was the big, blowhard bully. Edith Underwood."

"The one who recommended Blue Plate for the job," said Del.

"Yeah. Mulcahy really had her buffaloed."

Del swung his legs down and began spinning the chair slowly. "She didn't know about that poor Leilani, about her and the Dean? How old is Edith, anyway?"

"Early fifties? Around Mulcahy's age."

Lyle studied Jewel's head critically. "You'll do."

Jewel saw her dark red hair spiral in soft waves. "Nice. How come it looks longer? Del, if Edith Underwood knew what the Dean was up to, how could she defend him?"

"That's all I have time for, you two," said Lyle. "I got customers coming."

Jewel got up from her chair, untying the white smock and throwing it into a hamper. "But what if she *found out!* She thought he was the king of the world and found out he was shtupping students and poisoned him!"

They walked past the front desk.

"I'm going to see Edith Underwood and make her confess. And then I'll get more university work and make the Zoo animals a walnut-glazed ham!" She shook her fist in the air.

Lyle went to the door, unlocked it, and turned the Closed sign to Open.

"So!" she continued, all business, bright with purpose. "What do I owe you, Lyle?"

"Nothing, doll. It's a public service. And call an exterminator about that rat."

"Great!" said Jewel, not tracking. She pulled open the door with spirit. Del sailed through. "Later!"

Chapter Eighteen

"Leo Wallinsky, of course." Edith Underwood announced the killer's name with the same ringing certainty she'd ordered a cream-cheese whole-wheat bagel frothy with sprouts. Her face might bear the marks of grief—and strain—but her voice was unafflicted.

"Oh!" Jewel's eyebrows headed north for the Arctic. "How do you figure?"

"He *hated* Dean Mulcahy. He was *obsessed* with the Dean. According to Professor Wallinsky, poor Matthew was guilty of everything from vendettas to embezzlement. A feverish and violent imagination! It would have been simply *grotesque,* if it weren't so dangerous."

Edith's dramatic gestures captivated Jewel, even as they threatened her water glass.

The Antique Sandwich, a sprawling restaurant two blocks from campus, was a curious choice for the Religion scholar. Equal parts hippie, yuppie, and boho, the Sandwich's patrons wore Birkenstocks, jeans, and T-shirts; long hair, if they were male, and hair as short as animal fur, if they were female. Professor Underwood's loopy, honey-gold hairdo and flame-red dress, accented with black slashes at the collar, cuffs, and hem, stuck out. Maybe she liked being a pineapple among organic tomatoes. Or maybe she had a jones for sprouts and olives—every dish was buried in one of the two.

Jewel had no kick. Her benefactor-suspect had been sympathetic: "Oh, my *dear!* Anything I can do to help! Such a *tragedy* for so *many!*" And the Sandwich was a sweet place, with Chinese robes adorning the walls, shared newspapers traveling from table to table, overstuffed couches where intense young students could nurse their apple-cherry juice and write in their journals for hours at a time.

But here amongst the big-boot granola-heads, rare winter sun streaming through the windows, the idea that Edith Underwood murdered Mulcahy seemed ridiculous. She sat across from Jewel, a plain, tall woman who wore her grief like a badge of honor, pinned invisibly to her scarlet dress. She admired him, she defended him, she looked like she brought turkeys to The Poor on Thanksgiving Day, offensive but well-meaning. But what *did* killers look like? Jewel admonished herself. Was she expecting a skull-and-crossbones tattooed on the woman's forehead?

Bold with espresso, Jewel decided to give Edith a little push. "So—Wallinsky was wrong about the Dean sexually haras—"

"This is *just* the kind of rumor-mongering that Leo Wallinsky has fomented." Edith squared her shoulders for battle. "Dean Mulcahy is—" the big voice wobbled, "—*was* a complete professional. Occasionally students would develop crushes. Entirely natural, of course—he was a charming person—but when *unstable* or *malicious* students learned that the Dean was not 'available,' they struck back. Indeed, they are more to be pitied than censured; Leo Wallinsky put them up to it." Her voice and words were angry, but her face was only haggard with loss. Jewel had the feeling that Edith had said these things before, part of her usual defense of the Dean. There was no flicker or shadow, no liar's deliberate eye contact or shifty look away. If Edith believed Mulcahy had drop-kicked Leilani Summer to an early grave, Jewel would eat her car. Damn it. It had been a great idea.

"The man has long been a *menace* to the academic community at CBU," continued Edith. "It is no surprise that he has finally committed *murder*. I cannot *imagine* why he is still at large."

Jewel squashed an unnerving impulse to defend the police. None of that. "What did he have against the Dean, anyway? Why did he hate him so much?"

"There were many reasons." Edith leaned forward, planting her elbow deep in sprouts. "Professor Wallinsky curries favor with undergraduates. He gives high grades and little homework. This makes him *popular,* of course, but it earns him no respect. As a classroom teacher, he is nothing but an *entertainer.*" She said the last word scathingly, as though Wallinsky were sacrificing goats in the Faculty Club. "He loathes participating in university governance—he'd far rather stay home writing his *plays*. Yet he's always happy to waste time on *student causes*. Of course the Dean had a responsibility to criticize lax teaching methods and improper professional conduct, and he did so. Leo Wallinsky *deeply resented* this criticism."

"He killed the Dean because—"

"Not that alone, of course. Leo Wallinsky—" she never used either name separately, like Penn and Teller or Sacco and Vanzetti, "—was jealous of the Dean. He knew he could never have the professional success that the Dean enjoyed, and he *hated* him for it." Edith tossed her hair behind her, in a strange gesture, both imperious and feminine.

"Hmmm." Jewel bit into her pineapple-bran muffin. It was really very good, if you went for fructose instead of sugar, which she didn't, but hey—this was America. Citizens had the right to the sweetener of their choice.

Most of her brain was surfing the tidal wave of accusation that Edith was pouring over Wallinsky's head. This was a pretty damning indictment of the loud, profane, big-bearded playwright. Of course any fool could see at the dinner that Wallinsky hated Mulcahy—he'd accused him, with great fanfare, of molesting students. And Jewel remembered his bright-eyed, smothered laughter on learning of the Dean's death. There was something else, too . . . Wallinsky's rage had almost petered out, when the Dean said something that inflamed it again . . .

"Professor Underwood, had he applied for some kind of special job or—"

"The Westerfield Grant!" The woman sat very straight in her chair, looking, in her papal-red dress with dark cuffs and collar, like some rogue nun who'd joined the Canadian Royal Mounties. "Yes! He had applied for it and been, of course, rejected. He held Dean Mulcahy responsible for that, as well."

"What is the Westerfield?"

Edith's face glowed with pride for her school. "A very prestigious award. It allows the winner a two-year sabbatical in which to pursue his research interests full-time. A rare opportunity."

"So Wallinsky didn't get it?"

"Certainly *not*. There are many *deserving* faculty members at CBU. There is no need to award the grant to a foul-mouthed rabble-rouser, no matter how fine his work."

"Hmmm." Jewel watched a couple of curly-headed children play on a small carpeted stage. By night, the stage was for open-mike folk musicians and their long, painfully detailed opinions. By day, the stage was transformed into a free-for-all toddler fest, complete with Sandwich-supplied toys and games. A couple of tie-dyed tykes moiled around up there, innocent of baroque university politics. "Couldn't Wallinsky apply again?"

"He could apply yearly. But Dean Mulcahy chaired the

Westerfield Committee and he did not mince words in drafting its rejection letter. No, he made it very clear that Leo Wallinsky and his proposal would have to change drastically in order to qualify for the Westerfield."

So, Jewel brooded over her juice, Wallinsky could kiss off the big-money grant, and with it the two years of freedom to be a genius, until Mulcahy retired. Or was retired. To death.

Edith's litany of motives—obsession, resentment, jealousy—bore no resemblance to those higher motives that Wallinsky seemed to claim for himself at the dinner: justice, honor, truth. The man Edith described was far from heroic.

Jewel wondered about his ambitions. He might have a better chance of getting the Westerfield with Mulcahy dead, but would he be a shoo-in? He seemed to bask in the limelight, the night of the dinner. Maybe he wanted to be king of the heap. "Professor Underwood, did Wallinsky want to be Dean himself?"

The Religion scholar snorted, her head high and proud as that of a full-blooded race-horse. "Good heavens! That would be a total disaster! He has no discipline, no sense of order. It would be like electing an anarchist to the Presidency!"

"But—did he want the job anyway?"

"In all justice, I don't think so." A cloud passed over Edith's good, innocuous face, the shadow of a compelling motive she could not attribute to the enemy of the late Dean. "He wants to write great plays. Indeed, to give the devil his due, he is a very talented person. His work has been well-received in San Francisco and elsewhere. Of course," her disapproval reasserted itself with a louder contralto, "he has written *very little new work* since he received tenure, next to nothing, in fact."

Jewel finished her muffin. Mentally she was debating

whether to pull the Murder Suspect Statuette from Frances Carlotti's mantel to put it on Wallinsky's. The man was a powder keg. Even Jewel had seen that on the night of the dinner. Whether his purpose was noble or low or somewhere in between, he had motives enough to kill several Deans, with a few left over for the odd barroom brawl with assorted strangers. What Jewel didn't get was, why now? What was the urgency, what would have pushed Wallinsky over the edge? What else was the Dean going to announce, besides the death of the Women's Studies program?

The idea almost broke Jewel's coffee cup into bits. Who knew what the speech would include? Did anyone get a gander at the speech? If it were anywhere near as important as he thought, the secretive bastard would have had it under lock and key. Was it possible to keep secrets at Zoo U? The grapevine had telegraphed eight kinds of news across campus in a heartbeat—Ben told Wallinsky that Blue Plate was innocent, Wallinsky told Nick Mariani, everyone told everyone. Yet Mulcahy would not have had to ask anyone permission for what he was going to say at the dinner. She'd bet her pizza oven that he'd enjoyed dropping as many nasty hints and threats as he could until the witching hour.

But what about the trusty Muriel, Gal Monday-through-Friday and smart cookie? Jewel couldn't imagine the bastard doing his own typing under any circumstances, even under enemy gunfire, not when he had a secretary to do it for him. Muriel must have it in her computer. Did Muriel know what was in the speech? Was Muriel the *only* one who knew? Jewel put that on the back burner to simmer.

She didn't like Wallinsky as a suspect. Someone who hated the Dean so openly. Of course, that in itself could be good cover. Everyone would be looking for a secret hater. Someone like Underwood, who appeared to be Mulcahy's biggest fan. Or Lesley DeLaMar, the Baby Dean. Yeah, DeLaMar got a big prize with Mulcahy dead, ten years ahead of schedule. Wallinsky might not get anything. And he'd lose an enemy he seemed to need.

"How badly did DeLaMar want Mulcahy's job?"

For the first time, Edith's spate of chat dried up. She reached for her tea, then noticed it was long gone. Her eyes met Jewel's. "May I borrow your water, dear? I'm terribly thirsty." Edith Underwood drank, but not for long. "Lesley DeLaMar is ambitious, certainly, but she is only in her thirties. She would have been a fine age for the Dean's position when he retired. And she cares deeply about CBU—and would never—the idea is unimaginable."

Yet Underwood was imagining something. Her fingers crept almost involuntarily to her black collar. She straightened it, although it hadn't been crooked. Had Edith remembered something about DeLaMar? She looked sick. Her face almost crumpled.

"I'm sorry." Edith smiled wanly. "I can sail along, almost forgetting, for minutes at a time. And then—Matthew Mulcahy and I were friends for many years. I still can hardly credit—I can't believe that he's dead." Her eyes welled up. She dabbed at them with a napkin.

Jewel felt like a pig dog. She had seen Underwood, just a few days ago, wailing for Mulcahy as though she would never stop. "I'm the sorry one. You've been so helpful—recommending me for the job, and now today. I wasn't thinking."

Edith shook her head. "No, dear. We none of us can go on until we find out who did this terrible thing. And I appreciate your business dilemma. I will *certainly* advise Acting Dean DeLaMar to give your Blue Plate Catering the next two Humanities Dinners."

Unworthily, Jewel wondered whether she'd do better

without Underwood's recommendation. Pig dog worm. But she could hardly be worse off than she was right now, the jobless subject of stinky innuendo, poking around in a mystery that got more complicated with every poke.

Still more unworthily, she thought of Hartsock. That no-poke.

Professor Underwood whirled her head to look at the wall clock. "Oh, my! The senior seminar starts in fifteen minutes." She plucked itinerant sprouts from her clothes and stood.

Wait. Jewel had a feeling that things were slipping away from her. Edith shouldered an immense black leather bag and made some minute adjustment to her hair. She was going. But Jewel had something else to ask—what—

"Oh, Edith!" The woman's eyebrows shot up, but her smile was unmarred. "I mean—Professor Underwood—I understand what you say about Wallinsky's motives, but why would he do such a thing now, why in front of so many people at the dinner? Do you think he's crazy?"

Professor Underwood paused for a moment, for once silent and still. "Oh, no, dear," she said at last. "I don't believe in psychological explanations for human behavior, not ultimately. These are moral issues."

"Then—"

"He's wicked." She looked down at Jewel, her eyes tired. "Mine is an unfashionable opinion, I know. But I'm older than you are, my dear, and perhaps, in my own way, more experienced, if you'll forgive me. My work is with ancient mysteries, both Christian and pagan. I believe that evil exists."

Edith Underwood left in a whirl of red and black, her gold jewelry warm in the midday sun. Jewel stared after her, chilled to the bone.

★ ★ ★ ★ ★

It took more than a half hour's thought and a double shot of espresso for her to rise, swift with fear and purpose.

There was no one in the Dean's palatial outer office. The lights were on, but Muriel's computer screen was dark, her desk blotter neat. Untouched. Only eleven fifteen—early for a lunch break. Maybe DeLaMar was at some meeting and brought Muriel along to take notes. Maybe Muriel had taken a few days off, upset about Mulcahy's death.

Jewel stood uneasily, shifting from foot to foot. Her heartbeat thudded in her ears like a funeral march. Underwood knew something. She had sung like a canary until DeLaMar's name came up. Then suddenly she needed a moment, a glass of water, to collect herself. Grief for her fallen friend?

"I believe that evil exists."

Jewel was getting creeped out, standing irresolutely in a deserted office. She'd feel a lot better if Muriel were here.

Where was Muriel? Was Mulcahy's speech in Muriel's computer? Did anyone know it was there? What if someone didn't want people to know what Mulcahy had been about to say? What if he'd been killed to stop him from saying it? Was Muriel the only one who had the speech at her fingertips?

No noise came from the inner office.

Something had happened to Muriel.

Bullshit. The chatter of printers came to her from across the hall. People were beavering away, hard at work. Students, staff, faculty, and play-Deans were moiling all over the building.

Like there'd been people all over the Faculty Club when Mulcahy was murdered.

Don't get hysterical, Jewel told herself. Nothing could happen to Muriel, even if she were the only one with a copy of Mulcahy's speech. Acting Dean Lesleyface was probably right inside, perusing Mulcahy's files, shaking out his Rolodex, running her long nails in that ominous sofa, looking for spare change.

Unless DeLaMar was the one with the reason to kill Mulcahy before he made his announcements to Zoo U. Had he known something bad about her? Was that knowledge in Muriel's computer?

Muriel! Jewel leaped into the hallway, ready to go on a massive woman-hunt, call Ben Hartsock, scream, all of the above.

She stopped.

There, at the far end of the hall, tootling along in a gray-and-green flowered dress and sensible shoes, laden with fresh Xeroxing, was Muriel herself. Normal, hard-working, lady-like Muriel. She looked frazzled. Jewel could have sung with relief. As it was, she waved wildly, then dipped back into the outer office as Muriel disappeared around the corner. Ecstatic and over-caffeinated, Jewel decided to throw the Baby Dean a curve ball, to saunter in without being announced. It could give her just the edge she needed to jerk some information from the woman. Maybe even a confession. Jewel was safe as houses—Muriel was on her way, for gawd's sakes. Even if DeLaMar *was* the killer—what knowledge of her had crossed Underwood's face?—she couldn't kill both of them.

Chin high, Jewel swung open the massive inner door.

Acting Dean DeLaMar had been propped up in her vast leather chair, her body slumped in a horrible parody of rest. Her head hung to one side at an impossible angle. Diamonds at her ear beckoned, as in a child's nightmare of witches. Her legs were splayed. One hand rested in her lap. The other dangled off the arm of the chair. Her skin already looked like it had never been the skin of a living woman. She was not killing anyone.

Jewel screamed.

Chapter Nineteen

"She'll never be deader," said the Medical Examiner to Ben Hartsock.

The M.E. stood, sunny and substantial, in the hallway outside the Dean's office, pushing his half-glasses up. He looked like someone's grandfather in an orange juice commercial. By contrast, Hartsock looked like he wanted to bite someone's nose off. Jewel wondered whose. She and Muriel huddled a few feet away, within a sprint of the restroom. Good. Jewel had almost decided not to throw up, but she wanted to leave her options open.

That she'd had the choice was due to Muriel, who was able to carry on in the face of catastrophe. She'd set down the Xeroxing, pulled Jewel from the inner office, and pushed her at a phone. By the time Jewel had hung up from a brief but pungent chat with the 911 operator, Muriel had mustered a cup of coffee. The two of them waited in the hallway for the medics to come, Jewel gulping her coffee like it was water in the Gobi. Good Lord—Muriel had mustered brandy, too. She wondered whether DeLaMar had appreciated Muriel's treasure-like qualities.

Too late now.

The Medical Examiner and Hartsock consulted in low tones, Ben nodding, his face dark and drawn. He listened to the white-haired, stripe-shirted M.E. as though he were the only person in the world. A few words wafted Jewel's way: "head," "pushed."

Several Zoo animals tried to gather in the hallway by the Dean's office, including two suits with briefcases and a reporter from the student newspaper, but Hartsock had hustled them off. A group of ill-assorted corduroy-pants-wearing people, all victims of haircuts that looked as though they'd been done on the roof of a pick-up during a high-speed chase, had been especially indignant. "But we're the Petitions Committee!" protested their leader, brandishing a yellow legal pad as he retreated down the hall.

The brandy settled Jewel, sending rays of warmth to her fingers and toes. She was thinking, thinking. She thought: How terrible. She thought: Damn! My prime suspect. She thought: Zoo U's going to be a regular stop on the ambulance milk run. And: Was some loon picking off Deans until his own name—or hers—got to the top of the list? That was crazy. She hoped that this wasn't about crazy. If it was, she might never figure it out and get Blue Plate cooking again.

Edith Underwood's dowager voice came back to her: "I don't believe in psychological explanations"—her red dress vivid in the warm light of the Antique Sandwich—"these are moral issues."

Frances Carlotti had vibrated with fury. Over moral issues? Political questions? Could you even separate them? Jewel thought of the winsome historian's strong hands. Carlotti wouldn't be the next Dean. She'd just been hired. Way too young to be in the line-up, even if people with opinions like hers were in the running.

Leo Wallinsky's brawling public rage. Was that about morality? But even Edith Underwood, who would proudly throw the electric-chair switch with Leo in the hot seat, said he had no ambitions to be Dean. Yet he wouldn't have had to—he'd hated Mulcahy for any number of reasons.

It wasn't just about Mulcahy anymore, though. Lesley

DeLaMar was dead. Acting Dean DeLaMar. She'd never be the real thing now. Jewel was shocked—was this going to go on and on?—but also ashamed. She should probably be more sorry that DeLaMar was dead. There was some sorrow there, down in the murky sediment of emotion that felt like the bottom of a Turkish coffee. But it was any-human-being sorrow. The woman had made her blood boil, after all. And Jewel was running out of nice feelings.

She tried not to think of what the two technical people who came with Hartsock might be doing with DeLaMar's body in the Dean's inner sanctum. Don't be a cretin, she thought, just doing their jobs.

She finished off her brandy-soaked coffee, watching Ben Hartsock nod while the M.E. spoke.

It didn't make sense. She knew that people killed each other over spare change, but she just couldn't see someone murdering two people to become Dean of Zoo U. There was something else here, something simmering just below the surface motives, like a foreign flavor she couldn't identify. Saffron, cumin, Edith Underwood, Leo Wallinsky, Frances Carlotti, Tyler Seito, Leilani Summer, Ace, Helena Moore.

Now why did she think of Helena?

The M.E. bestowed a warm smile on Hartsock, whose face was all thundercloud. "At least you won't have to drag the Sound for the murder weapon. You've got it right in the office. The little lady hit her head on the desk and that was that." He pushed his glasses up again. "Fell or was pushed is the tricky part. You have a nice day, Benny. The fog's supposed to burn off."

"Thanks, Jim."

As the M.E. ambled away, Hartsock's bottomless brown eyes were unreadable. He stood for a moment, looking inward.

Jewel's musings felt feverish. Her head wouldn't stop. It

was an Indy 500 of colliding high-speed crashes. She had to get out of here.

"I want to go back to work now." Her voice was surprisingly loud and strong.

Hartsock stared at her for a moment, as if he'd never seen her before. Then his vision cleared. "Go. No, wait." He colored. "We need to talk."

She didn't like the sound of that. She'd told him everything she'd seen when she sauntered into DeLaMar's office. Told him twice.

"I talked already," she said. "I want to go now. I saw a dead body."

"Yes. Your second. That's why I—" Hartsock almost moved closer, but stopped himself. There was something in his voice she didn't recognize.

"Are you all right?" She couldn't help asking. Then remembered that she'd asked the same question the night before, as they tore off their clothes. She felt her face get hot.

"Yes and no," he said.

She wanted to stay. She wanted to leave. Uncertainty alarmed her. "Okay, bye."

"Later, then." He turned to Muriel, stalwart in her gray-and-green flowered dress, alert as a spaniel. She didn't seem overwhelmed by grief at DeLaMar's death. Muriel's readiness cheered Jewel more than the brandy. "Could you run through the list of Dean DeLaMar's scheduled appointments for me one more time?"

Muriel nodded briskly.

Jewel walked away, her legs unsteady. Benny! The nickname made her think of a ten-year-old in a shirt with lifesaver stripes, running, running.

Office workers crowded out the street dwellers on Pacific

Avenue. Lunch hour, still. Jewel had lost all track of time. Almost four P.M. in New York. Daph would be at work, still, head full of software and meetings. Damn time difference. Shocked and unnerved, Jewel had instinctively begun to bake.

She worked the pie dough quickly, so that the heat from her hands wouldn't melt the shortening. That was the difference between a huckleberry hockey puck and one as light as an angel's wing. She knew cooks who kept their hands out of the dough entirely, for fear of meltdown. But Jewel wanted to feel the dough under her fingers, however briefly. Something real.

The chilled utensils waited their turn on the butcher's block. The little radio murmured away, just loud enough to make a noise. The oven hummed slightly as it heated. Apple cider with cinnamon sticks and lemon warmed in a pan on the stove. Jewel was slightly embarrassed by this last note, a comfort drink from childhood, but she needed something warm, and if she drank any more coffee she would implode. The events of the last hour blurred like pine trees on the North Dakota highway that had taken Jewel to Washington at a minimum of seventy-five miles an hour to this gray and mountainous land of car trouble, bankruptcy, and violent death. Oh, none of that. She'd gone west, youngish woman, on purpose, and she wasn't giving up.

The dough gave up its secrets and waited for illumination or huckleberries. Jewel could use some illumination, although berries were always welcome. Her dizzying thoughts had slowed to merely disoriented. Some had vanished. Others returned with growing insistence. DeLaMar. Mulcahy. Helena Moore. Keeper of secrets. That moment between her and Lesley DeLaMar at the Humanities Dinner. Helena had wanted Jewel to be a witness to the conversation.

Student complaints, covering up a death. Had Helena known what Dean Mulcahy was going to say at the dinner?

The huckleberries glowed dark in the wooden bowl. Where had Del found them this time of year? She wanted a straight answer out of him, no mystical byways. She loaded the pie shell with layers of berries and brown sugar.

Lesley DeLaMar, protector of Mulcahy and the Zoo U flame.

A small, fiery light on the counter caught Jewel's gaze. The answering machine had two calls. Two! Wonder of wonders.

She wiped her hands on a towel and hit the button. Ben Hartsock's low, liquid voice made her want to hop in the answering machine, as though he lived there and she could shrink herself, Alice through the Looking Glass.

"Jewel. I have to talk to you about something important. Not about the murder. At least, not directly. Damn." He seemed to be swearing to himself. "I wish—this isn't the kind of message to leave on a machine, but I don't know when I'll see you. I can't see you while this case is pending." A pause opened up like a canyon. "Except as a witness. It's unethical. I shouldn't have—I'm sorry. I'm sorry to say it like this." There was a clattering on the tape, as though someone had dropped something metallic far away. Perhaps a suitcase full of iron filings on someone's chest. Jewel's. The image of the boy in the polo shirt came back. He was still running. Now he was only a blur of color at the road's end.

She felt tears rising, unbidden, behind her eyes. Had Hartsock hung up? Wouldn't he have said—

"I have to go. Be careful, okay? I'm speaking as a cop here, as well as a—look, this killer has done two people, and you're in the way."

The dial tone signaled a new chapter in the book of outrage that was Jewel's life. Whose way am I in? she wanted to scream.

So she did. "You lying, cheating, chicken-shitting, dry-humping—you can go—" she couldn't think of an acrobatic act of self-abuse that was bad enough, "—fish!" But Leo Wallinsky's buccaneer growl filled the room, costing her several valuable years of life.

"Feynmann! Wallinsky! Meet me! It's critical! I have to tell you something! And you have to tell me something! Not on campus, the hellhole is lousy with spies! Les Bailey Pier at seven tonight. Come alone! I didn't kill that bastard Mulcahy, although I'll dance on his newly-dug grave, once I find out where it is—that closed-mouthed California bastard of a brother of his won't tell me! I didn't kill DeLaMar, either. Haven't decided what to do on her grave yet! Pour a quart of scotch over it, maybe—filtering it through my kidneys first! Ha ha ha! And Feynmann, don't be late! I wait for no one!"

The dim roaring sound that filled Jewel's ears could have been the void left by Wallinsky's bear-like commands. Yet, with the part of her brain not yet fogged by fury, she thought not. It was the noise of a woman who had been pushed too far.

Mulcahy's murder.

Blue Plate's death throes.

Hartsock's kiss.

DeLaMar's killing.

Hartsock's kiss-off. And now, some brawling mean-mouthed bully of a playwright-professor leaves a stupid, tyrannical, bossy bunch of orders loud enough to make her eardrums bleed. That was it. She'd had enough.

She ripped the apron off, shut the oven down, and grabbed her car keys. She cast a swift look of longing back over her shoulder at the bowl of huckleberries. No. Jewel was going to get ready to meet Wallinsky on Les Bailey Pier tonight. And she knew just what she had to do. Pie or no pie.

Chapter Twenty

Jewel had sworn to herself she wouldn't wait more than fifteen minutes for Leo Wallinsky, tops, when a chugging noise drew her gaze from the Sound. A sparkling red Studebaker pick-up came to a halt, parked lavishly across two parking spaces, and disgorged a bear from the driver's seat. No, it was Wallinsky, massive and hairy in a long fur coat.

Jewel stared at him from the pier, lost in scorn and wonder. Fur coat! Who did he think he was, Nijinsky? It was cold but it wasn't *that* cold.

Wallinsky powered through the parking lot like a gust of wind, his beard and wayward hair making him look, at this shorter distance, like the mean giant from "Jack and the Beanstalk." A mean giant in a ten-thousand-dollar fur.

He covered the distance at a great pace.

Jewel's pulse bumped up six beats. No reason for alarm. Lamps on poles lit up the night, casting funhouse shadows on the pier.

She wasn't alone. An old man fished. A few teenagers smoked in the parking lot.

Wallinsky stomped down the pier, big and loud enough to scare dead fish in a bucket. "Feynmann!"

Jewel waved, wondering whether Leo Wallinsky greeted children the way he did adults. Did they flee into the woods, leaving behind a trail of stones and the memory of an ogre?

Suddenly he was almost on top of her, all out of scale.

His face was red. He stared down at Jewel like she was a tick. "You," he said, "are fucking everything up."

Jewel had to lean back to look him in the face. She couldn't see anything but beard and fur and eyes. "Yeah?" She squinted at him. "Like how?"

"Like," he mimicked unkindly, "flailing around, looking for Mulcahy's killer to save your pathetic business. It's got to stop. There's more at stake here than catering." He said "catering" the way Jewel would say "doily-tatting."

Then he halted abruptly, mid-growl. "Not pathetic," he corrected, with the precision of a writerly sheep in wolf's clothing, "irrelevant."

"Easy for you to say!" Fear made Jewel angry. Her temper cracked and split like firewood. "You're got a paycheck coming, no matter what you do, Mr. Job for Life! Mr. Fur Coat! I work for a living!"

With the unsettling mood shift she was beginning to see as the norm, Wallinsky let loose a big, operetta laugh, a pirate king laugh.

"Feynmann! You have a terrible temper! You probably didn't have any customers anyway, you harridan! But look, if you lay off this 'investigation' of yours, I'll give you the damned coat. Deal?"

Jewel advanced, her chin at a pugnacious angle. "Who are you to talk about my temper! You went off at that dinner like an electrical fire! And what's with the Westerfield Grant, anyway? Edith Underwood thinks you did Mulcahy, you know. Why did you call me out here to begin with? What do you want from me?"

A pleased look crossed Wallinsky's broad face, as though a dim student had said something unexpectedly provocative. "She does, does she?"

The fisherman left the pier, bucket in one hand, line in the other.

Now Jewel and Wallinsky were alone. The teenagers were a city block away, smoking and talking, backs to the water. The *Titanic* could rise without their noticing.

Wallinsky turned towards the Sound, leaning over the railing on his elbows. This signaled to Jewel a companionable mood, or at least a few seconds of one. She faced the water, too, although it was too dark to see anything but the outline of land on the horizon.

"Feynmann, let me explain the Texas Defense."

Her heart sank. "Did you drag me out here to talk football? I'll kill myself and name you in the note."

"In Texas, a man who confesses to first-degree homicide can walk freely from the courtroom into an all-night whorehouse if his lawyer convinces the jury that he was an instrument of justice. The Texas Defense is: the man needed killing. In the nineteenth century, when your ancestors were still being purged and massacred back in the old country, horse theft was a hanging offense. Homegrown hangings—"

"It doesn't matter how rotten Mulcahy was," snarled Jewel. Her feet were beginning to chill, even in her brown leather boots. "He shouldn't have been murdered, and—"

"He was a brutal fuckstain. Terrorized students, staff, faculty, anyone without the spine or the rank to walk away. He enjoyed it, too."

"What about Lesley DeLaMar?"

He rolled his eyes. "What about her?"

"Did she deserve killing? Is anyone else going to die?" She made a violent, ineffectual gesture in the air. "Until the killer is caught, the crimes might continue. And I can't afford it. My business is going under. *You* may have family money,"

181

she said, taking a shot in the dark at that black llama coat and his easy confidence, "but I *don't*."

He turned on her savagely, rocketing to his full height. "What do you know about my family's money, you nosy bint?"

She jumped back, which made her madder. "Nothing! I am *not* a bint!"

"It's Arabic for 'daughter,' " he growled, moving closer to her.

Wallinsky was ruining her nerves. "What are you so touchy about? What did you want to tell me? What do you want to know? I'm freezing. I saw a dead body. I had a bad day."

He narrowed his eyes. "I want to find out what you know and tell you to lay off."

She sighed and told him what she'd learned: Leilani and Tyler, Mulcahy's lie about the dinner delay, Carlotti. It might turn the conversation, which was so far pointless. Maybe Wallinsky would offer her some information in exchange. She hoped her impetuosity would anger Hartsock, her lavish shower of information on a violent-tempered murder suspect alone on a night-time pier.

The sooner she solved these murders, the sooner Ben Hartsock could see her again. Then it would be her turn to kiss him off.

If she lived that long. Was Wallinsky wearing a weapon under his coat? Was that why he put it on? She shivered with cold and frustration. She trusted the big-mouthed blowhard, but she didn't know why.

"That's what I know," she said irritably, "jack."

"That's *all* you know?" He looked suspicious.

"I don't *know!* I might know something that I don't know I know!" Strangely, this lame outburst seemed to answer a question he hadn't asked.

Wallinsky slammed his hands together and muttered. He walked away from her, down to the end of the pier, then walked back.

"Goddamnit." He stared glumly out at the water again. "I'll tell you why I want this to end, if you swear you'll never tell another living soul."

"Oh, fine. Then we'll be blood brothers." She was tired of men. The women she knew never made her stand out on a dock in the winter night while they threatened her, laughed at her, and extorted blood vows from her. She must have been a Pharaoh in another life and this was her punishment.

"I am," he began in a voice of a man reading children's Christmas stories on public radio, "a man of prodigious appetites: food! clothes! wine! travel! And I am a man of expanded responsibilities. I have an ex-wife on alimony, and child support for three kids. They live in New York." He made a scornful noise. Jewel couldn't tell its target—his ex-family, New York, himself. "I don't care about the money. Back when we were together, I was kind of an asshole to live with."

You amaze me, she thought.

"But I don't have enough money, nowhere near. So," he looked at her with a mix of defiance and shame, "I moonlight. Mulcahy found out about it."

"Yeah?" She was lost. "Is that illegal at Zoo U? To have a second job?"

"Nah. Dumbbutts in Business moonlight their collective ass off, consulting like mad hens." He bucked up briefly, then subsided. "It wasn't that. I was writing confessions."

Now she was really lost. "For Catholics?" She couldn't see any money in it.

"Imbecile," he said absently. "For women's magazines.

'Married Three Times and Still a Virgin.' 'I was Born Without a Vagina.' You know."

"*I* know?"

"It was the best legal scam I ever came up with." His voice held self-contempt and pride in equal measures. "I could crank them out like grocery lists. Watching baseball on TV. In between classes. I made steady money, easy money. I wrote plays in the summer. The confessions kind of warmed me up for the real writing."

"I *guess*." Jewel was fascinated. She forgot to be cold and furious. "No *vagina?*"

"Swear to God," he said, laughing again. "I persecuted this gynecologist in University Place until he said it was possible."

"I still don't get the problem. If it wasn't illegal, what could Mulcahy—"

"Christ on a pogo stick!" He smashed his hand down on the railing, all laughter gone again. "I'm one of your post-post-avant garde big-dick intellectual playwrights, get it? I'm seven kinds of Eugene Ionesco by way of Irene Fornes, get it? My work is just beginning to get performed at the theaters that matter! If I were writing pornography, it'd be one thing. But confessions!"

His massive shoulders sank.

Unaccountably, Jewel felt sorry for him. "Some of them sound pornographic."

"Mulcahy found out. I still don't know how. Maybe the squid got into my office computer. Who knows? He used what he knew to turn me down for the Westerfield. And every time I'd drag his reactionary, felonious, child-molesting ass close to the fire, he'd threaten to tell everyone."

Jewel gnawed at her lower lip. This sounded like the Mulcahy she'd heard about in other stories—Carlotti's,

184

Mariani's, Tyler's. Not just a tyrant, but a tyrant who liked watching his victims squirm. But—

"At the dinner, you threatened him with the student group against sexual harassment—weren't you afraid—"

"Fuck." He dragged out the word in his baritone so that it sounded four miles long. Jewel wondered if his plays had much dialogue. "Just calling his bluff. Christ, if he told, he wouldn't have anything left to tell. I figured he'd rather keep my balls in a vise than blow my cover."

"Huh." The man wasn't a bad psychologist, for all his profane and unreasonable antics. Yet something was wrong here.

Jewel shifted from foot to foot, trying to get blood to circulate again. Maybe Wallinsky had called Mulcahy's bluff in a burst of outrage and bravado—and maybe he knew that the Dean would not have time for any damaging revelations. "He might have been going to tell everyone in the speech that night."

The big man snorted.

"Did you know he wasn't going to?" A dimly-burning lightbulb in Jewel's brain began to blaze. "Hey! Why did you tell me about the confessions, anyway? No one would have to know—Mulcahy's dead. You're safe."

He turned to her again, head dropped low like a bull about to charge. "He couldn't shut me up by threatening me with the confessions. The night he died, he found another way, one that would have worked."

"What?"

"Not what," Wallinsky spat. "Who."

"Your family? But—"

"Not them. Listen to me. I didn't want anyone to know about my confession writing, but I could have weathered it. Others had even more at stake. Mulcahy told me that if I didn't knock off 'agitating students' as faculty advisor of SSH, he'd lower the boom on—one of these people."

Wallinsky's face darkened with the memory.

"Who?"

"Whoever poisoned him was pushed too far for too long. Mulcahy needed killing. The murderer deserves a purple cross and a Cadillac SUV. You just lay off. I'll get you some customers, if that's all it is. I'll have a party. I'll have a fucking party every night."

So Mulcahy had begun using Wallinsky's loyalty to a friend. He must have been afraid of the lawyer that Wallinsky had helped the student group to hire. Jewel wondered how many more students besides Leilani Summer had been victimized by the Dean.

She stared at Wallinsky, running through the names and faces of the Zoo animals she knew. Who had his loyalty, his sympathy? Helena Moore, Lesley DeLaMar, Nick Mariani, Edith Underwood . . .

"Please—who?"

He looked ferocious. "Are you deaf? I'm not saying any more." He glowered at her, hoping for a fight.

"But the person could still be dangerous—"

"It was Mulcahy who was dangerous! And DeLaMar, that weasel—she probably knew all about it! Tom Pearsall wouldn't hurt—"

They looked at each other in horror. Wallinsky hit his forehead with a slab-like palm, roaring in wordless frustration. Tom Pearsall. The older, bitter man who'd led the campus protests about Vietnam. The man who drank hard and steadily throughout the evening. The man with the glamorous wife.

Jewel could pinch herself for being so stupid.

She and Wallinsky were alone on the pier. The big man

could pick her up by the scruff of her neck and drop her in the Sound as easily as she'd throw an artichoke into a pot of water.

Wallinsky stopped bellowing. He eyed her malevolently.

"Now you know and you'll tell the world." Wallinsky grabbed her arm.

"No touching!" She reached into her purse and hauled out a canister of pepper spray. She held it aloft and pointed.

He roared and lunged for the canister, throwing off her aim.

Jewel sprayed his coat with pepper. He roared again. She began to run, her boots clattering on the wooden slats of the pier. The instructions on the can she'd bought at the sporting goods store that afternoon only got as far as spraying, not pursuit.

He caught up with her at once and spun her around by her shoulders. With a single smash downward, he brushed the canister from her hand. It rolled across the slats in the dock.

Jewel felt stupid with fear.

"You ruined my coat!" Wallinsky said in high indignation. "You animal activist! Did you really think I was going to hurt you? What the hell is that shit?"

"Pepper spray."

He released her and studied the stain. "Christ! You're paying my dry cleaning bill. If they can't get this mark out, you are death on a soda cracker."

He abandoned his stain analysis and glared at Jewel. "Don't tell anyone or I'll kill you."

Jewel was tired of being threatened. "Go ahead, it would be a relief."

They stood uncertainly on the pier.

"Did Pearsall tell you—"

"Fuck, no! He's no whiner! But he did it. I would have, if I were him. Everyone making jokes about Mulcahy and his wife. He's not well, or else I'm sure he would have done it sooner."

Jewel's brows furrowed. "So you don't know this, you're just guessing—"

"I am *never wrong.*"

"You don't have anything to tell, just a guess. Everyone has a guess."

He looked shocked. "I'm not everyone!"

"Oh, give it up. I'm going home." She turned from him and began walking unsteadily down the pier, towards the parking lot. With a brief thrill of panic, she imagined the sound of huge, running footsteps, then the feel of being tackled from behind.

"Don't tell anyone!" he shouted after her. "I could use a caterer! I might remarry! You never know! Just give me a couple days to line someone up! Also I'll have an end-of-term party, a big party!"

His voice got smaller as the Duster got bigger. She never thought she'd be so glad to see the wretched lemon.

"No, I know! A Dead Dean Party!" He laughed hugely from the pier. "It'd be great! Hundreds of people! I'll sell the coat! You'll be rich!"

As she unlocked her car door, she turned to look at him, a giant bear or sprite waving his arms over his head. "You *are* an asshole!" she called, from the safety of her open car door.

It was time to visit the Pearsalls.

Chapter Twenty-One

An hour later, Jewel put her palms on Blue Plate's counter as though to repel invaders. But there was only one in her lair, and he didn't repel easy.

Ben Hartsock stood on the customer side of the counter. His face was gray as ash. Jewel, who had been trying to get the Pearsalls' unlisted number when he walked in, slammed the phone back in the cradle and used Blue Plate's front counter as a shield. Coldly, she reported her meeting with Wallinsky. Words were exchanged on the advisability of meeting murder suspects at night on deserted piers armed with nothing but pepper spray.

Hartsock was against it.

"Gaudy way to get yourself killed," he said, voice low and full.

"I knew Wallinsky hadn't done it. I was safe," she lied. Her ineffectual run down the pier sprang traitorously to mind.

"You knew he hadn't done it." Hartsock was as restrained as Wallinsky had been uncontrolled, but his shadowed eyes and angry jaw said he was moved by something. Whether anger or passion or contempt she could not say. Besides, as with the diamond in Tiffany's window: if she had to ask, she couldn't afford it.

"Have you never been wrong?" he asked.

"More than once. I was wrong about you."

She could have cut her tongue out and baked it in a meat

pie. Ben—Hartsock—was a whole other matter. This was about saving her business, untying the dead weight that Zoo U had anchored around her neck, swimming to the surface.

"You weren't wrong about me."

The sudden softness of his tone unnerved her more than his rebukes. She broke eye contact and made for the refrigerator.

"And don't blow smoke." He raised his voice again. "You were wrong about meeting Wallinsky."

"So you keep saying. But here I am, big as life, making a pie."

Del had refreshed the huckleberries she'd left earlier by pouring water into their bowl, then covering them. The pie crust was beyond hope, of course, but Jewel liked the way he'd saved it, anyway. He had tidy, winning ways.

Hartsock, she saw from the corner of her eye, looked like the winner in a game of statues. If he had moved an eyelash, he'd done it when her back was turned. She did not slam the bowl of huckleberries on the butcher's block side counter.

She knew she was right. He could wait for an apology from her until the rains stopped.

Jewel began assembling the utensils to chill. She scooped them up and stuck them in the freezer, glancing at her watch. Once she'd left the knife and rolling pin and spatula in there so long that they'd been heavy with ice shards.

Flour. Butter.

"Take this seriously."

"I do." She was stung into looking at him. "Why do you think I'm baking?"

"To give yourself time to think. And to avoid me."

Astonished, she abandoned the pie.

The counter still separated them, their Great Wall of China. Hartsock's dark gaze bore down on her. His receding hairline made his eyes more . . . central. He wore a black shirt under his brown corduroy jacket. Black brought him into focus sharply. His cheekbones. His mouth.

Jumping penny toads! Get back on track.

"So what if meeting Wallinsky wasn't the best idea I ever had." She surprised herself as much as she did Hartsock. "It wasn't the worst, either. It's my business and my life. I found out things that matter. Wallinsky's not a killer. He's a brawler and a loudmouth bully, but—"

"He did a good job of throwing you Pearsall."

"That was an accident."

"An accident." Hartsock's eyebrows rose a fraction of an inch.

"Yeah." She leaned towards him, over the counter. "The man isn't built for secrets. He says whatever he wants. He seemed half-relieved to have the confessions stuff out. He wanted to tell it."

A thought struck her. "Maybe it wasn't all accident. Maybe he wanted us—" uh-oh "—or someone to prove that Pearsall couldn't have done it, to get him *off* the hook, not on."

"So Wallinsky's a brawler who favors the triple quadruple bluff," said Hartsock. "Fancy." A grin broke out. Jewel grinned, too.

Something in the air between them shifted. She remembered the feel of his half-day beard against her collarbone. Her face grew hot.

He wasn't the enemy. Her body was.

Hartsock opened his mouth to say something. But she didn't want to talk about ethics or the two of them or why he was right and she was wrong.

"Why *couldn't* it be Pearsall?" she said. "Wallinsky said he had reason, and I know he hated the Dean. And—" Suddenly she remembered the taut conversation with Helena Moore in her darkened car. "And people on campus said Mulcahy had been having some big-time affair with a married woman. Melisande Pearsall had been a student of Pearsall's and of Mulcahy's, too."

"You've forgotten DeLaMar. What reason would Pearsall have to kill DeLaMar? And if Mulcahy's been seeing Melisande Pearsall for years, why would her husband kill him now?"

"Oh. Good question."

Hartsock's smile had some steel in it. "Thank you."

But Jewel was now too jacked up to give him the swipe he so richly deserved. "There were so many people with reasons to hate Mulcahy, but I don't know why anyone would have wanted to kill DeLaMar, unless the idea was to be Dean."

Hartsock leaned his elbows on the counter. Their faces were close, but she didn't notice. Although he did smell good. "And you think it wasn't? People kill each other for less than that."

"I know, I know, but this just doesn't feel like it's about work. Or not only about work. It feels personal." She shrugged and headed for the cupboard to pull out brown sugar and nutmeg. Were there almonds or pecans? The pie would need some crunch. She began scrabbling in the far reaches of the cupboard. Whole walnuts. That would do.

"Everything people say," she said, pulling a nutcracker from the utensil drawer, "makes it sound like Mulcahy always found a way to mix up the two, personal and work."

Hartsock walked through the opening in the counter into the kitchen. He leaned against the sink, watching as she began cracking nuts on the butcher's block. For a moment there was a comfortable silence, filled only with nut-cracking.

"I don't know enough about DeLaMar." Jewel remembered the woman's diamond earrings and narrow pumps, her nasty niceness and her loyalty. "Just that she was a real puppy dog around Mulcahy, liked to be near him . . ."

"Romance?"

She didn't look up. "No. More like scoring points, sucking up. Everyone else she likes—liked—to one-up." She remembered the spare, elegant woman's antipathy to bad press for Zoo U. Her argument with Helena at the dinner about keeping scandals quiet. Her criticism of the press on the morning after Mulcahy's death. "Loyal, really true to her school."

"Used to be, maybe."

"Used to be." The itch at the back of her mind got bigger. Lesley DeLaMar, sprawled in her armchair like a broken doll. What had Jewel been so heated up about when she sauntered into that office? Fear for Muriel, but also— "Hey! You know anything about the speech Mulcahy was supposed to give that night?"

"A bit." Hartsock looked up from the pie-in-progress. "He didn't have anyone type it up. He liked changing things until the last minute."

"Like do you know what was in it and who knew about it? Because I keep wondering why he pretended dinner was late. He wouldn't have blamed Blue Plate for the bullshit dinner delay just to jerk me around. He acted like he had something to spring on people. He wanted that wait. I think he wanted to make everyone wait for that stupid speech . . . until something happened or . . . I don't know!"

"Mmmm." Hartsock looked far away. It wasn't cologne or anything, just his natural smell. She policed her thoughts. He returned to the land of the living. "Pearsall's out. He was in the hospital at the time DeLaMar died."

She was appalled. "Someone tried to do him, too? How—"

"No. He's got cancer. He goes in for chemotherapy about once every eight weeks."

She stopped working to stare at Hartsock. What she saw was Pearsall at the dinner: haggard, once-handsome, bitter, and sad. Surely he shouldn't be drinking. Unless it no longer mattered. "That poor guy."

"He's got motive enough, Wallinsky's right there. Pearsall believed Mulcahy and his wife were starting up an affair that had finished years ago. And Mulcahy was giving him a lot of static about his health. Are you doing a lattice top-crust?"

"No. What kind of static?"

"That's what I want to find out. Guy was too weak to talk much yesterday. I'm heading back today."

She straightened up and wiped her hands on a towel. She tried to look responsible. "Take me with."

Hartsock eyed her with dismay. Even exasperation. He began shaking his head no, no, no.

The door swung open and Del swung in, tie-dyed and sunny. He was carrying an armload of fresh asparagus. "Hi, you two! I'm doing a bisque! Ben, can you stay?" He loped past the front counter to drop his greenery on the far end of the butcher's block. "Guess what! I found out some stuff about the murder! Good stuff! Remember how I was going to go to the Triple-A Artwalk to see what I could find out?"

"Yeah, and . . . ?"

"I met this woman there who's a sculptor? She makes these big half-lizard, half-human things? I told her I worked for Blue Plate and how we didn't murder the Dean and she was real interested. She'd read about it in the papers and everyone was talking about it—"

Jewel's eyebrows drew together to form a single, stormy line.

Del hurried on. "And this friend of hers who's a travel

194

agent said Dean Mulcahy had called her just a week or so before he died. Guess what else!"

"Del—"

"He was trying to find out the best rates on flights to Puerto Vallarta."

In the complicated silence that followed, Del began trimming the asparagus. Jewel gave up on the pie. "What the hell?"

"Was he a regular customer of hers?" Hartsock asked, pulling up a chair from the wooden table. He sat so that he could see Del and Jewel at the same time.

"Not really. He'd call once in a while to price stuff, but he never bought anything through her."

"Why'd she remember him at all, then?" Jewel said.

"Because he always said, 'This is Dean Matthew St. James Mulcahy,' like it was her lucky day. Also, he liked deals, always had all these questions about cheap flights, coupons, discounts, you know. He was real interested in the companion ticket thing this month."

"The companion—" Jewel's head began whirling. "He was going to Mexico with someone else?"

"I guess," said Del.

Hartsock slid his notebook out of his back pocket. "She know who?"

"I don't think so. I think she told me everything she could remember that her friend said."

"Del," said Jewel, momentarily diverted. "How come she told you so much?"

"Um." He rinsed the asparagus at the sink. "She felt bad that we were innocent and she wanted to help us."

"Uh-huh," said Jewel. "And?"

"And . . . she's looking for a model. For this series she's doing." He wouldn't look up.

"You're going to model for her? Naked?" Jewel decided she was scandalized. He was a cute kid, but she was a kind of third parent. Del went pink.

"When was he traveling?" said Hartsock.

"Spring break, he said." Del sounded relieved. "I don't know when that would be. At the seminary, it was the end of March."

Hartsock was scribbling. "Did the artist mention her friend's name?"

"Nope."

"What's the artist's name?"

Del wiped his hands on his jeans. "Ariel Something. She gave me her card." He began emptying his jeans pockets, dumping pennies, gum wrappers, erasers, and scraps of papers onto the counter.

Knowing that Del's journey through his clothes and backpack could be longer than a winter night in Anchorage, Jewel turned back to Hartsock. "Take me with, to the hospital."

"No."

"I could help. Maybe Pearsall would say more if he knew it would help other people."

"No."

"Maybe I could talk to Melisande while you were talking to Pearsall. She'd say more to a woman."

Hartsock rolled his eyes. "The way Acting Dean DeLaMar opened her girlish heart to you? No."

Jewel marshaled her thoughts. There must be something she could say that would persuade Ben—Hartsock—to bring her along. She couldn't miss this chance. They were close to finding the killer. She could feel it.

Del was now halfway through the zippered compartments of his backpack. On the counter stood a mountain of flotsam and jetsam, including a Pez dispenser and a green feather.

"If you don't take me, I'll go by myself."

"You're a free agent."

"If I get into trouble, it will be all your fault because you didn't take me with you."

"Lame. No."

Suddenly she lost her taste for the game. She shook her hair out of her eyes. "I don't need you or your permission, either. I'll follow you there in the Duster. If you lose me, I'll go to every hospital in town looking for the Pearsalls. They'll tell me more on my own, anyway."

"I found it!" Del waved the card triumphantly, then loped up to Ben and handed it off.

"You tell me not to meet murder suspects alone," she said. "And then you tell me not to meet murder suspects with you. What am I supposed to do? I mean, what's that leave?"

Hartsock rose. His broad face was long-suffering. "It's interesting," he said, "that your parents didn't drown you at birth."

"I'll put a lattice crust on the top! Let me just get my coat." Her high-beam smile went to parking lights when she looked back at Del. "Model if you like, but keep your clothes on, little mister. You hardly know the woman."

Hartsock snorted.

Chapter Twenty-Two

The IV cart at the side of Tom Pearsall's bed stood as straight as a French headwaiter and as forbidding. Even with tubes, Pearsall managed a shadow of his usual irascibility. He lay propped on the white bed so that he had a dead-eye view, wan and sardonic, of everyone who came through the door. Jewel and Hartsock were not, she guessed, the tail end of a throng.

A bunch of pale, early daffodils stood in a glass vase by the window, overlooking a view of a Dumpster alley. The single-bed room boasted no balloons, no rhyming cards or well-wishing dolls. A tray of white and yellow foods had been abandoned. There were lines as deep as wells in Pearsall's face. His blue eyes were pale but keen. "No grapes?"

Jewel smacked her forehead. "I'm a fool! We passed Firmani's Market—"

A wheezing noise filled the room. Pearsall, laughing.

"I'd only throw them up." The wheeze turned into a cough, dry and painful.

"Should I get—do you need anything?"

He gestured dismissively at her concern, still coughing.

"I hate hovering," he said at last. "Sit down, Hartsock. And you, Blue Plate, what are you doing here?"

Jewel took the armchair by the bed while Ben pulled a straightback chair in from the wall. She stumbled through a few words about her business. Pearsall seemed unoffended and uninterested. She couldn't blame him.

"I'm sorry to bother you again," Hartsock said when

Jewel ran out of steam. He leaned forward in the chair. "And I'm sorry for the kind of questions. But homicide investigations—"

Pearsall rolled his eyes. "You said that yesterday. You have to turn over a lot of stones and sometimes bugs crawl out. Mulcahy. Mulcahy and DeLaMar. I bet you've seen enough insect life to start an ant farm." His hands, white and thin, moved fitfully on the top sheet. An old man's hands.

"Professor Pearsall, you said yesterday that Mulcahy had been giving you static about your health."

"The bastard was trying to force me out. He said I was too sick to teach." Rage stained his weak voice like blood. "It was more of his hypocritical bullshit. My teaching hadn't suffered. I only have to miss a few days a month."

"Could he have fired you?"

"I didn't think so. It bothered Melisande more than it did me. She—" he changed tracks, "—the Italian-shoe-shod son-of-a-bitch just wanted to roust me."

"Why?"

"Christ, why do you think?"

"Professor Pearsall, *was* your wife seeing Dean Mulcahy?" Ben's voice was steady and uninflected. Jewel flinched anyway.

"Spit it out, man. You don't care if she *saw* him. You want to know if she had *sex* with him." He tired of the lesson at once. "I don't know. They had an affair years ago. She ended it. When she met me." Pearsall stared out the window for a minute, as if searching for the energy that drew Melisande to him years ago.

"Yesterday you said you thought they might have started again. What made you think that?"

"Melisande had grown . . . secretive and nervous. Not like

her. She's . . ." Words failed him. He scowled with the frustration of a general whose soldiers had retreated ignominiously. "Poised. Even serene."

Hartsock nodded. Jewel thought the two men had some sort of connection. Whether from their session the day before, or from some instinctive man-thing, recognition or respect, she couldn't guess. But Ben knew what he was doing, how to question Pearsall. She wouldn't have, despite her big talk back at Blue Plate.

"So what did you think made her secretive and nervous?"

"Boredom, maybe. She quit her paralegal job a year ago, when the first round of chemo started. I thought she wanted out and was afraid to tell me. You saw her, man. She wasn't born to be an old man's nurse."

"You didn't ask her why she was nervous?"

"No."

Hartsock let his next question hang in the air. Pearsall heard it. The IV seemed to suck the color from his eyes. Not that there had been much left. But he wasn't looking at them, at the room, at the wan daffodils or abandoned tray. The landscape he saw was bleaker and private.

"I won't ask her," he said at last.

"Why not?" Ben sounded like he knew the answer and maybe he did. Jewel looked at him sharply.

"When she keeps something to herself, it's for a reason. Her reason. Not mine."

"Noble."

The faint question in Ben's voice stung Pearsall into brief anger. "No! Damn it. It's not about me. She's an independent woman, my wife. I won't rush her into . . . telling me anything she isn't ready to tell me."

"Respectful."

"Yes." Pearsall smiled at the good student. For a moment,

his grin gave Jewel a look at the man Melisande married, smart and canny, comic and handsome.

But his restraint maddened Jewel. Was it weakness or strength? How could you live with someone you loved and not ask them if they were about to leave you for your detested boss? It would be like standing on the edge of a crumbling cliff, waiting for the world to fall in. Jewel would rather jump.

She wanted to ask Pearsall about his restraint, if that's what it was. Unfortunately, Ben had wrung a vow of silence from her as they had jog-trotted down the hospital hallway. He wanted to question Pearsall without her interference. But vows were provisional, one of the reasons she'd never married, and her plastic wristwatch said it was time to break one.

"How could you not ask?" she said.

Hartsock's laser-gaze bored into her skull, but Pearsall didn't seem to notice. "She was in my survey class. It's not just that she was the most beautiful woman I've ever seen, before or since, although she was. It was her freaking intelligence. Unreal. Self-contained! I couldn't teach her shit. Her writing, her world view—she had her own rules, her own way of seeing. You couldn't judge her by the same standards as you did other students' work. Christ!"

For a moment, the hospital room faded, along with twenty-five years, and they sat with Pearsall, stunned before a brilliant and beautiful woman years his junior. His student. Mulcahy's lover.

"I still don't know why she married me."

"Tom." The crystalline voice cut through the memories like diamond. Melisande Pearsall stood in the doorway, elegant in a cinnamon-colored skirt and cinnamon- and black-patterned sweater, her white-blonde hair glowing. She carried a take-out cup of coffee with a bagel balanced on its plastic lid. Her peach-colored skin was wan. With what, Jewel

201

wasn't sure. Tea leaves made for easier reading than Melisande Pearsall.

Ben rose with instinctive good manners, Jewel from a sense of disquiet. Melisande Pearsall telegraphed anger with restraint. She had put the coffee down carefully, straightened her husband's sheets efficiently, and began cutting the bagel in half with a knife from the tray. "You're a fool, Tom."

Oddly, her anger cheered him. "That's the news? What's the weather?"

She refused to smile, handing him half a bagel as though it were alive with flames. He took it, but not as though he planned to eat it.

Hartsock remained standing. "Ms. Pearsall, I'm sorry— but would you mind waiting outside for a few minutes until we're done talking?"

Jewel saw a colder anger in the woman's eyes as she nodded at Hartsock, then turned from the room, chin high.

"I'll wait outside, too." Jewel gathered her coat and bag in a hurry, hoping that Ben wouldn't force her to stay. She made the hallway without hearing his voice. Probably he was happy to get rid of her.

Melisande stood at the hallway's end, incongruous among the low beige armchairs and old magazines. She stared at the window, although, as with Tom Pearsall, Jewel didn't have the feeling she was looking at the view. There was silver in Melisande's hair, mixed in with the white-blonde. Either a woman without vanity or one who knew that silver and white became her. Jewel hesitated. She tried to imagine her as a twenty-year-old, tried to imagine what she'd have seen in the Dean, why he closed in on someone so strong. Would he have gone for any good-looking student? Maybe she wasn't strong back then. Or just being a student, and young, provided enough of an imbalance of power. As a bastard, Mulcahy had been an overachiever. Jewel noticed again how he rampaged over the lines between sex and work, ethics and excess like a *Tyrannosaurus rex* stampeding over the plains. Imagine threatening a sick man with losing his job. But Pearsall at least could hold his own.

The Dean's abuse of power over students was worse. His long history of sexual bullying had gone unchecked. The shadowy line of young women would have been considered "conquests" back then. The students wouldn't complain. There had been no such thing as sexual harassment, not in law. But the crime existed before the law did. And it was hardly historical. All the contemporary legal debates, newspaper articles, and talk shows hadn't helped Leilani Summer.

Other people got hurt, too. Leilani's family. Tyler Seito. Frances Carlotti and Leo Wallinsky were strung tight with outrage at the Dean's misconduct with students. He found other ways to yank their chains, honing the same skills of manipulation that worked Leilani Summer into her grave. Jewel couldn't believe the man had even one relationship that wasn't stained with abuse of power. But Edith Underwood had the loyalty of an old-time family retainer—how had he worked her?

And, Jewel reminded herself, Pearsall. Melisande had been his student. For all Jewel knew, he had hit on young women, too. His philosopher friend had mentioned "groupies" at the Humanities Dinner. But Pearsall didn't seem to hate women or to care about scoring like Mulcahy had. If he had affairs with willing women in his classes—wasn't that different? Was it? All told, Zoo U was a crime scene long before the Humanities Dinner.

Melisande stood smoking, back as straight as the last poplar on earth. Whatever Pearsall had been doing twenty-five years ago, and with whatever license, he met Melisande and that was that. Italian great-aunts had an expression for love that struck you with such force: the thunderbolt—brilliant, illuminating, dangerous. Mulcahy had been cut out. Or had he?

Jewel knew the ending: Mulcahy, dead on the hardwood floor. DeLaMar, killed and flung into an armchair. What had Lesley DeLaMar done? Or seen? What did she know? Jewel knew the beginning: here, in the quarter-century-old mirage of young Tom Pearsall and even younger Melisande.

Jewel approached the woman with unaccustomed caution. "Ms. Pearsall?"

"I know." She didn't turn from the window. "Your business. Leo told Tom." Why Zoo U bothered with a telephone system while Wallinsky was on the payroll was beyond Jewel. Telephone, telegram, tell-a-Leo.

"It's not just about my business anymore," Jewel said.

"It never was."

"I know. I'm sorry."

Her sympathy whipped Melisande Pearsall around. She stared at Jewel with ice in her eyes. "Are you? What for?"

"Because this is a hard time for you, and—"

"Really. Do you imagine that I'm in mourning? That I'm mourning the death of my lover?"

"No! Who could mourn—I mean, your husband's sick and these murders have dug up the past—"

"Go away." Her voice, light and musical as it was, did not invite debate. Close up, Jewel could see the faint lines at her eyes, as delicate as Japanese brush strokes. Then Melisande's gaze returned to the window, as though Jewel had never existed.

But Jewel did exist. And the faceless figure at the edge of her consciousness existed. People were dead. Maybe others were in danger. Murder blasted the right to privacy out the hospital window and into the parking lot. It wasn't Jewel who'd wrested Melisande's past into the present. It was the murderer.

Jewel wanted the middle of the story. For Blue Plate and for her own satisfaction. To stop the murderer. It was urgent. Now, before Melisande returned to the hospital room. She took a deep breath.

"Mulcahy wanted you to go to Puerta Vallarta with him, didn't he? But you didn't want to go."

Melisande gasped. Her shock was palpable, bone-deep. "How—"

"He'd called a travel agent, trying to cop a deal on a companion ticket rate. He didn't use your name or anything. But it had to be you. I'd heard—well, things—" Jewel didn't want to get Helena in trouble for spreading rumors about Mulcahy carrying on with a married woman, "—and I'd seen him with you at that dinner. But I couldn't see you going with him. Not for that reason, anyway. He didn't act like a guy having an affair."

Melisande stared at Jewel. She'd recovered a little. Jewel found her luminous attention encouraging.

"He acted like he was trying to get you or get at you. Not like he already had you. You know. I mean, sometimes people will try to cover up an affair by pretending to dislike each other, but he wasn't doing that. He seemed really pissed that you weren't laughing at his jokes and acting impressed."

A long sigh escaped Melisande.

"You seemed—you didn't care about him. But something was going on. What was it? Were you going to go? What was his problem?"

Melisande's reply was elliptical. She slipped a suede jacket over her shoulders and began walking down the hall, away from Jewel. Even her back had authority. A beat late, Jewel understood that she was meant to follow. She scurried behind, addled with exasperation and wonder. Imagine commanding obedience with silence and a swish of a skirt. And she didn't even know the woman. What had Mulcahy been willing to do for Melisande—or to her?

With a cigarette in her hand, Melisande Pearsall looked like a film noir glamour-puss. Or she would have, if it weren't for the quick, angular intelligence in her eyes. She cupped her hand around a lighter, then slipped it into her jacket pocket.

The outdoor entrance to the hospital had one other smoker huddled in the night air, a large black woman who looked as though she'd be a good time on a good day. But this wasn't it. Her eyes were watery. Smoking, she pulled a ball of Kleenex out of her purse.

Jewel must have stared at Melisande's cigarette a moment too long.

"I like bad habits to be clearly defined," said Melisande, inhaling deeply.

"Yeah?" Jewel hoped the backchat wasn't going to stay this abstract. She was chilled, but not by the weather.

A car door slammed in the distance. Jewel waited. This one would talk when she was good and ready, and not a millisecond before.

Melisande took another drag and let out the smoke slowly. "He wanted to marry me."

"You're kidding! When you were a student?"

"Oh, no. Not then. Now."

"I don't get it. You've been married—however many years. Why now and not then?"

The hard fluorescent light of the entranceway made Melisande whiter, her eyes larger and darker. She paused. Not, Jewel thought, to find an answer but to word one.

"Years ago, I left him. For Tom, in a way, but I'd have left regardless. After a few months with Matt, I could see no reason to stay. I was deeply bored."

She watched a pair of twin girls holding get-well balloons. They raced up to the electronic doors, trailed by a grandmotherly black woman. They disappeared inside the hospital. Melisande turned back to Jewel.

"Matt never believed me. He thought it was a stratagem to win his sole attention. He wanted me back because I left. But then, over the years, he saw that I was wholly engaged by Tom. By my work."

Jewel was shocked to realize that she didn't know what the woman did for a living—or used to do, before she quit to take care of her husband. Was she a paralegal then? Or? Somehow, approaching midnight, with one man sick and three people dead, with the murderer alive and thinking—who knows? maybe smoking a cigarette just a few miles away—this seemed an appalling gap in knowledge. Melisande had been discussed as a lover, an ex-lover, a wife, a long-ago student. As though she only existed in relation to the male animals of Zoo U. Jewel would ask, but not now.

"Then he half-understood that I was truly gone." She spoke without vanity or modesty. "He wouldn't accept it. That's not fair. He couldn't accept it. He offered me marriage as though it were the greatest gift. Matt had always relished his reputation as an eligible bachelor, a man out of reach. Having the power to withhold was important to him."

She exhaled. Even played out, pressed to her limits, Melisande Pearsall looked like some wonderful dessert, champagne and peach and brown sugar. Jewel had never stood so near someone who could have been beautiful for a living.

But what she was saying was more compelling than how

she looked as she said it. For the first time, Jewel could see Mulcahy's limits, his bafflement at a woman who defied his definitions and experience. His cruelty, from this perspective, was a kind of freakishness. Like being morally stunted.

"In recent years, he'd grown more desperate. Partly because of Tom's illness. He didn't want to court a widow. He wanted to win me from my husband. Perhaps he also sensed that I would not be here, in Tacoma, forever. He thought he loved me."

Jewel no longer felt the cold or the night or the smell of death from the hospital. She was captured by the story Melisande wove of memory and smoke.

"If I married him, he would, out of consideration for me, ensure that Tom qualified for retirement with full benefits earlier than usual."

Jewel thought she would burst. "And if not?"

"He didn't say, not to me. But he told Tom that his job was not secure, that he was too ill to teach anymore. He told Tom that he'd make an announcement about him at the Humanities Dinner. Either early retirement or resignation for health reasons. I doubt he'd have done either, but Tom was worried about it."

"Your husband knew that Mulcahy wanted to marry—"

"No," said Melisande, quite sharply. "He knew only that Matt was snapping at my heels. Not about the proposal or the threat. I would not have him worried any further."

"So Mexico—"

"I told Matt I would marry him. That would have been a kind of wedding trip. He thought it would be amusing, a honeymoon in March, then a wedding in May."

Jewel was staggered. "You'd have—"

"I'd have said and done anything. In fact, though, I only had to wait for Tom's retirement package to go through. A few more months. Meanwhile, I'd have found a way to postpone the trip. Once Tom was safe, with the pension and health insurance of early retirement, I would tell Matt I lied."

Jewel felt the concrete of the entryway at her back. She needed something solid behind her. Even so, she felt unsteady, as though the ground might crack beneath her feet and float away.

"Mulcahy thought you would marry him."

"Yes."

"But to keep everything from Tom—and to lie to Mulcahy like that—didn't you think that—"

Melisande's clear gaze stopped Jewel. "I'd have said and done anything."

"But wasn't there any other way—"

"I do things my own way."

Jewel's breath came ragged. "Had Mulcahy told anyone? Was he going to make a big deal out of it at the dinner?"

"Mmm. He told me he would announce our engagement that night. Without naming me. To build suspense, he said. That wasn't the only reason. He was afraid that if he went too far—naming me, humiliating Tom—I would change my mind."

Jewel was staggered. This brave, stupid, lawless woman—what had her husband called her? "Self-contained?" The understatement of the century. But that was the least of it. With Melisande's bombshell, the murders seemed to shift, to slip into place with a terrible finality. Terrible because she suddenly saw the shape of the whole. Love and work, ethics and excess. The shadowy face—

"What would you have done? If he'd done some kind of announcement?"

"I'd have thought of something. Perhaps told the truth."

"He was going to announce his engagement, hinting

around—" She had to get out of there. Maybe Hartsock had already gone. Where had she left her car?

But first, a sudden spurt of anger at Melisande overpowered her. She wanted to shake the woman until her head fell off.

"Melisande Pearsall! Why didn't you tell all this to someone sooner? It's important! It might have saved Lesley DeLaMar! Didn't you think for one second about who killed Mulcahy and DeLaMar and why? Don't you have any curiosity? You and your husband aren't the only two people in the world. Don't you know you're in danger? I'm amazed you aren't dead already. You get back in there, where there are a lot of people." She snatched the cigarette from Melisande's hand and stamped it out.

Half-pushing, half-dragging the woman through the doorway into the check-in area, she continued haranguing her. "Don't be alone anywhere until someone's arrested. I'm serious."

She broke for the door, then remembered something else and turned back. An orderly and a man in a wheelchair were staring at her.

"And your marriage! Get a grip on it! You think you're saving Tom worry, but he thinks you're ready to leave him! Talk to him, for Christ's sake! And tell Ben Hartsock to call me at Blue Plate when he's through in there; I know who the murderer is. I'm going to close the deal."

Before running for the pay phones, Jewel was rewarded with a round-eyed look of pure blonde astonishment.

Chapter Twenty-Three

The door to Blue Plate was closed but unlocked. That was one thing.

A single overhead light burned at the back of the kitchen. The rest of the space was dim. That was another thing.

Del could be holed up inside, cooking, reading, or sleeping. Jewel didn't think so. She hesitated on the threshold for only a second. Whether or not she was right about the murderer, she refused to be afraid of entering her own place of business. All this fear, this maligning, this murdering, had to end somewhere.

It was going to end at Blue Plate. She swung in.

The pungent aroma of cumin assailed her. Had Del changed his mind about the bisque? Smelled like Indian food instead. That was the third thing. Three strikes and . . .

Jewel threw her bag on the front counter and made for the stove. The rolling pin and pie dish sat on the butcher's block, still waiting. They'd have to wait another day. So would the answering machine, with its red blinking "one."

She followed her nose. Sure enough, a creamy bisque filled the middle-weight kettle on one of the front burners. Asparagus and crab, although the smell of both was submerged in cumin. Instinctively, she checked the flame. Off, but the kettle radiated heat. She took a ladle from the stovetop to taste Del's project.

A scrabbling noise in the wall made her drop the ladle. She froze.

The noise sounded closer than it had before. The rat must be right behind the lower cabinets, next to the stove.

Probably her imagination, making the noise closer, louder.

Jewel gripped the stove and concentrated on her breathing. In. Out.

The scratching continued. Was the rat making progress?

She thought about visualizing something peaceful. But there was no time to visualize. She'd have company any minute.

Jewel made herself pick up the ladle again and try Del's bisque. Every taste molecule in her mouth seized up. At first she was afraid she would die. Then she was afraid she wouldn't.

She raced for the refrigerator. There was milk in it. Luckily. She drank straight out of the carton. Funny how most people would try to douse the flames with water. Yet dairy worked best, coating the fiery taste.

She stood for a moment in front of the open refrigerator, gasping. Another gulp of milk brought her mouth down from red alert to yellow warning.

That was the hottest food she had ever eaten, in a lifetime of eating spices. Del must have lost his mind. There was chili pepper in there, tossed with a generous hand. Chili pepper! In a bisque!

Appalling bisque. No Del. And he'd even forgotten to lock the front door. He'd be the death of her.

The silence in the room was suddenly oppressive. Why had the scratching stopped? No, she wouldn't panic. She would stick to her plan. The first person she'd called from the hospital would be here any second.

She shut the refrigerator door. The plan: to draw the missing answers from the killer's mouth. And to keep the conversation going until Ben checked his messages, got hers, and showed up with handcuffs at the ready. Jewel didn't think there'd be violence, but she'd been wrong before.

This was not, she understood, a perfect plan. If she were wrong about the murderer, she'd look like a moron in the middle of the night. But nothing was perfect: not plans, not Ben, not Jewel. At worst, she'd grovel to her former suspect, then report her conversation with Melisande Pearsall to Ben.

Her face was still hot with pepper and fury when she thought about the self-contained blonde cucumber. When was independence selfishness? When was self-containment criminal?

She was compelled by the murderous geometry of love and work, sex and power: Pearsall and Melisande, Melisande and Mulcahy, Mulcahy and . . .

The click of the front door shattered her thoughts like glass.

Edith Underwood.

They stared at each other.

The older woman didn't look cold or bustled, as though she'd just swept in from Pacific Avenue. Not a honey-colored hair was out of place.

After an endless moment, Professor Underwood's strained face eased into a smile. "Hello, dear. A rather *late* time for a phone call. Luckily I'm a night owl. You, too, I take it."

This time Jewel knew enough not to be distracted by the highly colored clothing—green wool winter coat, purple pants and matching sweater, the large necklace of beads and bones. Christ, not bones—bamboo.

The middle-aged Religion professor with her plain, good face, excessive clothing, and mild eccentricities. The loyal, slightly ridiculous college professor. That's what everyone saw. There was more, though, too much more.

"And your young colleague? Is he a late-night worker, too?" Edith Underwood scanned the kitchen quickly, with an intensity around the eyes that Jewel didn't like, not even a little.

Yet even now, past midnight, alone together at Blue Plate, Del gone, Ben gone, Jewel felt only shock and exasperation, not terror. She might be wrong. Even now, she couldn't credit Edith Underwood with two murders.

"I suppose that caterers, like college professors, are working at *all hours*." She smiled as though they shared a secret. Which they did.

"Del had some sort of vigil to attend, in protest of—he's coming back any minute." Jewel spoke with a confidence she almost felt.

"I see." Underwood walked through the opening in the front counter to the kitchen and put her bag down on the table carefully. "My goodness, something smells good! Don't tell me you've had time to whip something up since calling me."

Jewel sighed. If she thought that lunatic bisque smelled good, she probably ate five-alarm chili for breakfast and murdered seven people before lunch. Jewel noticed that she had magnificent posture, standing as tall as a lighthouse, not touching or leaning anywhere.

Then she had an idea. People relaxed when they ate. And when they sat. "No, this was started before. Would you like some? If we're going to talk, we might as well eat."

"Why, that's a lovely idea." Underwood looked merry, as though she were about to laugh. Was the woman unhinged? Shouldn't she be afraid of what Jewel had called to tell her? Unless she had nothing to be afraid of.

Jewel drew two bowls from the cabinets over the sink, loaded them with the noxious bisque, and sat at the wooden table. Underwood lowered her bag to the floor, then looked down at Jewel. She was a tall woman and solid. Even kind of shapely. Jewel wondered who else had noticed that, amidst the dither and color of Underwood's effect.

Not Mulcahy. She steeled herself. At best, this was going to hurt.

"Professor Underwood, when did you find out that Mulcahy had had an affair with Melisande Pearsall?" Underwood reeled slightly back, then sat down in the chair. Her smile fractured but did not fall. Woman knew how to take a punch, Jewel noted. Plenty of practice, if she'd been any kind of friend to Mulcahy.

"Oh, dear." The professor's voice remained strong, if flutier. "It was—let me see—a week before the Humanities Dinner. Matthew and I were planning the Curriculum Review and he—he used to confide in me, you see, because there were so few people on campus he could trust."

Jewel could hear the distant echo of Mulcahy's voice, the confidence given like a gift. Even now, she felt sorry for Edith when she heard the pride in her voice.

"He trusted me with the news of his impending—his—" Edith Underwood blinked several times, as though a speck of dust had blown into her eye. "His impending marriage," she continued firmly. "It was a secret, of course."

"Why?"

"Matt did not want the announcement to travel the campus unofficially. It would not have been—he wanted the information to come in a proper way, formally, at the Humanities Dinner."

"So he told you that he and Melisande Pearsall—"

The woman's name infuriated Edith. She lifted her chin like Marie Antoinette on the way to the guillotine. "That woman! Married to poor Tom Pearsall while she inveigled

Matt. He was a sophisticated man, of course, attractive to women and used to putting them off, but somehow—" She took a deep breath. "He was not *sensible* where she was concerned. I told him that the divorce—Tom's illness—a former student—that the whole situation was *unseemly* and would reflect poorly on him, but he only . . . laughed."

Her eyes glittered. Jewel could almost hear that laugh, laced with contempt and triumph.

"I was . . . rather shocked, actually. She was nobody, nobody at all. And a former student—people would take advantage of that to say that all those *terrible* rumors were true. I told him, of course. It was my responsibility . . ." Her voice trailed off and her mouth curved in a rictus of a cordial smile.

She looked over at Jewel's bowl, then at her own. "Perhaps," she said, in a grotesque imitation of her normal manner, "you would be so kind as to fetch me a new bowl of bisque, dear? This seems to have some sort of skin on it. I suppose because it's been sitting out? I'm no chef, of course."

"Yes, all right." Jewel's voice sounded tinny in her own ears. She didn't move right away. "You explained to him how, um, inappropriate the marriage would be, and—"

"He did *not* seem to understand. Distressing, really, as he was a man of such ready intellect. And he had always said he would never marry, but if he did, he would choose someone like himself, a scholar who could be his intellectual equal, a partner—I—"

Jewel tried to keep the pity and rage out of her face, to look merely neutral. It wasn't easy. He'd bought Edith's loyalty with cheap hints about marriage and even cheaper confidences. She'd believed that he was a man of integrity, of principles. It was time to cut to the chase.

"He slept with Melisande when she was a student."

"She was the only one!" Edith snapped, as though disciplining an insolent sophomore. "He was young, then, and she—he never—" Tears began running down her cheeks. She seemed unaware of them. "He was an honorable man. You wouldn't understand that, of course. Being at best a mediocre caterer, at worst—" She sniffed.

A dim suspicion took shape in Jewel's mind. "I was hired on your recommendation."

Edith chuckled unkindly. "Yes, because of that *disastrous* shower you catered for my niece. No offense, dear, but your incompetence was perfect. It was so easy for people to believe you could have added a poisonous ingredient by *accident*."

She smiled condescendingly.

"You planned all along," Jewel said, anger staining her voice, "to kill Mulcahy and blame—"

"Not really, Jewel. I thought if that woman were to die, then Matthew wouldn't be at risk. He wouldn't appear to be a man who'd abandoned his principles or even a ready target for those who wanted to *vilify* him with their rumors, that terrible Leo Wallinsky or *fanatical* Frances Carlotti."

Jewel felt cold and afraid. But she couldn't stop. "You were going to kill Melisande and blame Blue Plate?"

"It would not have been first-degree murder," Edith explained in her lecturer's tone, "but some lesser charge of involuntary manslaughter, even criminal neglect. You would not have gone to jail, or at least," she corrected, "not for very long."

Jewel wanted to gag. Edith Underwood's eyes glittered and her face was wet with tears. The purple sweater, the green coat, the honey-colored hair assaulted Jewel's vision, but she didn't take her eyes from Edith's face. This was no time to give up. She had to know everything.

"Why the Dean? Instead of Melisande?"

Edith's face clouded in memory. "I spoke to him one last

time before the Humanities Dinner. He was . . . almost rude, really . . . I *quite* forgave him, of course, as he had a lot on his mind. I urged him to reconsider, for the sake of his reputation. He laughed and said that marrying . . . her . . . would improve his reputation, rather than otherwise. A younger, beautiful woman . . . he told me not to make myself ridiculous with . . . things I didn't understand."

"That pig," Jewel said involuntarily, then flinched at her own big mouth.

"No, dear. Although I appreciate your . . ." Edith foundered for a moment, then started over. "I couldn't let him do that to himself. It was easy to add the water hemlock to his salad while he moved through the crowd. No one noticed me."

Jewel saw the Faculty Club in her mind again, people laughing and talking and shouting, Underwood strangely invisible in her bright colors and dithering.

"Or," the murderer corrected herself, "so I thought at the time."

One person saw Underwood, one sharp-eyed woman, too sharp. "Lesley DeLaMar."

"Lesley DeLaMar." Edith took a small spoonful of bisque. Without flinching, Jewel noticed. More disturbing was the openness of her confession. Why was she telling all this? Expiation? Rehearsal for a confession to the police? Or—

"Lesley made an appointment to speak with me in Matthew's office the morning that you and I met for lunch. She told me what she'd seen. I was *quite* taken aback, as you might imagine. She insisted that I resign from my position and confess to the crime. She said that she did not want the University's reputation damaged further. I believe that she wanted to claim some sort of credit for bringing me to justice, as she had it. Certainly there seemed to be no personal grief to expunge. She seemed delighted with her promotion."

Jewel recalled the way DeLaMar had seemed to expand with pleasure and righteousness in the Dean's armchair. No, no grief there, for all her sucking up. Yet she tried to do the right thing, for whatever motives.

"Professor Underwood." Jewel picked her words carefully. "Why didn't you confess?"

The older woman sighed with theatrical impatience. "Haven't you been *listening*, dear? Have I been *unclear*? I couldn't *tell* Matthew's secrets or have him made ridiculous in the eyes of his colleagues, much less the ordinary newspaper reader. It was imperative that none of this sorry episode become public. I didn't have time to think what to do. Lesley threatened to expose—everything—if I didn't do so myself, but she wanted me to resign first. I'm afraid I rather *impulsively* pushed her down, hard. Her head hit the corner of the desk. She seemed to die very quickly." Jewel watched in horror as Edith poked around in her bowl with a spoon. The double murderer seemed relaxed by conversation and confession, but the glitter in her eye did not dim, and Jewel sensed that time was short.

"I thought I was safe then. That is, that Matthew's reputation was safe. That policeman seemed uninterested in me as a suspect. Of course, I was Matthew's dearest friend. But then you kept asking questions . . ." Edith gazed speculatively at Jewel.

"Oh, you wanted bisque without skin on top! Here, I'll bring you some! Sorry! I'd forgotten!" Babbling, Jewel snatched Edith's bowl from her and walked to the stove. Before ladling up the bisque, she glanced back to the table, wanting to ask—she saw Professor Underwood dropping something powdery into *her* bisque.

Jewel turned back to the stove fast. Her hands were shaking. No expiation, no confession to Ben, no remorse. Another poisoning.

Mentally Jewel cursed herself, in a long monotonous string of profanity, beginning with the day of her own birth in Bayonne and ending with her warning to Melisande Pearsall at Group Health Hospital. She shouldn't have called Underwood for a meeting. She shouldn't have come back on her own. Too late, too late.

The rat scrabbled again. This time it sounded close enough to be in the cabinet itself, with the sugar and flour. Horrible. Jewel gripped the edge of the stove, immobile.

"Are you all right, dear?" Edith asked.

"Yes." Jewel cleared her throat and forced herself to finish reloading the bowl. "Peachy."

Jewel put the bisque carefully in front of Edith, who looked extremely pleased with herself. Good. Edith hadn't heard the rat.

As though keeping the rat a secret was the most important matter Jewel had on her plate at the moment.

The ridiculous thought jump-started Jewel from fear to fury. Enough, she thought. No one's poisoning me in my own place of business. And this homicidal fruitcake was going to wake up tomorrow in jail as long as Jewel had a breath left in her body. Underwood had to pay. Pathetic though she was, the woman was also a two-time murderer, going on three. And what about Leilani? Edith's self-deception and her staunch support of Mulcahy helped him drive Leilani over the edge into oblivion.

But Jewel couldn't stand for Edith not to know the man she'd sacrificed her freedom for.

"Mulcahy used you," she said.

Underwood stared up at Jewel, bisque forgotten. Her

smile broke into a thousand pieces. "It was foolish of me to expect someone like you to understand."

"I understand, all right. He took you for all you were worth—your loyalty, your friendship, your faith in him—and he threw them all in your face! Melisande didn't want him! She wasn't going to marry him! She was just stringing him along until Tom got his retirement package."

Edith's eyes narrowed. She rose, shouldering her bag, as if to leave. "That's a vicious lie. She was besotted—"

Jewel couldn't stop. "Mulcahy slept with every student he could scare into his office! He had no reputation to save! He preyed on people who couldn't defend themselves. Some hero! Edith, how could you?"

The gap between the two women closed faster than Jewel would have believed possible. Underwood could move when she wanted. Her kindly middle-aged face was mottled with grief and rage.

She put a strong hand on Jewel's shoulder. Jewel twisted away.

The woman's face struggled into a parody of her outside self. Her purple sweater rose and fell like ocean waves until she was calm enough to talk. "Jewel—we're both—over-wrought—let's sit down."

"No! And I'm not eating that damned poisonous bisque, either."

"Perhaps it *is* a bit spicy—"

"I saw you poison it! I won't eat it!" Jewel glared at Edith defiantly.

The honey-headed woman came up with Blue Plate's best cook knife. Where—when had she . . .

"I think you'll find that you *will* eat it." The big triangular knife was pointed at Jewel's stomach, two feet away. Edith's hand was steady. "Sit down, Jewel."

Jewel sank into the wooden chair. Edith stood over her, knife an inch from the side of Jewel's neck. "Being poisoned will be better than being stabbed, I think. And who knows? You may live. It's impossible to get the amount of water hemlock exactly right. Much depends on a person's size, condition . . ."

This was, Jewel thought in her terror, a fucking ridiculous way to go, sliced with your own cook knife by a woman old enough to be your mother. Why couldn't she peg out like Julia Child, ninety-something, in her sleep, a bowl of her famous French onion soup on the nightstand?

"No one will believe it's me." Her voice shook. "Why would I kill DeLaMar?"

"Because she saw water hemlock in some of the salads, an ingredient you denied using. Of course, people will believe me, even if you live. A professor of Religion—an incompetent caterer."

Jewel turned angrily. The blade nicked her neck. She cried out in pain and shock. A really bad way to go, being poisoned with an inedible bisque. What would happen to Del? Who would laugh with Daphne on the phone? What would Ben think? Who would make grits for Lyle, the way he liked them? What about Daphne, marooned with her sister Nadine, the wedding planner, for the rest of her life?

"Now eat, Jewel. I don't have all night."

The rat-scratching sounded like a car horn.

Jewel jumped. This time Edith had heard it, too—her chin lifted—but she didn't take her eyes from Jewel. The knife remained steady.

"What's that, dear?"

Even at knifepoint, faced with an unhinged killer, Jewel didn't like to say that there was a rodent living in Blue Plate's wall. "I'm not sure."

But Edith caught Jewel's hesitation. "Squirrels? Or perhaps a mouse? Even better." She chuckled. "If you have any insects or rodents in your place of business, my story is even more credible. Now eat up, dear. Hurry."

Everyone would know about the rat. Jewel was incensed.

She got an idea, born of desperation. She lifted the spoon to her lips and ate a tiny amount of bisque. She began to cry. It wasn't as hard as she thought it would be, crying.

"Jewel, I'm out of patience. Eat faster, dear."

"I can't. I mean . . . the bisque is so awful. Couldn't I—if this is my last—my last meal—couldn't I fix it? Or something?"

Underwood pursed her lips, considering. For what felt like hours.

"How Foreign Legion," she said at last, with a kind of laugh. "You don't smoke, I suppose? Yes, by all means."

Jewel stood, slowly. She didn't want to alarm Underwood, who had only moved the knife back a few inches. There was only going to be one chance, a single moment.

She took her bowl in both hands and moved towards the far counter. Edith followed her.

"It's just—my spices—I can correct—" Jewel gulped. If she didn't watch it, this crying would get out of hand. She had to see what she was doing. "I'm sorry."

Her tears seemed to calm Edith Underwood, who half-smiled with regret and condescension. "That's all right, dear. Just hurry."

Jewel turned to the counter. Edith was less than a foot behind her, watching. The knife was pointing—Jewel could feel it—just behind her shoulders.

She opened the lower cabinet and, without looking, reached for a small jar. Cayenne. Out of the corner of her eye, she could see the pie-in-progress she'd abandoned. The bowl. The rolling pin. Had Edith seen the rolling pin?

Jewel sprinkled a bit of cayenne on the top of her bowl.

"Cayenne pepper, do you really think so?" Edith tittered. "It is rather *lively* as is, dear."

A rat ran from the open cabinet across Edith's shoes.

Involuntarily, Edith dropped her eyes.

Jewel lunged for the rolling pin, spun around, and swung hard.

It connected at the side of Edith's neck. She screamed and staggered. But she didn't let go of the knife. Jewel swung again, this time at her head, as hard as she could, with her whole body behind the swing, the rage of her fear and fatigue. There was a thud, dull and solid. The rolling pin on Edith's skull.

Edith crumpled. An ungainly heap of purple and bone necklace. Knife still gripped in her hand.

There was wailing. How could Edith be wailing? Her eyes were closed. Her mouth. She looked dead.

It was Jewel. She was crying as though her heart would explode. Oh God, she thought, her whole body shaking, I killed her. "Don't—don't—don't be dead."

Her legs shuddered so violently she almost fell.

"Christ! What—" Another voice, from the front door. Ben Hartsock, looking fearsome, moving fast. Behind him, Del, ponytail flying.

"It was her," Jewel cried, still holding the rolling pin, sick with shame and pity and the end of fear. "She killed them. I killed her. I did it. She would have—I'm sorry. I only wanted to stop her."

Ben glanced down at the body with pitiless speed. He put his hands on Jewel's shoulders and looked straight into her eyes. "She's not dead."

"Not?"

"She's breathing. Her chest is moving."

Del edged closer to the scene, squeamish but determined. "Oh, man. Bad karma. Not yours, Jewel."

Edith wasn't dead.

Jewel's tears stopped. Her face was wet. Her nose was running. Time to get a grip. She grabbed a dish towel and wiped her face.

"Ben," she said. "What took you so long?"

Chapter Twenty-Four

Jewel stumbled to her kitchen in a tangle of bedclothes. Easier to rise up wearing a top sheet than to sort herself out.

There would be plenty of time to sort things out. The sheet was the least of it.

She hadn't slept that long since she was a teenager, recovering from a double shift working the fryolator at Stewart's Root Beer Truck Stop. Prom night. Onion rings were in vogue. Jewel hadn't had an onion ring, french fry, fried shrimp, or chicken drumette for seventeen years.

The window over the kitchen sink showed the morning still blanketed in fog, even though it was almost noon.

Jewel didn't care. Blue Plate Catering was closed this morning.

She knew she'd have to go back to the storefront, to make meatballs or truffle-hunt for wedding receptions. She would go back, maybe even this afternoon, but not this morning.

She sighed and opened the refrigerator.

Last night re-ran in her skull. Edith Underwood splayed on the floor. The rolling pin hitting her hard on the side of the head. The rat running across her shoes. The film in Jewel's brain showed backwards, out of order, fast-forward, every which way.

Only three things would scrub those pictures out of her brain. Time, most of all. Weeks and months of time. The second was food. That she could start with immediately. The third was sex. A lot of it. Slower than honey. No pager.

Jewel shut the refrigerator door, gently, shook off the top sheet, and made coffee. Time, food, and sex. Start there. She imagined herself turning off Ben's pager, then reaching—

The phone rang.

Jewel cursed. Couldn't she have uninterrupted sex, even when she was the only one there?

Daph's voice filled the room and warmed it.

"Girlie, are you there? You haven't called in a couple days, and with all those poisoned professors falling from the barn house into the pig trough—"

"I'm here." Jewel clicked off the answering machine, one-handed the coffee pot, and poured herself a giant cup. Strong enough to eat with a fork. Good.

"Well, thank Christ for that. I tried Blue Plate already. Isn't it nine A.M. there? Why aren't you at work already?"

Jewel filled her in. Daph was gratifyingly avid for details, priming the pump with searching questions whenever Jewel took a sip of coffee. She was aghast at Jewel's danger— "Poison *and* a knife? Why couldn't she use a gun like a normal person?"—and riveted by Ben Hartsock. "A fucking hero," Daph marveled. "I bet he doesn't live with his mother, either."

Jewel liked reliving that part, where Ben and Del flew in the door. Ben had made her tea with lots of honey in it, for shock. After calling the medics, he kept his hand on her—her shoulder, around her back—at all times. He asked a few questions, but mostly the story had poured out of her at sixteen knots an hour. Then he drove her home and left her.

She had slept for ten hours. In her clothes.

"How are you, really?" Daph was saying, serious.

"Really? I'm okay."

"A little too fucking close for comfort, alone with a double murderer late at night in your storefront." Daph was slam-

227

Beth Kalikoff

ming something around in New Jersey—cabinet doors, Jewel imagined, or stacks of magazines. She was frightened for Jewel, even though the threat was over.

"Hey, it's not a hobby with me."

Daph snorted. "Anyway," she said, "I also called to give you the heads-up."

"Uh-oh." Jewel lined up garlic cloves on the counter and began peeling them. Garlic mashed potatoes for breakfast. Why not?

"You know how Bathroom Bob has all these broken blossoms he daddies?"

Jewel nodded, then remembered she was on the phone. "Sure. He's great that way." Her father, wide of girth and large of spirit, was a sweet man who had all but adopted a number of sad young women, lost souls without fathers of their own, who just needed, he said, a little kindness.

Everyone called him Bathroom Bob because he owned a bathroom fixture store famous throughout the Brunswicks for the quality and quantity of its stock. Bob's humor was also a draw. He had taken down the wooden sign decades ago, but people still remembered it: "Bob's Bathroom Supply: We Cheat the Other Guy and Pass the Savings Along to You."

"So," Daph continued, "one of them wants to move to Tacoma and come out, and you're supposed to help her adjust to life outside the closet."

"I'm what?" said Jewel in wonder, pausing over the garlic slices.

Daph hooted. "It'll be a nice little project for you, Jewel. Do they have Pride Parades out there, where the buses don't run?"

"Dad told you this?"

"He told Nadine, and she told me."

Jewel exhaled in relief. "Daph! You scared me. I don't

228

want to adopt a woman my age. You know your sister's the original unreliable source."

"Yeah," said Daph, "but it sounds just like him, doesn't it?"

The trouble was, it did.

"You know what? I can't have this conversation right now." The potatoes were on the boil. Jewel needed two hands and an empty brain.

"Guess what else!" Daph was winding up, Jewel could tell, and wanted a parting shot. "You're going to get a call from the Brown and Haley people out there."

"The candy factory?" Brown and Haley's Almond Roca was Tacoma's pride, exported over the seven seas.

"They need a caterer. But they don't want a big-deal caterer, because—oh, shit, I got a call on the other line, catch you later."

"Daph!" But Jewel was once again talking to a dead line. How on earth could one of the Jersey Feynmanns have an inside scoop on Brown and Haley?

She could imagine Daph's Mrs. New Jersey pageant smile, ear to ear, like a Cheshire Cat who just ate a mouse and T-boned Mrs. Texas in the talent competition.

Chapter Twenty-Five

Three days later, Helena studied the red, green, and white crepe paper dangling from Blue Plate's ceiling lights. Orange and yellow plastic flags were strung from one corner of the ceiling to another, like at a gas station opening. "Happy Birthday," said silver letters on the refrigerator door. "Happy St. Patrick's Day," crowed green letters taped over the oven fan.

"Goodness," said Helena, returning her gaze to Jewel, who was drizzling caramel sauce over homemade vanilla ice cream on raisin-bread pudding. "I thought color-blindness only struck men."

"The banners were on sale."

"I certainly hope so." Helena toasted her with a martini. Jewel grinned. She was happy to see Helena looking relaxed, without the murders casting a shadow between them.

They'd spoken on the phone earlier, swapping details. Helena's warning in the cold car had been just that. She had known enough about Mulcahy's misconduct and Leilani's death to know there was a lot to cover up. She didn't trust people like Edith Underwood and Lesley DeLaMar to do the right thing, and few other staff members knew enough about what the Dean was doing to stop it. Rumors, Helena had said, don't cut it.

Leilani's death had raised the stakes even higher. Helena had wanted Jewel out of the middle, while she talked to

Tyler Seito, trying to get him to go public with the story of his girlfriend's death without urging him beyond comfort or ethics.

Now, in honor of the Blue-Plate-Back-in-Business party, Helena was even more elegant than usual. Her golden high-necked blouse and piles of chains made her look like an empress.

"Jewel, what do you think?" Del held a tray of rhubarb tarts aloft like a church offering. Their lemon-sugar glaze glowed in the fluorescence. Their crimped crusts were just right. The boy was an artist.

She smiled up at him. He had donned his best T-shirt for the occasion, a peach-colored Triple-A Artwalk sketch that he called Dali on Downers. A raspberry head-rag kept his ponytail out of harm's way.

"Del! Don't go into business for yourself! Swear to me!"

He shone with pleasure. "I'll check the meringues." He bounced back to the refrigerator, his long stride covering the kitchen space in microseconds.

Helena leaned against the chrome counter by the sink, her drink in hand. "Well, she isn't the first woman to crack wide open over a worthless man."

"No," agreed Jewel. "She knew better and she didn't know better. Edith had to believe the cartoon cut-out of Mulcahy she'd invented. Otherwise, she'd have to see she'd thrown away all that love and loyalty. You know what still makes me mad?" She stuck spoons in each bowl of bread pudding. "The way he used her loyalty to him."

Helena took a sip. "Yes. That was very ugly. Just like him, though. Poor woman. Poor Lesley DeLaMar, too."

"I know." Jewel gnawed her lower lip. "If she'd only told Ben instead of trying to play everything herself! But she wanted to put the p.r. spin on it."

"Mostly, I think about Leilani."

They sighed.

Helena roused herself from contemplation to give Jewel seventy-five watts of her glorious smile. "Did I mention that the SSH brochures are at the printer? Or that I intend to make sure that the university honors its responsibilities?"

Jewel held her orange juice and vodka aloft. Helena smiled, then frowned. "Why was the front door open when you came back the other night?"

"That was Del."

"Yeah, it was me." He looked up from the meringues. "Edith Underwood got to Blue Plate before Jewel even left the hospital. I was still here."

"Oh my! She must have moved fast when you called her, Jewel."

"Uh-huh. And she lives close."

"She was acting weird," said Del. His face clouded in memory. "She's, like, making small talk with me, but all the time, her eyes are going everywhere: the doors, the stove, you name it."

"Mmmm," Helena said.

"It made me feel funny, late at night, her waiting for Jewel. I didn't know if Jewel had really called her or not. So I went off to find Ben. I left the door unlocked because Edith was still here."

"Couldn't you have left a note or something, hon?"

"He did!" said Jewel. "The bisque! He spiced the living bejesus out of it! Helena, it almost busted my sinuses open."

"I didn't want to write anything down," said Del apologetically. "I didn't trust her to leave it. I got a real bad feeling from her. So the bisque—it was the only way I could think of to tell Jewel to watch out."

"So if Edith had been alone here, why didn't she drop the poison in the soup then? Instead of waiting?"

"I think she was going to play it by ear," said Jewel, pausing as she put out the napkins. "She didn't want to kill me unless she had to, and she wanted to find out what I had to say."

"Spontaneous."

Edith's fractured smile came back to Jewel with heart-stopping clarity. The sight of the knife in her steady hand. That scream, as the rolling pin connected. If she could, Jewel would scrub out the mental images with a Brillo pad. As is, there was a lot of cooking in her future. Now that she had a future.

"Spontaneous," agreed Jewel sadly. "After Del left, she waited in her car across the street, to see if I'd brought anyone with me."

"Ben and I called Jewel from the police station," added Del.

Helena wrinkled her brow. "You didn't check your messages? Why ever not? Jewel—"

To Jewel's relief, a young man in a brown uniform stuck his head in the front door.

"Ma'am?" The guy from the exterminator's.

Jewel met him at the door.

"Ma'am, everything's fine now. Just get someone to patch up those holes within three days. You should see the teeth marks on 'em." He reached in his back pocket for a business card.

Jewel, smiling, took it, although she knew the rat was still alive.

It was all Del's fault. He'd become the rat's death-row advocate: "Stop the killing," he pleaded. Del had argued that this particular rat had helped Jewel rescue herself with the

233

rolling pin. Maybe he was right. Maybe he wasn't. It didn't matter. She'd been too tired to protest. Del could adopt the rat and name it Del Junior for all she cared. As long as it was gone.

Yesterday, while Jewel was buying new bags of sugar and flour, Del lured the rat out of the storefront with rotting kitchen scraps. Then he had transported it, who knew how, to a bird sanctuary south of Olympia. Jewel had her doubts about whether a city rat could survive in the country but kept them to herself. Once Del had freed the rat into the "wild," he permitted Jewel to call an exterminator. Just in case.

"I'll bill you," said the man.

Ben Hartsock slipped into the foyer, eyes bright.

He unzipped his brown leather jacket. He wore a white shirt underneath. And undershirt. He was clean-shaven, unlike the night of the peppery bisque, when he'd rushed into Blue Plate like a dirty avenging angel. Jewel liked the fact that Ben had called the medics, made her tea with honey, asked her a few questions, and sped her home. Competent. Capable. She had especially liked the feel of his hand on the back of her neck. The small of her back. The memory made her kind of swoony. Like she wouldn't mind taking his clothes off with her teeth.

Jewel handed Ben a rhubarb tart. He smiled. "Thanks." His voice held promise. She studied his chocolate eyes.

Nick Mariani and Del Troutman were deep in conversation, Nick's dark head and Del's sandy one as close as sunflowers. "I'm almost twenty-five," Del was saying. "I mean, I'm older than I look."

"How is she?" said Jewel.

Ben leaned against the counter, his face serious. "All right. She has a mild concussion, but no permanent damage, they say."

"Good," said Jewel. "I wasn't trying—" she said for the fiftieth time.

"I know you weren't," said Ben for the fiftieth time. "The shrinks are waiting for their turn with her. I spoke to Edith Underwood's sister a few days ago. She said that Underwood's work was like a vocation, that she had blocked out everything else in her life. Her sister thought that vocation idea came from the Dean. I was getting ready to arrest Underwood when Jewel . . ."

Jewel wasn't surprised. Dedication to your craft was one thing. Cutting off everything else was another, as bad as making a person your life's mission. Edith had done both.

"Jewel," Ben said, in a lower tone.

"Hang on," she said, "there's one more thing."

Frances Carlotti was sipping a glass of seltzer sparingly. ("I don't drink alcohol," she'd said.) Her ethereal beauty had a touch of color today, honey and sand, rather than the invalid's pallor the night Jewel had found her collapsed on the Faculty Club hallway carpet.

"Frances," said Jewel. "Are you pregnant or what?"

All eyes turned eagerly towards the historian, who blinked once, twice. "No. Why—"

"Why did you faint? The night of the Humanities Dinner. You were looking for Mulcahy, and I found you—"

"Oh." Frances looked chagrined, although she kept her chin up. "He said he would announce the dissolution of the Women's Studies program, and with it a few faculty lines, at that dinner. My line, he told me, unless I wanted to work part of the time in History, and part of the time in the Dean's office as a—factotum."

"Helper," said Nick to Del, unasked.

"I wanted to try and persuade him not to, one last time. I was concerned, and I'd forgotten to eat that day. I have a con-

235

dition called *vasovagal syncope,* which is exacerbated by stress. If you also forget to eat or drink, you faint. Although you do recover very quickly." She ducked her head, as if she'd just confessed to pederasty.

"Huh," said Jewel. "So what's the big-dog mystery?"

Frances colored. "I hate it. It's so . . . feminine. I don't tell anyone unless I can't help it. It mortifies me."

"You should eat," said Jewel conclusively.

"Yes. I always mean to," said Frances, without contrition.

"Carlotti," said Wallinsky. "Overcome your deadly pride. Why, I myself have poor depth perception, if you can believe that. Routinely I mow down mailboxes and children's bicycles because I can't judge distances. Fuck it, right? I can't be wearing glasses, can I? Or contacts? Right?"

Frances almost smiled.

Conversations began again. Under cover of chat and beneath the orange flags, Ben came close to Jewel.

"I'm sorry. I got carried away, that night. I shouldn't have, it was unethical. And I'm sorry I told you the way I did."

"Forget it," said Jewel masterfully. She wondered at this strange, new, forgiving impulse in herself. "Could have happened to anyone."

"Well," said Ben, assessingly, "I hope not. Anyway, it's not unethical anymore. The case is closed."

"How about dinner?" she said.

"Tonight," he said. "Out or in?"

"Lunch hour's over," Helena stood. "Back to work, folks."

Everyone started foraging for their coats and bags.

"Jewel!" Del scrambled to his full height and gestured at Nick, who was bringing empty plates to the sink. "Nick is going to photograph our food! He's curating this show at the Museum of Glass and we can be in it!"

"Great, Del. Thanks, Nick."

"Food—that reminds me." Frances was putting on her gloves. "The Women's Studies Conference? We'll be taking bids for a caterer. And we'll need lunch at our planning sessions."

The guests spilled through the foyer onto Pacific Avenue.

"Jewel," Helena turned back to Blue Plate in a glitter of gold and necklace. "My stepbrother's girl is managing this Tacoma Dome show on health and diet, and she wants you to do a Blue Plate booth there."

Nick tore his gaze from Del. "The Tacoma Men's Choir—"

Ben slid his eyes over the crowd, then back to Jewel. She barely saw him. Visions of sugar plums crowded her view. And salmon croquettes, and glazed ham, and fettucini almondine . . .

Tacoma lay before her like a jewel.

"Call me," she said, to the world.

About the Author

Beth Kalikoff grew up in New Jersey and Connecticut. She's worked as a short-order cook, restaurant host, and waitron. Her poetry and nonfiction have won national awards. Currently, she teaches writing at the University of Washington's Tacoma campus. Although she has a Ph.D. in English, she's normal. Unlike Jewel, she's not much of a cook; her specialty is "three things on a plate." She lives with her husband and dog.